a Face in Every Window

OTHER NOVELS BY HAN NOLAN

A Summer of Kings

When We Were Saints

Born Blue

Dancing on the Edge

Send Me Down a Miracle

If I Should Die Before I Wake

a Face in Every Window

★

HAN NOLAN

HARCOURT, INC.

Orlando   Austin   New York   San Diego   London

Requests for permission to make copies of any part of the
work should be submitted online at www.harcourt.com/contact
or mailed to the following address: Permissions Department,
Houghton Mifflin Harcourt Publishing Company,
6277 Sea Harbor Drive, Orlando, Florida 32887-6777.

www.HarcourtBooks.com

First Harcourt paperback edition 2008

The Library of Congress has cataloged the hardcover edition as follows:
Nolan, Han.
A face in every window/by Han Nolan.
p. cm.
Summary: After the death of his grandmother, who held the family
together, teenage JP is left with a mentally challenged father and
a mother who seems ineffectual and constantly sick, and he feels
everything sliding out of control.
[1. Family problems—Fiction.   2. Mentally handicapped—
Fiction.]   I. Title.
PZ7.N6783Fac   1999
[Fic]—dc21   99-14230
ISBN 978-0-15-201915-0
ISBN 978-0-15-206418-1 pb

Text set in Minion
Designed by Trina Stahl

A C E G H F D B
Printed in the United States of America

For Grace Adams,
and for her son, Brian,
with all my love

a Face in Every Window

Chapter One

★

ONCE WHEN I was seven years old, my grandma Mary knitted me a blue sweater. "Blue," she said, "because yer a boy and to match the color of yer eyes." Every time I wore the sweater, though, it grew. I had to roll the sleeves up so much they looked like fat doughnuts hanging from my wrists. When the sweater got to looking like a dress it had stretched out so much, I decided I would shorten it by unraveling it some. The more I unraveled, the more I wanted to, and I told myself I was knitting backward. I watched how each stitch linked with the next slipped out of its loop with just a gentle pull. I was fascinated with it and fascinated with the pile of yarn that had accumulated on my bed. When I had finished my little project, I brought my blue bundle to Grandma Mary and said, "Look, I knitted backward."

Grandma Mary stood at the kitchen counter mixing batter for a chocolate cake. She turned off the mixer, lowered her head, and took a deep breath. I could see by the tight-lipped expression on her face that she wasn't as pleased as I had been with my discovery.

"James Patrick," she said, finally looking up at me. "You know, don't you, lad, it took me four months to knit that sweater."

"Well, then, knitting backward is faster," I said. "It only took me this afternoon."

Grandma Mary came away from the counter and took both my arms, pulling me to her. She looked me in the eyes and said, "I created something when I made that sweater, and when you took it apart you destroyed it. Creating is better than destroying. Remember that, James Patrick. Destruction leaves you with nothing. We just have a pile of yarn now and before you had a nice warm sweater. You understand now?"

I nodded, but it wasn't until she died, two years ago, when I was almost fifteen, that I really understood. Our family was like that sweater—created, held together by Grandma Mary's hard work and love. We were linked together because she linked us, she gave us our place, our roles. We were her children, dependent on her to hold us together. After she died, it was like we were knitting backward, the three of us— Mam, Pap, and I—unraveling, but this time it was Grandma Mary who pulled the string, destroying what she had created by dying.

Chapter Two

★

THE DAY AFTER Grandma Mary's funeral my father, my dear Pap, dug holes in our yard with one of Grandma Mary's serving spoons, as if, with his heart broken, he needed someplace to spill its contents. Neighbors, hurrying past the small clapboard houses and chain-link fences on their way to the train station, would come upon our scratch of lawn with all its holes and dear Pap carving out still another, and they'd shake their heads and ask themselves, "Whatever will become of the O'Briens now that Mary's gone?"

My mother, Mam, reacted to Grandma's death the way she reacted to anything stressful—she got sick. She fainted on the bus on her way to work and an ambulance brought her to a hospital in downtown Philadelphia, where she struggled for the next three weeks to get over a case of pneumonia. The school principal, the neighbors, my aunt Colleen, and I feared she, too, would die, leaving me to tend to Pap for the rest of my life. Pap was, as Grandma Mary liked to put it, "a wee bit slow in the head," and he spent the weeks Mam was in the hospital going out of control—out of *my* control. Of course, Aunt Colleen, who lived in a mansion with her husband, a brain surgeon, and had a cook and a housekeeper to run her house, had to stop by and check up on us just when things were at their worst. Grandma Mary had always kept her kitchen tidy, with the coffee and flour and sugar and pastas in jars on the counter, her pots lined up by size hanging on the wall next to the stove, and her dish towels stacked in the drawer next to the sink, but the day Aunt Colleen stepped into the kitchen she found the place turned upside down. Pap claimed he had been trying to invent a flying saucer, but what he'd ended up with was sugar all over the floor, soaking-wet dish towels in clumps on the counters, SpaghettiOs in the dish-towel drawer, and all the pots under the table filled to overflowing with water. I was standing in the midst of his mess, my hands full of soggy spaghetti noodles, and Pap long gone, when Aunt Colleen happened to enter.

"Well, what is going on here, James Patrick? Do you know your father is up on the roof singing to that cheap plastic Nativity set some idiot has hoisted up there? He could fall off."

"Larry Seeley," I said.

"What?" Aunt Colleen took another step into the kitchen, her high-heeled shoes making crunching noises in the sugar.

"Larry Seeley put the Nativity set on the roof."

"That friend of yours? Why—"

I turned to face her. "No, not Timmy—Larry, the older brother. The one on drugs. And who knows why around here anymore. Pap said something about wanting Mary and Joseph and the baby in heaven with his mother, so Larry gets

4

the great idea of putting them up on our roof for all the world to see. I was at school when he did it."

Aunt Colleen, who dressed in what Mam liked to call the Queen Elizabeth style—suit, hat, and purse—set her purse on the table and tiptoed over to me, shaking her head. "If your grandmother could see this place now...I told your mother at the funeral and now I'll tell you, you should put your father in some kind of group home. It was a crazy idea, her marrying Patrick in the first place. She married your grandmother as much as she married Patrick, anyway."

I'd heard all this before, how Mam had been born with a hole in her heart and was always so sickly as a child. I knew the first ten years of her life were spent indoors and mostly in bed. I'd heard how Grandma Mary, neighbor to Mam and her family, used to walk over to their house with Pap in tow and give Mam her lessons at home so she wouldn't have to go to school and pick up any new germs that might have been floating around. Aunt Colleen made it sound ugly, saying that Mam married Pap so she could be cared for and comforted by Grandma Mary the rest of her life, but Grandma Mary had always made the story sound sweet and good.

"Yer mam loved spending her days with yer dear pap and me," she'd say in her high Irish voice. "Even when she went off to college she never forgot us, and when she came home for the holidays we'd build us a tent out of old sheets and some chairs, same as we did when yer mam and dear pap were young things, and the three of us would sit under it and tell stories and eat chunks of chocolate fudge, yer mam and pap's favorite.

5

"Now, I remember very clearly yer mam sayin', 'Oh, I wish it could always be like this, just me and you and Patrick. I wish the whole rest of the world would just go away.' And I says, 'Aren't ya happy then, Erin,' and she frowns, almost ready to cry, and tells me about college and her family and how she just doesn't fit in anywhere. I hugged her and said how we'd always be there for her, and I could see by the grateful look in her sweet blue eyes that she knew it was true."

Mam got sick again just before her college graduation ceremony and had to go back home to recuperate. That's when Pap proposed to her. He'd seen the movie *The Sound of Music* and had the idea that he could be the captain and Mam could be Maria. Aunt Colleen made Pap's marriage proposal sound like a whim, but again, Grandma Mary made it sound sincere and good.

"I told yer dear pap how marriage was different from the way him and me lived together," she'd said. "I told him it was the way his father and I lived together, but yer dear pap was set on marrying yer mam and one day when I thought he was just in the garage tinkering, the way he does, it turns out he'd gone over to yer mam's with a handful of weeds and flowers he'd picked along the way, and he just went up to her bed, where she was resting and sipping on some tea, and asked would she marry him, and lo and behold if the child didn't say yes."

I didn't know what to say to Aunt Colleen when she suggested putting Pap in a group home, so I didn't say anything. I just gritted my teeth and cleaned up around her while she stood in the kitchen, never offering to help, and telling me how we were going to have to shape up, face the music, get with the program, step up to the mark, and every other cliché she could think of along those lines.

That night, after Aunt Colleen had left and I'd straightened out the kitchen, more or less, I went outside and joined Pap, who lay on the grass staring up at the now-lighted Nativity set. Grandma Mary had purchased the life-size set with the lightbulbs inside each figure one Christmas when I was about five years old. Dear Pap and I loved to stare at it all lit up at night so much that Mam and Grandma Mary decided to leave it out year-round. Eventually the paint wore off and I grew up and got tired of seeing the white plastic figures clumped on our back lawn like a mound of snow that never melts, but dear Pap loved it still.

That night I sat on the grass next to Pap's long body, the heels of my feet resting in two of the holes Pap had dug, and stared up at the glowing white shapes. For a long while we just stayed together, watching the Nativity scene, and the spring air grew thick and damp around us and I got cold. Still, with the seat of my pants getting wet and the chill bumps hard and sore on my arms, I found myself feeling calmed, my anxieties about Mam and my frustrations with Pap melting away, as if Grandma Mary were there resting her hand on my shoulder and whispering to me, "Hush now, hush now, James Patrick." I wondered if Pap felt it, too, if Pap heard Grandma Mary speak to him, if that's why he hung around the Nativity set so much. Then I asked him, my hand pounding the cold, damp earth in the hole next to me, "Pap, how do you feel now that Grandma Mary's gone to heaven?"

Pap didn't say anything right away, and I dug my fingers into the dirt and ran them up the wall of the hole, feeling the grit clumping beneath my fingernails. At last he said, "I'm thinking I'm all alone now me mam is in heaven. I'm all alone now, James Patrick."

His words startled me, stabbing into the night air the way they did. With those words he cut out of me that chunk of truth I had been hiding from myself, the truth everyone else seemed to know—neighbors, Mam, Aunt Colleen, even the teachers at school. The whole meaty truth was that without Grandma Mary, we, each of us, felt left all alone. We had no safe place anymore. Grandma Mary was our safe place, our warm hearth, our helping hand, our listening ear. She was the open arms welcoming us home, the gentle heart, the bountiful pantry, the loving voice. Grandma Mary was everything good that touched the deep-down goodness of our own souls and brought it to light.

Pap's words were so true that I couldn't even lie and say to him, *But, Pap, you have us, me and Mam. We're still here, we're your family, too.*

We weren't a family anymore. We were like three abandoned children wandering the house and the halls of the hospital, each one orbiting in his or her own misery. Since I couldn't lie, I didn't say anything to Pap that night. We just stayed there side by side, each alone, and like everyone else, I wondered, *What's to become of us now that Grandma Mary's gone?*

Chapter Three

★

WHEN MAM CAME home from the hospital after a three-week stay, I tried to put all my anxieties behind me. I thought now that she was home we could begin to put our lives back in order, and Pap would settle down.

I'd never seen him act the way he acted those first few weeks after Grandma Mary died. One time when we went shopping I asked him to get us some laundry detergent and he dashed off down the grocery store aisle with coupons from Grandma Mary's coupon wallet flying out behind him. Ten minutes later I heard his voice at the other end of the store shouting, "Hail Mary, where's me boy gone? Hail Mary! Hail Mary!" and when I caught up to him and tried to get him to hush he said, "Hey, yer not me mam, and I'll be doin' what I please." Then he took off down the aisle again and crashed into the creamed-corn display. I had to pick up all the cans, so people gave me, and not Pap, their dirty looks when they had to navigate their carts around them.

At night Pap would climb up on the roof and sing Christmas carols at the top of his lungs, and again, if I tried to get him to come down, he'd shout, "Yer not me mam down there, so go away." "Yer not me mam" had become his response to every request I made. Worst of all for me was that he'd take off on his bicycle early in the morning before I woke, instead of going to mass the way he used to do with Grandma Mary, and he'd stay away for hours. I'd have to go looking for him, sometimes missing my classes at school, which made me furious. I had final exams coming up and I needed to ace them.

I had to ace everything, always. It was the only way I could prove to myself and everyone else in town that I wasn't Pap. People thought because we looked a lot alike that we were alike. True, we were both thin and had long bodies. We both had blue eyes and wild hair that could only be tamed by shaving it all off, but neither one of us, with our long faces, looked good in hair cut too close to the head, so we kept it long. There were differences, though. My hair was red and his was brown, I had freckles and Pap didn't. Beyond that, if all a person did was look in our eyes they'd see right off the difference between us. My gaze was keen, focused, and Pap's glance was slow, his focus just off center, as though he could draw in the object to be seen only so far, and no farther. You could never feel satisfied that he had taken in the whole picture, the total view.

However, during those three weeks that Mam stayed in the hospital, we were alike. If Pap ran, I ran after him. If he shouted in a public place, I shouted for him to keep quiet. We were acting just alike, and I couldn't wait for Mam to get well, but it didn't take long after her return to realize things would not get back to normal.

I had had Pap bake a loaf of soda bread for Mam's homecoming. Grandma Mary had taught him how to bake the bread, and he could do it on his own as long as someone reminded him to take it out of the oven when it was done. The bread baking calmed him down so much I wished I had come up with the idea sooner. I would have had him baking bread all day. I cooked Mam SpaghettiOs, just about the only thing I knew how to make; but Mam barely touched her food that first night home and she left the table early, saying she still had unpacking to do. I followed her and watched her from the doorway of her bedroom. She moved from suitcase to closet, bent forward as if her back hurt too much to straighten. She'd lost so much weight that the pants she wore had bagged out at the hips and thighs, and her shoulder blades poked out beneath her spring sweater like elbows. Worse than her thinness, though, was the way her whole personality had changed. She had become quiet and withdrawn, even secretive, and she seemed to want nothing to do with cither Pap or me.

The old Mam was open and lighthearted, always happy to see me, to spend time with me. My favorite times were when Mam would invite Pap and me to go with her to the creek. It curved around the back of our small neighborhood like an arm gathering and caressing our tired homes, and to us it was paradise. We would tuck the peanut-butter-and-jelly sandwiches Grandma Mary had prepared for us into our jacket pockets and spend the day there. In the summer we'd go to the deeper section and swim or fish. Pap was a good swimmer and loved it more than anything. Mam didn't swim but sat on the bank drawing wildflowers in her sketchpad, happy just to be outside in the fresh air.

We'd examine every blade of grass, every clump of dirt, every wildflower. And I, loving order and rightness in all things, classified all our findings on index cards.

When I was six, I got hold of Grandma Mary's recipe file, dumped the cards with words on them in the garbage, and created our first file with the blank yellowed cards that had been crammed at the back of the box. I made a list of all the insects we had seen, working long and hard at keeping my words within the narrow lines of the cards.

Grandma Mary dug her cards out of the garbage and gave me a swat on my bottom for dumping her treasure, but the next day she bought me my own file box with two sets of index cards. I continued with my insects and then moved on through the animal kingdom, writing down names, habitats, diets, et cetera, and filing the cards alphabetically according to species. At eleven I worked on the plants, going beyond our little universe at the creek, and growing anxious at the thought of the existence of so many plants. If I lived forever, I thought, I could never list them all. Still, I continued to try—labeling and ordering the world, somehow believing if I could name it all, put it in its proper category, I could control my own fate. I believed I could understand the order of the world, God's order, God's reason, the way the nuns taught it in school, and then I wouldn't have to fear the chaos and randomness of life.

It was a fear that had grown out of my need to understand my dear Pap, and yet I couldn't understand. What had happened to him? Why was he born slow? Why couldn't he be like everyone else's father, like my friend Tim Seeley's father? How could it happen? How could I stop it, change it, fix it?

I thought I could order the world, write it down on a piece of paper and file it away. Then Grandma Mary died. I dumped all my index cards, sixteen packed file boxes' worth, into the garbage. I realized life was all about randomness and chaos.

Mam continued to ignore us those first few days after she came home from the hospital. She acted restless. I'd see her pacing in front of her bedroom window, standing beneath the crucifix over her doorway, staring at it for long periods of time, and then wandering outside to stare at Pap's holes, scooping up the birdseed he'd dumped in them from Grandma Mary's forty-pound bag, and running it through her fingers. She took long walks and wouldn't say where she was going or when she'd be back. Worst of all, though, she'd race to the phone every time it rang, and I knew who she was waiting for. I'd seen it when I'd visited Mam at the hospital her last week there. I'd seen the way she'd get when it was time for Dr. Morris to visit.

"Hand me my makeup bag, would you, JP," she'd say, setting aside a well-read copy of *Philadelphia* magazine. Then she'd pull out her mirror and look at herself, powdering the freckles on her face, smoothing down her red hair, shaping it on her shoulders just so, and adding another coat of lipstick to her lips.

"What are you getting yourself all dolled up for him for?" I asked her once. "Why should he care what you look like? He's just your doctor."

Mam was still dabbing at herself, holding the mirror higher and closer to get a better look. "He's lifted my spirits the past couple of weeks, the very least I can do now that I'm feeling better is make myself presentable."

I didn't like it. I didn't like the way her eyes shone when he entered the room, or the new familiar way they talked to each other. He called her Erin and she called him Mike. Mike Morris, built like a soccer player, had dark curly hair, bushy brows, and broad hands with fingers that seemed to touch Mam too often and linger on her arm, her shoulder, way too long. He had a way of looking at her that I'm sure wasn't professional. His brown-black eyes studied her, stayed on her face so long it made me squirm and sweat. There were three other patients in the room with Mam, but when Dr. Morris was there, you'd never know it. She had me draw the curtain, for privacy, she said, for when he listened to her heart—another thing he did way too often, all of a sudden.

I felt like a helpless kid, dancing around the bed, talking too much, interrupting their conversations, sitting on the bed next to Mam so that Dr. Morris wouldn't. I talked about Pap as if he and I were just having the greatest time at home together. I brought up stories, Mam and Pap stories. "Hey, Mike"—if Mam were going to be familiar, so was I—"did you ever hear about how my mother and father got together? It's a sweet story, it really is."

Mike told Mam about the opera *Tosca*, which was playing in town that next month, and right in front of me he said, "We'll have to go, Erin. It's always nice to have an opera buddy. I hate to go alone, don't you?"

"Oh, she hears operas all the time, don't you, Mam?" I

said, jumping into the conversation before Mam could give her answer. "Yeah, she and Pap play tapes and dance all over the house to the operas, don't you, Mam? Tell him. Tell him how Pap will grab you and say, 'I love you, I love you, I love you,' a million times."

I had hoped Mam's infatuation would end when she left the hospital, but it didn't. It was as if she were walking around holding her breath all the time, only letting it out when the phone rang, then holding it again when the caller wasn't who she'd hoped it would be.

His call came three days after she got home. I stood close by, at the kitchen window, pretending to watch Pap staring up at the Nativity set while Mam talked, chattered, laughed, played with her hair, and said a couple of times, her voice lowered, "I can't talk about that now, I'll let you know later."

Finally, after several days of this kind of call, I figured it was time to have it out with Mam, to make it clear that she was a married woman and if she didn't like who she'd married, it was her own fault.

Mam sat at the kitchen table and listened to me rant, her hands folded in her lap and her ankles crossed, her feet tucked halfway under her chair. She acted patient with me, the way she often did with Pap, and this infuriated me even more.

"Okay," I said. "I can see you're not listening to me. You're treating me like Pap, but you're the one acting like him. You're the one who looks foolish, not me."

Mam coughed and closed her eyes a long minute. Then she opened them and said, "Come on, let's go on back to your grandmother's room a second."

She took my hand, but I pulled it away. "No, you go on and get what you need, I'll wait here," I said.

"I don't need anything. I just wanted to talk to you."

"I thought we were talking. Why are you trying to change the subject? Why do we need to go to her room?"

"Because her room will become your room. You're finally going to get your own room, a real room."

"No. Why? I like the room I have now. I like sleeping on the porch. I've never complained, have I? I don't want Grandma Mary's room."

Mam took a few seconds to look around the kitchen. She blinked her eyes several times and I saw the tears welling up. "JP, every room is Grandma Mary's room. This is Grandma Mary's house. Look at these stenciled cabinets, those lacy curtains—they're all hers, they're all her. You can't live in her old room, JP, and I can't live in her house. Do you understand?"

"No." I backed away from her. "What do you mean? You don't want to move, do you? That's not what you're saying, right? You want to change things some, change the wallpaper or—or the curtains." I looked around the kitchen at all of Grandma Mary's things, and I couldn't imagine the room any other way, with any other wallpaper, any other cabinets. I thought to myself how this was her house. I could still feel her presence in every room. I could smell her fresh-brewed coffee, her peach turnovers, her molasses cookies. The smells had wafted into every room, into every corner and crevice in the house, and settled on the carpets and curtains like a mist. They were there in the house forever, Grandma Mary was there—and that was all the more reason not to leave, not to move. We couldn't move. Where would we go?

"We've got to move, JP," Mam said, breaking into my thoughts. "I've thought about it, and it's the only right thing I know how to do."

"But it isn't right. You've lived in this neighborhood all your life, and Pap—Pap's lived right here, right in this house. How will he survive without— This is all he knows. This is my house, too. I was born here."

"JP, let me tell you something. When I married your pap—well, I married your pap because I loved him. I love dear Pap very much, you know that. But you see, I had been sick, I had been afraid, and I knew a safe place. Here. This was the safe place, with Pap and Mary. It was home because she was home. She created such a haven for us, for all of us, and Pap and I—we've lived like children, we've never had to grow up, have we?" She looked at me, her head tilted, a sad, please-understand-me expression on her face.

She continued, "Then you, JP, you came along and I thought, *Now, now I'll have to grow up, learn to cook, learn to be a mother.* But Mary took care of that, too. She was your mother and I was your friend, your best friend. 'Just you and me, JP,' remember? Remember how I used to say that to you?"

I didn't answer her.

Mam sighed. "I think Mary was just happy to let me take over playing with Pap, the everyday playing with Pap, and I've been happy to do it. I wanted to play, to spend my days outdoors with Pap and do all the things I missed out on when I was growing up. So that's what I've done. But then— well, then your grandmother dies, doesn't she? And here we are. Here we are without her."

Mam took my hand again and pulled me toward the hallway. "Come here, I want to show you something."

"I don't want to go in her room," I said, leaning away from her.

"No, not her room, the living room."

I followed Mam and she took me to the closet where Grandma Mary kept the vacuum cleaner. Mam opened the door and next to the vacuum were a pair of Grandma Mary's shoes. A pair of navy pumps, the shoes she died in, though Mam had had her buried in her white ones to match her favorite dress. I stepped back from the closet.

"I put them in here," Mam said. "I couldn't look at them. More than anything else in the house, her shoes make me the saddest. They're waiting for her, for her feet, and I'm waiting, too, for her to fill them again—because you see, James Patrick, I can't. I can't fill them and I know—I know you want me to, expect me to. Everyone expects me to, and I can't."

I shook my head and Mam nodded back at me. "Oh yes, JP, I've noticed you watching me, hating me almost. We were friends, you and I, but now what? What are we now to each other? I don't know how to be your mother. You want me to bake and say motherly things and knit sweaters and cook dinners just like Mary's, but I can't. I don't know how to cook. I never learned. I never had to learn."

Mam closed the door, and I stuffed my hands down in my back pockets. I didn't want her dragging me somewhere else that I didn't want to go.

"We need a fresh start, JP, and I have a plan. A really marvelous plan."

Chapter Four

★

"I'LL BE RIGHT BACK," Mam said, leaving me standing in front of the living room closet. I closed the door and waited for Mam. When she returned she had in her hands the *Philadelphia* magazine she'd thumbed to death back at the hospital. She flipped it open to a page in the back. "Read this," she said, handing it to me.

CONTEST. Send $200 and a 500-word essay: Why I want to own this house. 1840s stone farmhouse, slate roof, 6 bedrooms, 4 fireplaces, country kitchen, LR, DR, parlor, two-story sunporch all glass, some repair required, overlooking woods, small cabin, close to town—New Hope, PA. Winner announced Aug. 1.

I looked up from the ad. Mam's eyes danced, her face beamed like a child's. And I felt old, as old as Grandma Mary.

I handed her back the magazine. "This isn't real, Mam. This is one of those come-ons. You'd just be throwing two hundred dollars down the drain. Sorry. We'll get used to it here. I'll move into Grandma Mary's room and we'll be all right again, you'll see. You can learn to cook. All of the recipes are in her file, and—"

"No, JP," Mam interrupted. "No! I've already mailed off my essay. I mailed it yesterday, with the two hundred dollars. I wrote it in the hospital." Mam blushed. "Mike helped me. See, I've already made plans. That's what I wanted to tell you, what I couldn't talk to Mike about over the phone because I hadn't told you yet. He's going to send out a real estate agent tomorrow. He's going to help us sell this place, and we're going to move into that farmhouse."

"Mam! That's crazy. I can't believe Dr. Mike didn't stop you. Even if this thing's for real, what makes you think you'll win? You've just thrown away two hundred dollars. And what do you think 'some repair required' means? The place is a dump!" I spun away from her. "I can't believe this! I can't believe this! What are we going to do way out in New Hope? My school is here, your work's in Philadelphia. New Hope's at least an hour away from here. I can't believe this!"

Mam let me rant on, and the next day and the day after she let me sulk—while a couple of real estate agents walked through our home, while one man came out to make an estimate on the cost of fixing up the yard and another to make an estimate on painting the house. She told Pap her plans and the two of them locked arms and jumped up and down in the kitchen, and for the millionth time I wished Grandma Mary were still alive. They thought nothing about the reality of the situation. Mam acted as if she already owned the farmhouse, telling neighbors where we were moving, describing the house but not showing them the ad or the picture; she didn't want any more competition. She began to clean out our rooms, all except Grandma Mary's bedroom. She said she couldn't bring herself to go through all of that yet, and I said I thought she was probably feeling guilty.

"You go in her room and she's in there. You know it, you can feel it. You know she's angry."

"JP, that's nonsense," Mam said. "That's ghost talk and I don't believe in ghosts. I'm not feeling guilty at all."

Meanwhile the painter came and slopped white paint on our house. The house had always been yellow, but Dr. Mike's real estate agent said white would sell better, so they painted it white. The yardman dug up our whole yard, turning over the earth, planting grass seed, blocking off the area with a foot-high fence and a sign saying KEEP OFF. Pap ignored the sign and the fence, walking there often and lying out on the dirt every evening to look at the Nativity. He'd come in later with clumps of dirt dropping off his backside as he walked, and smelling of manure. Mam bought him a folding beach chair and told him to set it out on the sidewalk so the grass could grow; we couldn't live in the big stone farmhouse if the lawn here didn't look nice.

Then Larry Seeley, my good friend Tim's druggie brother, started hanging around Mam. He had been living in the city, but while Mam was in the hospital he'd come back home, claiming he was clean. Then his parents kicked him back out of the house when Mr. Seeley caught him in the bathroom popping some pills. I guess he had nowhere to go, so he came to our house. He sat in Grandma Mary's kitchen, puffing away on his cigarette, flipping back his long hair, or pulling on the strands of denim around the holes in his jeans, and talked to Mam about vegetarianism as if it were some kind of religion. He talked about cruelty to animals, fats and hormones and other serious problems associated with eating meat, and brought over some vegetarian cookbooks from the library.

Within a few short days, he had convinced Mam that meatless was the way to go. We became lacto-ovo vegetarians, which meant we drank milk and ate eggs but no meat, poultry, or fish. Mam started cooking us all kinds of tofu and seaweed foods Larry recommended, and I couldn't decide if Mam was a bad cook or the food just didn't taste good. But I did know that I didn't appreciate Larry butting into our business.

Mam had bought a wok to cook in instead of using Grandma Mary's frying pans, and a food processor to take the place of Grandma Mary's mixer, and I asked her how we could suddenly afford all these purchases, how we were going to pay the painter and the yardman when she hadn't even gone back to work. Mam said we had lots of insurance money from Grandma Mary.

We were using her money to buy our way out of her house. The whole thing seemed wrong to me.

When Aunt Colleen found out what was going on, she came over to set Mam straight.

"I hate to say it," she said, "but next to marrying Patrick, this has to be the stupidest thing you've ever come up with."

Mam took a sip of her coffee, nibbled on a fortune

cookie, then folded her hands back in her lap. She was giving her the Dear Pap treatment, patient, waiting, letting Aunt Colleen have her say.

"Really! A house in New Hope. Do you think they'll just give you a house for two hundred dollars? The whole thing is rigged. They collect the money from a few thousand people from all over the country, and then they give the house to a relative. Honestly, baby, you haven't got a prayer.

"Now, there are some cute little houses in Langhorne I could show you. Little Capes that are just as charming as can be."

Mam shook her head. "No, I'll take the stone farmhouse in New Hope."

Aunt Colleen stamped her foot. "But that's just it. You can't *take* it. No one's going to *give* it to you. You think it's just that easy? You think people hand over big old farmhouses every day, because you want one? You've got to earn it. You've got to go out and earn the money. You can't just sit here expecting everything to be handed to you. Mary O'Brien's dead. Our parents are dead, and our only brother's a monk locked up miles away from here. You're not going to be coddled anymore, Erin. It's time you woke up."

Dear Pap came into the house then and heard Aunt Colleen's voice. "It's Colleen!" he cried. He shuffle-ran into the living room and hugged Colleen, squeezing her around her arms and waist. Aunt Colleen squirmed in his arms, trying to break free. She made a face as if he smelled bad.

"Patrick, that's enough. I'm so very glad to see you, but that's enough." Pap let go of her and she pulled down her suit jacket and fussed with the bracelets on her wrists. "You need to learn to control your emotions better, Patrick. Do you know what emotions are?"

Aunt Colleen always tried to teach Pap something when she saw him. I believed she thought if she could just get hold of him for a couple of weeks she could turn him into a genius.

Mam told Pap to have a seat and help himself to a couple of cookies. Pap sat down and dug right in. He loved this new discovery of the fortune cookie. He hated the taste, said they tasted like soap, but he loved the fortunes. One day he got into the cellophane bag and broke open all the cookies, jammed the fortunes down in the pocket of his khakis, and claimed he had the most good luck in all the world. Mam said she wasn't going to buy another bag until every last broken cookie was eaten, so Pap got me to eat them all. Since then I've never cared much for the cookies or the fortunes.

Aunt Colleen watched Pap grab a handful of the cookies, examine them, and then put all but two back. She shook her head and said she had to leave.

"But think about what I said, Erin," she added, scurrying stiff-legged in her narrow skirt to the front door. "You could buy yourself a nice little home, a real step up from this place. I agree with you there, you do need to move. This neighborhood's been going downhill for years."

Even though she was somewhat on my side about the house issue, I felt glad to see her leave, and so did Mam. But still, Aunt Colleen was better than what came after her. The real estate agent set the FOR SALE sign up in our yard and we had a steady stream of nosy people touring our home.

I tried to make myself as scarce as possible. School had ended. I had taken my final exams, got my As for the year, and said good-bye to some teachers I prayed I'd get to see again the next year. I spent a lot of time playing basketball down at the school, or hanging out back at the creek with Tim Seeley, either fishing or pitching stones. When I got hungry or needed a rest, I went to the Seeleys' house, not mine. I felt like Pap, running off every day, but I didn't think anyone would miss me.

Mam had started taking driving lessons from Dr. Mike. She had gone back to work, so they met in the evenings three times a week. Mam even managed to squeeze a dinner into the deal, leaving me and Pap to fend for ourselves. Pap never thought about food unless someone called him in to eat, so I didn't concern myself with giving him dinner anymore; it was Mam's problem.

Then one night, coming home from the Seeleys' and feeling good about just sitting around having a real father-son–type conversation with Mr. Seeley, I discovered Pap sitting outside in his beach chair staring up openmouthed at the Nativity set, his back hunched forward, his hands dangling off the armrests. I remembered what he'd said to me the night I'd gone out to talk with him when Mam was in the hospital—"I'm all alone now"—and seeing him sitting there I felt his loneliness, and my own guilt at having been so happy to spend the evening with Tim and his father. I sat down on the concrete next to him. "Have you stopped roaming, Pap?" I asked. "I hope so. I've missed you."

Pap sat quiet for a minute, and then he said, shrugging, "I'm tired is why. That's all. I'm tired."

I looked at his face in the pale light of the Nativity, and he looked so serious, as if he were considering something deep, as if he were Mr. Seeley, and I felt more guilty than ever because I had wished earlier that night what I had wished a hundred times before, that Mr. Seeley, and not Pap, were my father.

Although Pap claimed he was staying home more because he felt tired, I wondered if Pap felt jealous of the amount of time Mam spent with Dr. Mike. I noticed that he didn't hug Dr. Mike when he saw him, and Pap hugged everybody. He hugged me just about every time he saw me, even if we had been apart for as little as five minutes.

Dr. Mike would ride up in his sporty BMW and honk the horn for Mam. He never came inside our house. At first Pap used to come out to greet him and try to talk to him through his car window. He even asked if the doctor would teach him how to drive.

"I can ride a bicycle, you know."

"Yes, Patrick, I'm sure you can," Dr. Mike said, running his hand over one of his curly eyebrows as though trying to smooth it down.

"Yes, I can, but you don't think so, and I know that you don't, but I can too ride a bike and I'll show you."

Pap ran to fetch his bicycle out of the garage and Mam came out of the house ready for her driving lesson.

Dr. Mike put the car in Drive and I told them to hold on, adding for Mam's benefit that Pap said he wanted to show Dr. Mike that he could ride a bike.

Dr. Mike sighed and Mam, looking first at him and then at me, said, "Tell Pap I'll watch him when we get back. Mike only gets a couple of hours, and it's so nice of him to spend them teaching me how to drive." Mam set her hand on Dr. Mike's leg—just for a second, but I caught it.

Dr. Mike pulled away with a nod of his head, and out came Pap on his bike. He raced down the street after them, his baseball cards sputtering in the spokes of his wheels. He called, "Hey, wait for me!" and Mam stuck her head out the window and said how great he looked and that she'd be home in a couple of hours.

After that, Pap stopped visiting with Dr. Mike when he drove up, and if Pap happened to be sitting in his beach chair at the time, he didn't bother to turn around and wave. He didn't even startle when Dr. Mike sounded his horn.

I tried to talk to Mam about the driving lessons and dinners, to question her about what was going on between her and Dr. Mike, and Mam said I read too much into things. "You watch too much television," she said.

"I don't watch any television, and you know it. Your saying that just shows how guilty you are. You're reaching, Mam. Pap knows what's going on, and if he knows then so does everyone else."

"What? What do you think is going on?" Before I could answer she said, "I'll tell you what's going on. I'll tell you what it's all about."

She started breathing hard and making this wheezing sound, gulping in air every few words.

"When Mary died, I didn't know—I didn't know what I was going to do. I don't know how to care for your father and you all by myself. I told you that. When I got sick I was so depressed, lying in that hospital bed. I'm always sick, always lying in some bed. I felt so desperate, I couldn't get well. To tell you the truth, I don't think I really wanted to get well, and then Mike—Mike saw—he knew what was happening, and he brought me the magazine, the one with the contest in it. He talked me into entering it. He gave me something to look forward to, and I told him I couldn't—I couldn't do it, I didn't know how, and he said, 'I'll be there.' Just like that. That's all it was, but I knew he meant it, and not in any wrong or sexual way, JP. He said, 'I'll get you through it. You don't have to worry.' And that's all this is. In a month or so he'll stop coming by altogether. But right now he's teaching me how to drive and he's just being there for me for a while. He's just being a friend."

Mam's voice had quieted down the more she spoke. When she spoke of Dr. Mike her voice got soft, and I tried not to read anything into the change in her tone. The wheezing had stopped, but then she got herself all excited again, the veins in her neck bulged out, and she said, "And I've heard enough about how stupid that contest is. Let me dream, JP! Why can't you just let me dream? What does it hurt anybody? Does it really hurt you for me to say we're going to win? If we don't win, we'll move somewhere else, but that dream has been the sole joy in an otherwise dismal spring. Let me have my dream!"

And so I did. I said nothing more about the contest or Dr. Mike, but I felt hurt that it was Dr. Mike and not me and not Pap who had made her happy, who had brought her her only joy in an otherwise dismal spring.

Chapter Five

ON SATURDAY MORNING, July 31, the day before the announcement of the winner, Mam couldn't sit still. She paced the floors from the kitchen through the living room to my porch and back to the kitchen. She answered the door when no one had rung the doorbell and kept dialing a number on the phone and hanging up halfway through, forgetting who she wanted to call. We were all on edge, even Pap, and when he came in from the garage and joined us at the kitchen table for lunch, he spotted the soy sauce bottle still on the table from the night before and, without thinking about it, shook it as if he were mixing salad dressing. The cap was loose and Mam had removed the little plastic piece inside that prevented her from pouring out too much (Mam loved soy sauce on everything), and the soy sauce flew out of the bottle and splattered all over the kitchen. It hit the lace curtains and the area rug, and seeing this, seeing the mess everywhere, Mam jumped up from the table and yelled at Pap for the first time in her life.

"How could you be so stupid? Look what you've done! This isn't our house anymore. We sold it. Can't you keep a room tidy for one minute? Must you wreak havoc everywhere you go? Digging up our yard and costing us a fortune, tracking in creek mud every day that I've got to clean up, over and over. Get out! Get out of the way and let me clean this up. Both of you!"

Pap had jumped out of his seat and was standing in the midst of the mess and Mam's tirade with his body hanging forward, his arms limp, his head drooping. Mam had said to get out and he just stood there, crying.

I got up and hugged him. I told him it was okay, it was an accident. His arms still hung at his sides. I twisted around to Mam and said that I'd buy some new curtains. I still had money left over from working at the skating rink over the Christmas holidays, money I had been saving to buy a computer, but it could wait.

"They're from Grandma Mary's *Country Curtains* catalog," I said, my voice a monotone. "I'll order us a set." I turned back to Pap, who had leaned his forehead down on my shoulder.

Mam came up to the two of us. "I'm sorry. Patrick, I'm sorry." She placed her arms around us, and Pap lifted his head. Sweat trickled down to the end of his nose.

"I hate you today," he said, wiping at his nose with the sleeve of his shirt. "I don't want to be here anymore." Then he pulled away from us and left the house. Mam and I followed his movements through the windows, watching him walking toward the creek.

I turned to Mam. "Nice going," I said. "I hope winning that stupid house is worth it." Then I left and headed for the Seeleys' house.

As I approached their front yard I saw Tim sitting on his steps talking with, of all people, Bobbi Polanski. I had never used the word *hate* much—Grandma Mary had always said it was an ugly word—but if ever I felt the emotion it was with Bobbi. She was a year ahead of me in school, two years older in age, and the neighborhood dictator. To get on her bad side was to find yourself the butt of her jokes and insults, and often in the creek fighting for your life. She was the only person I'd ever known who got kicked out of Saint Ignatius, and back when it had happened, rumor had spread around our fourth-grade classroom that Bobbi had said the *f* word to Sister Elizabeth.

Grandma Mary was the only one who felt sorry for Bobbi. She said it was a real pity, that Bobbi was a "smart wee thing," and she told me to be sweet to her because Bobbi had led a hard life. That was when I learned about her father. He'd always been scary looking to me, but I didn't know until then that he beat her—not that anyone had ever been able to prove it. Grandma Mary had called a state social worker once and had asked the worker to come out to the Polanskis' house, hoping she could get Bobbi's abusive father arrested, but Bobbi wouldn't admit anything to anyone and after two more visits the social worker never came back.

Grandma had warned me to be nice to Bobbi, but it was hard when she'd made it her life's mission to goad, tease, and otherwise make my life miserable.

Our most recent run-in with each other had occurred a few days before Mam had come home from the hospital. It was nighttime, well past dinner, and I hadn't seen Pap all day. Finally, when he did come home he stood in the kitchen doorway with his shoulders hiked and his arms held away from his soaking-wet body. He smelled of beer, but he didn't seem drunk, only cold and upset.

"Pap," I said to him, trying to sound calm, "whoever you're spending your time with isn't a nice person to you. I think you should make some new friends, but what do you think?" I added that last bit to keep him from responding with, *Yer not me mam!*

"He isn't a friend anymore to me, 'cause he's dead anyway."

"What's that supposed to mean?" I asked, the anxiety in my voice obvious.

"That Pauly Stinson boy fell over dead," Pap said. "I told her he was dead, but she says no, he's just passed out, but I don't think so."

"Who? Who, Pap? Who were you with? It's important, because we want to be sure no one is in trouble."

Pap stepped inside the kitchen and closed the door. "Pauly Stinson, I already said it was him already." He kicked off his shoes and water ran out of them.

"You been in the creek?"

"Yup. He tried to baptize me when I said I already been baptized, but he baptized me again and held me under the water a real long, long time. Maybe six hours I was under there, is how come I'm wet and all." He pulled off his shirt and wrung it out on the kitchen floor.

I reached forward and grabbed the shirt out of Pap's hand. I tossed it in the sink, saying, "Pap, you're making a mess on Grandma Mary's floor."

"Well, she won't mind," he said, tiptoeing out of the puddle he'd made.

I grabbed a sponge and got down on the floor to sop up the water. "Did you push Pauly Stinson in the creek?"

Pap sat down on the floor next to me and wiggled out of his pants. The dark hairs on his skinny white legs lay flat, as though they had been stroked with a comb.

"He was already in the water, 'cause when he baptized me he got in the water so he could hold me down good and long."

I took Pap's hands in mine and looked in his eyes. "Pap, tell me, when did Pauly fall over? When did he look dead?"

"After he baptized me with water he baptized me with beer and he was laughing and I was laughing and then he stopped laughing 'cause she was yelling at him and then he just fell over." Pap nodded. "He just fell over and he didn't say anything. He just fell over like me mam. Just like me mam." Pap looked at his feet, still in the wet socks covered in mud. He wiggled his toes.

"Who, Pap? Who was yelling at Pauly?"

"That pretty Bobbi girl that you don't like but I do and so does me mam."

"Bobbi Polanski was there?"

"Yup, and she said he's not dead, just passed out. But I don't think so." Pap shook his head.

I stood up. "I'm going to go talk to Bobbi. You stay here, okay?"

"Hey, yer not me mam, you know!"

I pointed my finger at Pap and exploded. "Stay here! You don't go anywhere. Just do it; Pap!"

Pap got onto his knees and crawled away from me. I left before I saw where he went. I stormed out of the house, intent on wringing Bobbi's neck. It was one thing giving me grief but another thing entirely to pick on Pap. How low could a person sink?

I didn't go to Bobbi's house. I knew it was too early for her to be there. Her father worked the late shift. He wouldn't be home until three in the morning, and her mother always went to bed early. That gave Bobbi four more hours to roam the streets.

I found her, as I did the afternoon Pap spilled the soy sauce, hanging over the railing of the Seeleys' front steps with a cigarette pinched between her fingers and talking to Seeley as if the two of them were great friends. Seeing them together infuriated me even more, and I clenched my fists and called out to her from down the street.

"Polanski!"

She and Seeley looked up at me, watching me approach.

"I figured you'd come looking for me, O'Brien. Nice zit," she said when I reached the steps and she could see me under the stoop light.

"Named it after you, Polanski," I said, my jaw set tight. "Now, what did you and Stinson do to my father?" I could feel my nostrils flaring like a bull's and I felt like one, as if smoke were coming out of my nose. When I said the word "father," my voice broke and I felt tears stinging my eyes. It made me even angrier. I asked her again, louder, no break in my voice this time, "What did you guys do to my father?"

Seeley looked at the two of us and said, "Hey, what's going on? What happened?"

Bobbi took a drag off her cigarette, then flicked the butt at me. "I just saved his life, pus-face."

She backed away from the railing and turned to leave, and I charged, tackling her onto the Seeleys' lawn.

Seeley stood up. "Hey!"

I sat on top of her stomach and pinned her arms back as if I were wrestling one of the guys, one of the stronger ones.

She kneed me in the back and I fell forward over her, but I held on, squeezing her wrists.

"Is Pauly Stinson dead?" I yelled in her face.

"No, you moron!" She spit at me, and I squeezed her wrists harder.

"Tell me what happened!"

"You won't find out this way," she said, bucking me off her with both her knees ramming into my back and both her arms jerking to the left, throwing me off balance. She twisted herself out from under me in one slick move and gave me a good kick in the ribs.

"Hey!" Seeley called again.

"I saved your father's life!" Bobbi shouted at me. "I found Stinson holding him under the water and I saved that retard's life." She drew in her breath, and I realized she was crying. "And don't you ever"—she kicked me again—"*ever* touch me. *Nobody touches me!*" She screamed this last bit and kicked me one more time before Seeley yelled for her to cut it out and finally pulled her away from me. I stayed on the ground tucked in the fetal position until I was sure she'd left. Then, without saying anything to Seeley, I limped on back home.

So that afternoon when I headed down the street, wanting to get away from Mam and the soy sauce, and found Bobbi hanging over the railing of the Seeleys' steps once again, hate and shame rose up in me so fast I stopped dead in the road and whipped around without saying a word and headed toward the creek. I couldn't run the risk of wanting to hit her again. As angry as I was, I felt guilty for attacking her—not that I didn't think she deserved it, but I hated the way I'd lost control that night.

I had always prided myself on being in control of my emotions, and my life. It's what I did best. I set a course for myself and I followed it: Get straight As, take every honors course, make the honors society, become class valedictorian, and attend Princeton University. These were my goals and never had I strayed until that night. I hated what she made me do.

Later, when I returned to the house, I found Pap and Larry sitting on the roof in the midst of the Nativity set.

Even from that distance I could tell Pap had a sunburn.

"Pap, you're frying up there."

"Hey, JP, it's Larry is here, look."

"Hey, kid," Larry called down, not looking at me but at the top of the Virgin Mary's head.

"Hi, Larry. What's up?"

Larry chuckled and smiled at me. "We are. Why don't you come up and join the party?"

"What's going on?" I asked, wondering if Larry was high.

Pap stood up and raised his arms and face to the sky. "I'm the Three Wise Man!" he called out.

I ran closer to the house. "Pap, sit down. You'll fall. Larry, make him sit down."

"Hey, down there," Pap said, "yer not me mam, you know, and I'll be doing what I please, 'cause yer not me mam."

Larry tugged on Pap's arm and Pap sat down. Then he called down to me, "Larry's a Three Wise Man, too, and so can you be if you come up here."

"Yeah, come on up," Larry called down. "You've got to see this."

"See what?" I asked, coming around to the side of the house where the trellis leaned against the freshly painted wall, its legs sunk into the ground much deeper on the left than the right. I shook it. "Is this thing safe?"

Pap stood up and walked to the edge and looked down at me. "You can do it, me boy, and I'll be here to catch you if you fall."

I started up the trellis. "Gee, thanks, Pap."

Larry laughed. I climbed up to the roof of the porch, which was as far as the trellis took me. Then I walked down to the edge where that roof met the main roof, careful not to look over. I grabbed on to the edge of the upper roof and swung my leg up, hoisting myself with my arms, and climbed on. "There's got to be an easier way," I said, crawling up the steep incline toward the top. I settled myself behind the Nativity set next to Larry, who slapped my back.

"No sweat, eh?" Larry said.

I took a deep breath and looked around. I'd never been

on our roof before. I loved climbing trees, but it had never occurred to me to climb on the house. Grandma Mary never would have let us.

Then I caught sight of what Larry must have meant when he said I had to see something. "Pap," I said. "What's all this stuff? Hey, there's my Swiss Army knife. I've been looking all over for that. And Grandma's shoes."

Pap nodded. "Her dying-in shoes."

"She really die in those?" Larry asked.

"Yeah," I said, looking over all the loot Pap had stashed back behind Mary and Joseph and the Baby Jesus. "There's my baseball cap Grandma Mary gave me for my birthday. And your good pen that she bought you. And the serving spoon. Mam's going to have a fit when she see's all this. Hey! The iron egg skillet."

Larry slid down toward the Three Wise Men. "That's not all," he said, standing and lifting up one of the figures.

"Your fortunes from the fortune cookies, and Grandma Mary's rosary beads, and her knitting needles." I turned to Pap, who was looking down on the objects with a strange, wistful smile.

"Pap, Mam would have let you keep these if you wanted. We don't have to get rid of all of Grandma's stuff."

He looked at me, his face brighter, his plump cheeks red from the sun. "Oh, I don't want to keep these, anyway."

"No, he doesn't want to keep them," Larry agreed, chuckling to himself and lowering the figure. He made his way, crawling, back up to us.

"I told you, I'm the Three Wise Man."

"Yeah?" I said, waiting.

"These are my gifts of treasure for the Baby Jesus, of course, James Patrick, and you should know that."

I smiled, looking over Pap's head to Larry. "Yeah, of course," I said.

The phone rang in the house. We all paused and listened. It stopped ringing after three rings and I asked, "Is Mam home?"

Pap stared down at his feet and nodded. There was a long silence and then we heard a scream. It got louder. Mam came running out of the house from the porch and screamed again. By then I had figured it was a scream of delight, an *Ahhhh!* kind of scream. The three of us stood up. Mam looked up, surprised to find that now we were three. Then she raised her fists in the air and screamed again.

"I won! I won the house. I won!" She started jumping and skipping, ignoring the stay-off-the-grass sign.

"I did it! I won the house! I won the contest!"

The three of us cheered and slid down the roof to the edge to get off.

When we'd all reached the ground, Mam stopped jumping around and ran to us, hugging the three of us, and we all laughed and cheered, and they jumped around in a circle as if they were playing ring-around-the-rosy bunny-hop style, while I looked on, the upsets of the morning forgotten. Even I felt victorious. Maybe Mam was right. Maybe this was exactly what we needed. We could move to New Hope and settle down to a new life, one without Grandma Mary but still a good life. Three cheers for us!

Chapter Six

★

THE OFFICIAL ANNOUNCEMENT of the winner came out the next day, August first, just as the ad had promised. Our local newspaper's reporters showed up at our house to photograph us and to get a story. Half the neighborhood got in on the picture. Nothing this great had ever happened to any of us, and it was a celebration for us all.

I caught Bobbi Polanski watching the action from her porch, half hidden by a post and peeking out from behind it, gnawing on a fingernail. I felt so full of goodwill, I almost called her to come on and get in the picture, but I caught myself in time and didn't.

Pap, who had spent most of the night in agony from his sunburn, still wore the wet washcloth that Mam had folded and placed on his forehead, pinning the cloth to an old apron string and fitting it to Pap's head so it would stay on without his having to hold it. Aspirin and the wet washcloth kept him cool and quiet. His nose had blisters on it. The newspaper reporter took Mam aside and asked if Pap were Mam's brother and did he have to be in the picture? Mam called to Pap, put her arm around him, and said he was her husband and that he would stand right next to her for the picture, washcloth and all.

I felt proud at that moment and wished Dr. Mike had been there to hear it. But then when they wanted a picture of just me, Mam, and Pap, I couldn't do it. I couldn't be in a picture with Pap looking like that, with the caption identifying the man in the washcloth as my father. I managed to wander out of sight for a while and then wander back around when they had given up on the idea of a family photo.

Mam had notified Dr. Mike that she had won soon after she had come out screaming to us. He said he'd meet us out at the farmhouse the next day when Mam went there to meet the owner and take the scheduled tour. That's when I found out that Dr. Mike, most conveniently, lived in Washington Crossing, just minutes from New Hope.

Larry Seeley offered to drive us up there for the house tour. I was surprised when Mam agreed to go with him, but then he had a large van, almost a bus, that seated eleven people. It was an old wreck of a thing, painted a dull flat brown, with a rag coming out of the gas tank, a major rust problem across the front just below the windshield, and several bumper stickers on the rear doors and windows asking us to save the environment, whales, earth, rain forests; ride a bike to work; love the color green; and be at peace. Mam, Pap, Larry, Tim, Bobbi Polanski, a couple of friends of Grandma Mary's, and I all rode in the van, black smoke puffing out the back, obscuring all the bumper stickers and Aunt Colleen, who followed behind in her Mercedes.

When Mam had called Aunt Colleen to tell her that she had won the contest, Aunt Colleen said nothing good would come of a house gotten by such means and Mam had better watch out. "Remember, if it sounds too good to be true, it usually is," she said. "I don't have a good feeling about this. No, not at all." Then she asked when she could see the house and Mam told her we were heading out there the next morning, so there she was, following the van in her Mercedes.

The greatest part of winning the house was seeing the change in Mam. She had become a new person. Overnight she had grown more confident. She stood tall, proud, her feet barely touching the ground. She had filled out her clothes since her illness, and the warm sunshine had given her good color in her cheeks. Her eyes, flashing first here, then there, smiling for the camera, smiling at her neighbors, held a light, a sparkle in them I'd never seen before. Mam had become this beautiful, gracious stranger.

We drove through the main street of New Hope, past the playhouse, the boutiques, and the art galleries, past the pricy restaurants and the bed-and-breakfast inns—and it was as if we'd entered another country, so different was it from our charmless street with its pawnshop and Laundromat, the car wash, the Chinese take-out, and McDonald's. What were we doing here?

More reporters were waiting for us when we rolled up the steep, tree-lined drive of our new home. Pap bounced in his seat and his voice croaked with delight. He poked his arm out the one window that was stuck halfway between up and down and waved to the people on the lawn.

The cameras flashed while Mrs. Levi, the cheery-looking woman who had placed the ad and chosen the winning essay, introduced herself to us. The reporters asked her why she chose Mam's essay over the more than 3,075 entries, and she said she liked the line Mam had used from Harpo Marx because it had always held a special meaning for her as well. She said, "Mrs. O'Brien wrote that she wanted a house filled with love, and when she came home from work each day she wanted to see 'a face in every window' smiling out at her." Then Mrs. Levi smiled openmouthed at Mam and grabbed both of Mam's hands and squeezed them. "I've had good times with my family here. I know you will, too. I knew when I read about you wanting a face in every window we were kindred souls." Mrs. Levi pumped Mam's hands and Mam nodded, tears welling in her eyes.

I thought it was a strange thing for Mam to have said, considering there were just the three of us, but it worked, and I liked the part about the house filled with love. It made me think of the old days with Grandma Mary.

We walked the grounds first and discovered that a cabin came with the property, along with a two-car garage that would hold all of Pap's junk, and then some, and that had a basketball hoop attached above the garage doors.

The cabin stood at the bottom of the sloping lawn, about twenty feet into the woods. The owner said it had been built in the early 1800s and had always stood right there on the property. The original family probably lived in it while they were building the main house. We peeked inside, saw some missing floorboards, among other things, and moved on; but

Larry stayed behind and I wondered if he had gone in there to pop a few pills or to sniff cocaine. He stayed in there during the rest of the outside tour.

We discovered that more woods, deeper and thicker, lay beyond the lawn at the back of the house. When we saw this, Mam and I looked at each other at the same time, both of us delighted, both of us thinking about our days at the creek, and Mam nodded and I felt a wave of relief wash over me. Everything was going to be all right. Mam, Pap, and I could settle down to a quiet life in our house with woods and lawns, flowers and fruit trees. We could roam the woods in search of deer tracks and raccoons, watch the changing seasons, hunt for interesting rocks and wildflowers. Yes, it would be all right.

Dr. Mike arrived in time for the house tour and I could tell by the quizzical expression on his leather-tanned face and his raised bushy brows that he was surprised by Mam's behavior. I think he believed he was going to be "Dr. Mike, action hero," come to rescue his damsel in distress. But Mam stayed in the lead, talking with the owner, asking questions, with the reporters and photographers trotting behind her scribbling in pads and looking for photo opportunities. The rest of us followed behind them, forgotten by everyone except Mam, who would turn to us when she saw something wonderful and exclaim, "Isn't this perfect?" or to me and Pap, "Won't we have fun picking our pears?"

There were three pear trees, a cherry tree, and a large and very old oak tree that stood near the cabin and had remnants of an old treehouse clinging to it.

We followed Mam up the stone walkway to the house, a light gray stone structure two stories high. Four windows jutted out from the roof, making me think that the attic space had been turned into more rooms. The house was longer than it was tall. It had black-painted shutters on the windows that looked as if you could really use them, and a deep porch running across the front of the house. The owner had set out rockers and other chairs, all painted a fire-engine red, and there was a table with a checkerboard painted on top. I wondered if we would get to keep them. Then Pap threw himself in one of the chairs and with great energy rocked back and forth and called out, "Is this mine, too? Erin, is this mine, too?"

Everyone laughed and so did Pap. He tried all the chairs out and asked again, "And is this mine?"

The owner, Mrs. Levi, said she was leaving some furniture and yard equipment behind, since she would be moving to a much smaller place; and I think both Mam and I were glad Pap had asked, since neither one of us would have and we both wanted to know.

Mrs. Levi opened her front door and stood in the entranceway, allowing us to enter ahead of her. Dr. Mike pushed his way through the group and caught up to Mam. Mam gave him a hug and introduced him as the one who had convinced her to enter the contest. The reporters gathered around him and he grinned and struck a few poses, hoping, I guess, that someone would take his picture. No one did, but he got to the head of the line and toured the house right beside Mam, as if they were husband and wife, as if this were their new home.

A couple of times I caught Dr. Mike gazing at Mam instead of the rooms we were supposed to be viewing, and I knew that he was seeing what I saw, the new Mam, the beautiful, well-mannered, most gracious and charming woman. And I saw, too, that he was in love with her.

I wasn't an expert on romantic love. I had had just two girlfriends in my life, both of them back in seventh grade. It didn't take me long to realize, though, that being in love had used up all my brain power and I was starting to make mistakes in my homework. I'd given up on love, but Tim Seeley fell in love all the time, and the expression he wore whenever he was smitten was similar to the one I saw on Dr. Mike's face that day, and I realized then that no matter how old you got love always wore the same face.

Watching Dr. Mike made me ill. I knew I needed to do something—attack the man, create a distraction, have a seizure—but these were just thoughts, ideas, plans I knew I'd never put into action.

I followed Mam and Dr. Mike like a shadow, knowing I was a coward and reminding myself that anytime I did confront something head-on, such as the time I attacked Bobbi Polanski, I came out the loser.

Mrs. Levi led us from room to room, upstairs and down, and out to the sunporch off the living room, which looked out over the backyard. I counted the fireplaces, making sure there were four, as the ad had said. I counted four, all right, but two of them, said Mrs. Levi, didn't work. The best one was in the kitchen, a tall, wide stone fireplace big enough to stand in, with black pots, the kind used for witches' brews, hanging over a stack of logs. Herbs collected from the garden just outside the kitchen entrance hung down in bunches around that fireplace. The fireplace also had what Mrs. Levi called a beehive oven. She said she still baked bread in it. Pap stuck his head inside it and called hello. He played with the door latches in every room, ran his finger along the stenciling on the walls, and stood where the wide pine floors creaked and he rocked back and forth on them, humming along with the noise.

Aunt Colleen, who had strolled through each room with her arms folded and a sour look on her face, decided it was time to take Pap in hand. But Pap had become overexcited by all the people and the trip out, and he broke free of Aunt Colleen, shouting, "Hey, yer not me mam!" and took off running through the house, squealing with delight.

Mam excused herself and asked if she could walk the grounds again with just Pap. Then she made her way past the rest of us and went to him. I saw the reporters shake their heads and one of them said, "That poor woman," and Dr. Mike replied, "Indeed."

Seeley and I went out onto the porch and found Larry sitting in one of the rocking chairs, watching Mam and Pap holding hands and walking toward the cabin. He looked up at us when we came out, nodded at his brother, and asked, "How's it going at the homestead?"

Seeley shrugged, and I could see that he didn't want to talk to his older brother. Larry had always been the misfit of the family, the poet in a family of football stars. Mr. Fresca, one of the sophomore English teachers, used to call him Hamlet because he was always so moody, and the nickname stuck. From there, kids started asking him where his tights were, since Hamlet wore tights, and then the rumor got started that he was gay. Tim Seeley hated his brother for the embarrassment he caused him at school and the turmoil he caused at home, fighting with his football-coach father all the time. Mr. Seeley called Larry a loser, the black sheep of the family.

When Larry asked him how it was going at home, Tim didn't answer. He jumped off the porch and headed down toward Bobbi Polanski, who stood at the bottom of the sloping lawn, shading her eyes and staring up at the house.

I looked at Larry, who watched his brother and fiddled with the hoop earrings in his ear.

"So, uh, I hear you're not living at your parents' house anymore," I said, preferring to talk to Larry rather than join Bobbi Polanski on the lawn.

He shook his head. "I'm in the doghouse."

I nodded, tried to chuckle, be cool.

He rocked back in his chair and pulled his hair forward and began braiding it. "No, really, I'm in the doghouse," he said. "I'm sleeping back of the McCloskys' place, in their old doghouse."

"Are you serious?"

He finished braiding his hair and tossed it over his shoulder. "Hey, I've slept in plenty worse. It's big enough. They used to have a Saint Bernard. I take a crap in the woods when I need to, wash in the creek—I do okay."

"Yeah, I guess," I said, not knowing what else to say.

He stood up and stretched, looking down at me at the same time. "Don't look so worried," he said. "I'm like a cat; I've got nine lives and I always land on my feet."

"Maybe," I said, wondering what it would be like to be someone like Larry, to have lived his life. "But how many lives have you already used up?"

He turned to me and made a fist, and I wondered for a second if he were going to punch me, but he smiled and just gave me a nudge. "You've got a point," he said, not answering the question. Then he added, "I like you, O'Brien. You're smart, aren't you?"

I shrugged, pleased for some reason that he liked me.

He stuffed his hands in the pockets of his cutoffs and leaned against a post. "So did Timmy tell you about what happened?"

Now I'd done it. I should have left with Tim when I had the chance. I didn't want to get in the middle of a family feud.

I looked down at the floor, pretending to study the gray-painted floorboards. "Not really," I said. "Just something about your father seeing you with some—uh—pills, I guess."

"Vitamin pills. They were vitamin pills."

"Maybe," I said.

He shook his head and pulled out a pack of cigarettes from the pocket of his T-shirt. "Man, I'll never be able to live there again." He took a cigarette out of the pack and lit it, stuffing the box back in his pocket. He took a few puffs and looked out at my parents. Pap was spinning around and around while Mam stood watching him, talking to him. Some of the other people had drifted out, coming from around the back of the house to where they stood. I looked for Dr. Mike but didn't see him.

"You've got great parents," Larry said, surprising me. That's one thing I never expected to hear from anybody and knew I'd never believe myself, much as I loved them. "They just let you be, don't they? They just kind of live for the moment. It's great."

49

"Your parents are pretty good," I said, and then added, "Your father's great."

Larry flicked his cigarette ash over the side of the porch and squinted at me. "You good at sports?" he asked.

I shrugged. "I'm okay, I guess, in basketball."

Larry shook his head. "No good, two strikes against you. You're mediocre, strike one, and you like basketball, strike two. Now, if you were really great in basketball, that would put you in neutral territory, but you see with Dad, with my great, wonderful, slap-you-on-the-back, how-ya-doin' father, you'd better be great at some sport, preferably football, because that's all that counts."

"I don't know. He's nice enough to me," I said.

"For a friend of Timmy's. For a neighborhood buddy. It would be a whole different story if you were his son."

"Yeah, maybe."

Larry tossed his cigarette down on the wooden floor and mashed it with his foot. "You say 'maybe' a lot. Aren't you ever sure of anything? Don't you *know* anything?"

I could hear the irritation in his voice.

"I know you're living in a doghouse," I said.

He snickered. "Yeah, I sure am." Then his expression changed. He looked worried, even scared. He looked out toward the cabin again. "They'll never let me change. To them I'll always be Larry the dropout, the dopehead.... They were just looking for me to slip up. I take a few vitamin pills and it's the perfect excuse to kick me out. I'm too much trouble, and I'm not worth the effort. Even I'll admit that."

Larry jumped off the porch. I watched him, long legged and lanky, walking toward Mam and Pap, and I thought

50

about the way he'd blown it, thrown his family away with the way he acted. I knew if I had his family, his parents, I'd do anything to stay with them. I'd do anything to keep a father like Mr. Seeley.

I looked across the lawn and saw Pap, dizzy from spinning, waver and then fall to the ground.

Chapter Seven

★

MAM AND THE contest were a one-week wonder, and then all the hoopla ended. Everyone went back to whatever they were doing, and we got down to the business of planning our move. Mam held a yard sale and sold at least half of our furniture.

Pap and I walked every day to the grocery store to pick up any cardboard boxes they were willing to hand us, and together we packed up the house.

Mam enrolled me in the public high school out in New Hope. I had never been to a public school before, only Catholic schools. Mam said it was too late for me to apply for a scholarship at a Catholic school nearby, which is the only way she could send me, so for at least my junior year I'd be attending the public school.

We didn't see Dr. Mike but a few times that August. He came to give Mam a few more driving lessons, but since we were so busy with the move he did most of his visiting over the phone, always late in the evening, always when I had gone to my room for the night.

Larry, who had never given me or my family the time of day until that summer, came over every day to help us pack and to talk to Mam. It seemed to me that in just a few short months, ever since Grandma Mary's death, she had replaced Pap with Dr. Mike and me with Larry. While Pap and I did the grunt work, sorting and packing the junk in the garage, arguing over what should go and what we should throw out, Mam and Larry sat laughing and talking over their plates of hummus and tabbouleh, figuring out the logistics of the move.

I never told Mam that Larry lived in the McCloskys' doghouse. I didn't want her feeling sorry for him.

I asked Larry once if he ever planned on getting a job to support himself, get himself out of the doghouse, and he said he still had plenty of money. I asked him where he got it, and he said he used to sell drugs on the streets. I didn't know whether to believe him or not. Why would a drug dealer own a beat-up van? I thought they drove around in Cadillacs or limousines. Why would he live in a doghouse instead of renting a place? But I told Mam about the drugs, thinking she ought to know what kind of a person she was really dealing with.

"Don't let him fool you, Mam," I said to her. "All the Seeleys say he's nothing but trouble. You don't know all the things I know about him, but believe me, he's dangerous. He could get Pap hooked on drugs. Think of what that would be like."

"Now, why would he want to do something like that?" Mam had asked.

I shrugged. "I don't know. Why would he sell drugs? He can't have much of a conscience if he's going around doing something like that."

★

ONE NIGHT LARRY came to the door. Mam and I answered it at the same time. Larry looked at the two of us, then said, wiping at his nose, that he'd come to talk to Mam in private. Mam shooed me out of the room. I didn't like it, but I headed back to the porch. I heard Pap come inside, and Mam told him to go on to bed and she would be there in a while. Pap left and the voices in the kitchen got low and whispery. I turned on my radio and flipped through a copy of *Sierra* magazine, waiting for Larry to say what he wanted to say and then leave, but after a couple of hours of flipping through magazines and then playing myself in a game of chess, I got tired of waiting and headed back out to the kitchen.

I could see them from the living room. Mam and Larry stood hugging each other, and I came to the entrance to the kitchen and just watched, waiting for them to realize I was there. Larry stood facing me, but he had his head buried in Mam's shoulder, his hair mixing with hers.

Larry lifted his head and saw me first, springing back from Mam as if there were a coil between them. His cheeks were wet and flushed. He turned away from me, holding his head down, not saying anything. He grabbed a napkin off the counter in front of him and blew his nose on it.

Mam turned around to face me, surprised. She grabbed up her hair and flipped it off her shoulders. I noticed a wet patch on her right shoulder.

"JP, is everything all right?" she asked.

I stared at her a good minute, saying nothing, amazed that she had asked me what I should have asked her. Then Larry, with his head still bowed, keeping his face averted, said he ought to get going and fled before Mam could stop him.

Mam looked at the door and I looked at her. She stood with her arms crossed, shaking her head and licking and biting on her lips.

I took a deep breath and let it out. Mam turned toward me.

"What's going on?" I asked. "What did he want?"

"He just wanted to tell me about himself, JP."

"What about him?"

"About his life, what it's been like for him."

"What what's been like for him?" I asked, knowing that through his brother, Tim, I probably knew as much as she did about him.

Mam massaged her shoulder. "I'm sorry, JP. If you want to know more than that, ask him yourself. Now, I'm very tired. I'm going to bed. We've got just one more day before the move, and I've got my driving test in the morning." Mam moved toward me, holding out her arms as if she wanted to hug me. I glanced at the wet spot on her shirt and backed away. I turned and shuffled off to my room. Then Mam called to me and I turned around, standing just inside the room.

"Larry's going to be coming with us," she said. "He's going to be living with us in New Hope. He needs a place to stay."

I looked at Mam standing in the light of the kitchen, and I stood in the light of my porch, but the room between us, the living room, was dark, and the distance across that darkness, immeasurable.

Chapter Eight

★

THE NEXT MORNING Mam set off with Dr. Mike to take her driving test, and since she planned to drive Dr. Mike's BMW for the test, I asked her at breakfast if she figured on buying a BMW after she passed. We'd never needed a car before, we had the train station and the bus stop at the end of the road, and most of what we really needed was within walking distance.

Mam said that Larry had offered his van in exchange for his living with us. She said this with her back to me, leaning over one of the last boxes left to pack. What little talking we'd done that morning had been like that, our heads turned away from each other, almost as if we were talking through someone else who would then pass our message on to the other person. I knew that this time Mam kept her back to me because she thought I would think a beat-up van in exchange for a place to live was a stupid deal. I did, and I told her so while spooning the last bit of my cereal into my mouth. We only had the one bowl and spoon left out, so we ate in shifts.

Mam turned from the box and looked at me, ready, I realized, for a battle.

"That van is all Larry has to offer, and so I'm taking it. He said he'd keep it in working order, so what more do I need?"

"We're moving to a rich people's town, Mam. Rich people like Dr. Mike and Aunt Colleen. What will those people think if they see you driving around town in that thing? And then when they see Pap act up, which he will eventually, and find out Larry the drug dealer's living with us, what are they going to think?...Larry will probably start selling drugs on the streets of New Hope."

Mam's face got red and I could see her chest heaving. She set her palms flat on the kitchen table and leaned toward me. "That was an ugly thing to say. You listen, JP. I've never cared about what other people think, and I'm not about to start now."

"Well, that's obvious," I said, grabbing the cereal bowl and moving toward the sink.

"JP, what's wrong with you? What's going on? We're moving to a beautiful new home with woods that go on for miles. What could be better? You and I can—"

"You mean you, *Larry*, and I," I said, turning on the faucet and letting the water run as if I could drown out the sound of her voice and the clamor of my own thoughts.

"Larry? Is that the problem?"

"No, just part of it." I turned around to face her, letting the water run behind me. "It's this Larry thing—and—and..." I shrugged. I couldn't think of what to say. I just wanted her to tell me, explain everything without my having to figure out what it was I wanted to know.

"I won this house, JP," she said. "A whole big dream house. Now, I don't deserve it any more than anyone else, but *I* won it. So I want to share it—with you and Pap and Larry, whoever, not grab it and sit on it and keep people away. I want to share my good fortune. I believe in doing that, JP. Larry's giving me an opportunity to do that. He's really giving me another gift."

I rolled my eyes and turned back to the faucet. Mam came up behind me, reached around my waist, and turned off the water. She grabbed my shoulder and turned me around to face her. "Do you think that's corny? Stupid? What? Don't just roll your eyes. Tell me."

I wouldn't look at her. I looked at the sink instead. I yelled at the sink. "I care about what people think. I care, Mam. You and Larry and Dr. Mike—what are you doing? What about me and Pap? What about *us*?" I lifted my head and saw Mam's bewildered face. I wanted to cry. I wanted to tell her I didn't know what I thought or what I was feeling. I just knew that things felt wrong and I wanted them to feel right. I wanted her to hug me the way she had hugged Larry, and yet I knew that if she tried to touch me I would push her away.

Mam must have seen it, my weak moment, the moment when I thought I wanted her to hug me, because she moved toward me, and she lifted her hand toward my face. But I couldn't let her touch me. I bolted from the kitchen, slamming the door behind me and running toward the creek.

I stood ankle deep in the water and listened to Pap and Larry talking in our yard. Larry stood on the roof and Pap stood down below, shouting warnings to Larry about taking down the Nativity set.

"Don't break the lightbulbs," he said. "See, they got light-bulbs, is how they light up. See them, Larry? Don't break 'em."

I heard Pap shout to Mam when she left with Dr. Mike to take her test, and then I walked on, down the creek, moving from rock to rock, past the Polanskis', the Wallaces', the McCloskys' houses, thinking how this would be my last time at the creek.

I spent all morning wading in the water and examining the flora and fauna around me. When I got hungry I wandered down to the Seeleys', realizing it would be the last time I could just walk over and spend the day hanging out with Tim and his father. Mr. Seeley didn't get home from work until after five, and I looked forward to it all afternoon. I wanted to spend one last good evening with him, but the evening didn't go well at all. He was upset about Larry moving out to New Hope. He said Mam wasn't right in the head, first marrying my "retard" father and then inviting his own drug-addict son to live with her. "She's just asking for trouble," he said. "How's he ever going to learn anything if people keep bailing him out?"

I cut the evening short and, feeling irritable and disappointed, said my good-byes to the Seeleys and wandered on back home.

No one was there when I got to the house. I found a note Mam had left for me on the kitchen table. It said, "Gone for a drive in Larry's van. I passed my test!"

A few minutes later the van rolled into our driveway and all the doors opened at once. Larry got out of the front seat with Mam, and Pap and Bobbi Polanski hopped out of the back.

I stood outside on the stoop with my arms crossed, watching the four of them laughing, each one carrying a bag from McDonald's.

Pap waved to me. "We're going to have a picnic for our last night. Come on, JP, to the creek."

"I've already eaten," I said, waving, trying to look cheerful, casual. When had Bobbi Polanski joined the crew?

"Well, come on with us, anyway," Mam said.

I glanced at Larry snitching fries from his bag, and then at Bobbi, who was hanging back behind Pap. I saw that she had her arm in a sling.

"No," I said. "No, thanks, I've still got a box to pack."

Mam handed her bag to Larry and told them all to go on without her, she'd be there in a minute. Then she headed toward the house. I went back inside and hurried toward my room.

I didn't want to talk with Mam just then, but she followed me back.

"How long are you going to act this way?" Mam asked when she caught up to me. She stood in the doorway in her jeans and a T-shirt, her hair in a ponytail, and I thought she looked young. She looked young enough for people to think Larry was her husband.

I turned away from her and chucked my basketball shoes, my basketball, and the book on chaos and complexity I had been reading all into my last cardboard box. "Is Polanski living with us, too, now?" I asked, keeping my back to her and not answering her question.

"No, JP, but she's eating with us."

"What's with her arm?"

"Why don't you come out and ask her yourself?"

I threw a sweatshirt into the box. "You know, Mam, you have a knack for choosing just the people I happen to hate, who the whole town hates. That ought to tell you something, don't you think?" I looked up at her.

"Yes, it does. It sure does." Mam nodded and crossed her arms in front of her. She leaned against the side of the doorway.

"Mr. Seeley was right," I said, setting her up, wanting to hurt her.

"Right about what?"

"You're not right in the head." I pointed to my own head. "You're not all there. Mam, you go for every misfit and odd-ball that comes along. No, you don't just go for them, you marry them!"

I gasped, realizing what I had just said. I had gone too far. I could feel my face burning. I took a step toward Mam and tried to speak. "I—I—"

"You've said enough, JP," Mam said, backing away, her voice quiet. "Finish packing and get to bed. You need your sleep."

She left and I didn't call her back. I didn't say anything. I flopped down on my bed and just sat, waiting for the dark.

Chapter Nine

★

WE MOVED ON a Tuesday, Dr. Mike's free day. Mam insisted we couldn't move without him. We used a U-Haul truck, and Larry, Pap, Dr. Mike, and I loaded it while Mam directed us.

I kept myself busy, trying, in a way, to make up for what I had said the night before. I acted extra-nice to Pap, even when he dropped my box with the microscope in it that Grandma Mary and Mam had given me for Christmas that past year. My only gift. I had written FRAGILE all over the box—not that Pap could read it, but Mam could, and Mam was the one pointing out which box went where and who carried it. Maybe she was getting even with me, having Pap haul my stuff, but I didn't let her see that it bothered me. I just picked up the box and said, "It's okay, Pap," and set it down in the truck.

I didn't speak to Mam except to say, "You want this in the back of the truck?" or "Should we set that box on top of the table?" I was all business to everyone.

Larry brought his radio and set it on the roof of his rusty van and turned it up full blast, drawing neighbors out of their houses to come watch the procession in and out of our front door.

Tim Seeley and Bobbi Polanski stopped by and helped awhile, Bobbi using just her one good arm. I tried to act more cheerful around them, as if I were having as much fun as the others. I didn't pull it off too well, though, and Seeley asked me at one point, "What's wrong with you, anyway?"

When it was time to leave we said our good-byes and Mam walked through the house one last time, dabbing at her tears with a McDonald's napkin left over from that morning's breakfast.

I said good-bye to Seeley. I told him to come visit and that next weekend wouldn't be too soon, and then I went down to the creek for one last good-bye. I stood looking down in the water, watching the minnows darting about in what appeared to be aimless activity, and I wondered if there were some creature larger than us, God maybe, who looked down on us and saw all our comings and goings and thought all our activities were aimless, pointless. I thought about randomness and chaos, my old fears. I thought about the way life was, and death. I thought about Grandma Mary just dropping dead in the middle of her bedroom, in the middle of blow-drying her hair, wearing her slip and panty hose and navy blue pumps. Her skirt and blouse lay on the bed ready for her, but *poof!* she dies before she can get to them. She dies with the blow-dryer in her hand and her hair half-wet and half-dry. She dies right in the middle of living. It made no sense. Life made no sense.

I turned around to leave and found Bobbi standing be-hind me. I hadn't even heard her.

"Hi," I said, and then added, "bye."

"Yeah, good luck in your new house," she said, shaking her head so her hair fell back behind her shoulders. I had always had the feeling that she did that so people would notice her beautiful hair, and it was beautiful. It was honey colored, like clover honey, and it was long and straight and looked very heavy, as if she had tiny weights hanging from the ends. She liked to swish it and swing it and toss it behind her with her head or hands, whatever got her the best effect.

I looked away, uninterested in her charms. Neither one of us said anything, and then I said, "Well, gotta go."

I passed her and headed for the truck. She said to my back, "You never liked me, did you?"

I stopped walking and turned around. "You never gave me a reason to, Polanski."

"Seeley likes me. You didn't know that, did you? We talk sometimes." She flicked her hair back again and adjusted the sling around her arm.

"I'm not Seeley," I said, catching sight of a bruise on her wrist. "So what happened to your arm?"

She laughed. "Fell. What else?"

"I can imagine what else," I said.

Bobbi studied the sling and I saw her expression change, turning inward, shutting down, and I flinched as if I'd heard the echoing slam of a dungeon door. I'd never seen a face change so suddenly. One second she was laughing at herself and the next she was gone—just gone. Then she became all smiles again, her dimples showing—more charm. "My dad rigged up this sling. Pretty nice, huh? Better than you'd get at the doctor's. Dr. Morris even said it was good work. He said Dad tied it just the right height for my arm."

Someone honked the horn and I looked back toward the house a second, then at Bobbi. "See you—sometime—then," I said, backing away.

She held out her hand for me to shake. "I just wanted us to part friends."

I stopped and crossed my arms in front of me. "Why?"

"Come on, O'Brien, we grew up together, that's all. No ulterior motive."

I leaned forward and shook her hand. It felt cold and dry and firm.

The horn sounded again and she squeezed my hand before we both let go. I stood there for a moment, puzzling over her gesture, but then the horn blasted three more times and I took off.

★

AT THE NEW house we discovered that Mrs. Levi had left us a heavy-duty riding mower, which Pap wanted to ride right away. He was supposed to be unpacking all his junk from our old garage into our new one, but he couldn't stop fooling around with the mower.

I got tired of arguing with him and went inside to unload some other boxes, ones without a lot of broken junk in them.

Mam told me to help Larry in the parlor. I didn't know which room she was calling the parlor, so I hunted for Larry and found him in the room with the piano. It was an old upright, taller than I and heavy looking. Mrs. Levi had said it was a Victorian piano. Someone had painted it a wine color. I went over and played a few notes. It sounded bad, as if I were playing it underwater.

Larry came up behind me and touched some of the lower notes. He had long fingers and the tips of them bent way back when he pressed a key.

"Maybe tuning it will help," he said, trying a scale.

"Yeah, maybe." I went over to one of the boxes and ripped the tape off the top.

"You know, I had this thought," Larry said, turning to face me. "We ought to get Pap to try this thing out. Who knows, he might turn out to be one of those idiot savants. You know, one of those people who have this one stroke of genius in them and then the rest of them is just—well— Anyway, I saw on TV this guy who could play the piano like Liberace, and he was retarded and blind but he had this one God-given gift, to play the piano. So maybe..."

I threw down the blanket I had pulled out of the box. "What do you think? You think you just discovered retarded or something? You think Pap's some new discovery? Don't you think Grandma Mary tried all those things long ago? He's forty-two years old. Don't you think Pap's already had a million tests? Pap is Pap, okay? You're not going to discover some hidden genius, or some great math skill, or...or... artistic ability. Can't you just let Pap be Pap?"

"Can't you?" Larry said, standing with his back to the piano, blinking at me.

"What's that supposed to mean?" I asked, but Larry didn't answer. He turned around and played "Three Blind Mice" with one finger. I went back to unpacking, tossing the stuff on the floor, and then Larry stopped in the middle of his tune and said, "Sorry, JP, you're right. I've never paid much attention to Pap before. Okay? But I like him." He turned and came over to the box where I stood and pulled out a picture of me, Pap, and Grandma Mary dressed up for my first communion. He studied it.

"I used to kind of pick on Pap," he said, setting the picture down on a side table that wobbled on the uneven floorboards. "Well, 'pick on' maybe isn't the right phrase. I used to like to fool him. Get him to believe things. I told him once that that set you've got, the Mary and Joseph and Jesus, the Nativity, came alive at night when we went to sleep. I told him we could never see it because they waited until everyone was asleep. He believed me."

" 'Course he did."

"Okay, I was stupid. Believe me, I've been paid back plenty in my life. Anyway, like I said, I like Pap. I'm not going to hurt him, if that's what you're thinking. I'm not going to give him drugs or anything."

I tossed the emptied box behind me and tore open the next one, happy to have something to rip into. "Did Mam tell you I thought that? Is she telling you everything I say?"

"I lied to you about selling drugs," he said, not answering me. He flipped his hair back off his shoulders and leaned over the box with me. He helped me to dislodge a rolled-up rug set in at an angle, pulling up on his end while I pulled on the other.

"I never sold, I just used, and most of the time I was too poor to even use. I came home because I got tired of living on the streets. I was a failure even at drug abuse."

We dropped the rug on the floor and unrolled it with our feet, kicking and stamping on it to flatten out the edges.

"I'm telling you this to make peace. I need a break, okay? Your mother's giving it to me. I won't mess up."

We both stared down at the rug, a braided coil of blues and browns.

"I need this family," Larry said, pointing his booted foot and smoothing down a section of the rug that had bubbled up.

I lifted my head. "We're not your family," I said. I left him then, returning to Pap in the garage.

The unpacking dragged on. Mam only got the one day off from her job, so we worked all day and into the night. The next morning Mam took Pap to work with her, driving the long miles into Philadelphia in Larry's van, and left Larry and me alone to finish unpacking.

I had saved my room for last. I wanted it to be just right. I wanted everything to have its own place, everything to be in order. I'd had first pick of the bedroom I wanted, not counting the one Mam and Pap chose. I'd picked one of the two attic rooms and prayed Larry wouldn't pick the other. I wanted to be as far away from everyone as I could get.

Mam had seemed disappointed. "I would think after spending your life out on that porch you'd want a real room, not some hot attic."

"It is a real room," I said, "and it has a fan and so does the room at the other end of the hall. I can set it up so one fan is drawing air from the other and it'll be plenty cool. Anyway, I like it up there."

Mam let me have the attic, and Larry, who said he had plans to fix up the cabin in the woods for his place, chose a large square room right next to Mam and Pap's.

My room had a slanting ceiling with a stone chimney sticking up through the center of it, dividing my sleeping area from my work area. Mrs. Levi had left behind two desks and three bookshelves. I got rid of the wobbliest desk and kept the other and the three shelves. I had plenty of books, my microscope, which Pap didn't break after all, a globe on a stand, my chess set, a rock collection, a small Indian arrowhead and artifact collection, and a bunch of medals and certificates I had won in school. I had parts of old science fair projects collected in a box and a topographical map of the creek and our old neighborhood that I taped to the wall. I fixed it so one side of my room looked just like a library, dark and hidden from view when I sat on my bed on the other side.

The house was the kind of place I figured would have secret passages, and although I had outgrown all the Hardy Boys stuff years earlier, I couldn't help but look around in closets and behind pieces of furniture, knocking on walls for a secret door.

I came backing out of one of the closets downstairs, one with built-in shelves that had the smell of a used fireplace in it, when I heard someone else knocking.

I decided it was Larry making fun of me and I called out to him. He came to the top of the stairs and yelled down to me, "What did you say?"

I stood at the bottom of the steps, about to answer him, then I heard the knock again.

Larry hung over the banister. "Go see who's at the door."

I saluted him and went to the door and opened it.

Bobbi Polanski stood before me on the porch, with one arm still in the sling and the other holding a grocery bag full of clothes.

"I lied," she said, setting her bag down.

"Huh?"

"When I said I wanted us to part friends. I did have an ulterior motive. I'm moving in."

"Huh?" I said again.

Larry trotted down the stairs and opened the door wider. "Bobbi? Are you okay?"

"Sure," she said, brushing past me and stepping into the house.

"Just come on in, why don't you," I said.

"Thanks. Get my sack, will you, JP?"

I left it on the porch and kept the door open.

Bobbi took a few more steps in and looked around at the living and dining rooms, neither one with any furniture in it yet, and then walked to the stairs and craned her neck to see up the stairwell. She had on a pair of low-cut jeans and a T-shirt that hovered just above her belly button. She sank her hand into her back pocket, turned around, and walked back toward us. She had a firm, square-shouldered, narrow-hipped body, and her walk was more of a stride, heavy on the heels. I'd always had the feeling that she'd make a great prison warden.

Bobbi looked at Larry. "Six bedrooms, right?"

"Yeah, uh, three unoccupied."

She looked at us both and grinned. "Nice place." She nodded. "Yeah, I think I'll like it here just fine."

"Not if I can help it, Polanski," I said. "What makes you think you can just shove your way into my house, anyway?"

Bobbi took her hand out of her pocket and set it on her hip. "I don't recall the newspapers saying your name was on the winning essay. Seems to me they said a Mrs. Erin O'Brien won this house."

I gripped the doorknob and wished it were her neck. "Nobody here likes you, Polanski, so why don't you just pick up your little shopping bag and get out."

Before Bobbi could snarl out her next retort, Larry's van rattled and quivered into the driveway and Mam and Pap hopped out.

"I got a job!" Pap called out. "I got a job. My first real-time job!" He looked up at me. "Going to the center is a job, isn't it, JP?"

I looked at Mam, but Mam wouldn't meet my eyes. She knew I'd be upset about Pap taking classes with her. Grandma Mary didn't want Pap taking those horticultural therapy classes down at the center where Mam taught, even if they were meant for people like Pap.

"He'd pick up nasty habits being around all those other brain-damaged people," Grandma Mary had said. "He'd start picking his nose in public or touching his privates, and we can't have that, you know. Anyway, they're not going to teach anything I couldn't teach him me own self, right here in me own home."

But, of course, Dr. Mike had to interfere, reminding Mam that Grandma Mary was dead now and that she needed to consider what was best for Pap and that Pap needed someplace to go during the day. He thought Pap really could get a job, someday, just as Larry had wanted Pap to learn the piano. Mam agreed, of course, and so it would be their own fault when Pap went along to the grocery store one day and decided to pull his pants down because he'd seen someone in his class doing it.

I was so upset just picturing the whole idea, I'd forgotten that Bobbi was with us. Pap came toward me with his arms out, wanting to hug me, and Bobbi stepped forward in front of me and hugged him first.

"Hey! It's Bobbi come to stay!" Pap said.

I glanced at Mam and I could tell she was surprised to see Bobbi, but she was also delighted.

Pap clapped and hugged me and Larry, then sat down in the rocker and began a rapid rocking, his fingers twitching on the armrests.

Bobbi walked over to Mam, who stood beaming at the top of the porch steps, and the two of them hugged. "I'm glad you changed your mind," Mam said, and then I knew that Bobbi had been invited. She had been invited behind my back, just as Larry had. Everything went on behind my back, mine and Grandma Mary's—a total betrayal.

"She can help me put up the Nativity," Pap said, rocking his chair hard enough to hit the wall behind him. "You know where we're going to put it?"

Bobbi turned from Mam, wiping at her eyes and said, "No, where?"

"Right above where you're standin' right now on this porch, is where. And it's flat up there so they won't fall off and get hurt. And you can be a Three Wise Man if you want to."

Bobbi nodded. "I can't wait," she said.

Mam twisted around, looking back at the driveway.

"Bobbi, how did you get here? I don't see a car."

Bobbi shrugged. "Oh, I just hitched a couple of rides." She set her gaze on me and added, "Thanks for *inviting* me to stay, Mrs. O'Brien."

"Well, we're glad to have you. There's plenty of room here."

Pap jumped up from his seat and hugged Bobbi again, squeezing her tight. "Isn't this so fun?"

Mam answered him. "We need to celebrate all this good news. Come on," she said to Bobbi, "let's pick out a bedroom for you, and then we can all go down to the kitchen and make ourselves a celebration dinner."

We all paraded back into the house, with Pap grabbing up Bobbi's bag and swinging it up onto his head.

"Hey," he said, "this isn't so heavy as the boxes we've been moving."

I entered the house last, kicking the front door shut behind me. The four of them continued up the stairs and I stayed behind watching them—this new thing my family had become, this monstrous entity with eight eyes and eight arms and legs, this oddball creature with one giant mouth that had devoured my real family.

Chapter Ten

★

WE ALL SPENT the next several weeks adjusting to our new lives. Everything was new: home, family, school, jobs.

I was the only one, however, who found the transition difficult. I felt as if I were drowning in a swirling pool of chaos. In school I stuck with what I did best, classes and homework. At home, though, life was a party that never ended, and Mam was the one keeping the party going. At first she just stayed up late talking with Larry and Bobbi, then she went out on more dates with Dr. Mike, coming in at all hours, and finally she created what she called all-night fun-a-thons. Mam, Pap, Larry, and Bobbi would dance to loud music all over the house, the way Mam used to do with Pap, or the group would read plays to one another, acting the parts, or watch movies, or play basketball. The next morning Mam would have to drag herself out of bed, gulp down several mugs of coffee, and set out for work exhausted before the day had even begun.

Then after one weekend when all she could do was sleep, I decided we needed some order around the place, and at my urging, Mam assigned us all jobs to do around the house. Mam gave me the job of head yardman, and I not only had Pap bugging me for rides on the mower, which I had to admit were fun the first few times, but I also had Larry telling me how to mow.

"If you mow it first one direction this week and then the other direction the next, you get a better cut. It's better for the grass," he said to me, hollering out the kitchen window. Making dinner was his job.

"You want to mow the lawn, be my guest," I hollered back. "Otherwise, lay off!"

That was Larry's and my new relationship. He kept trying to play big brother and because I didn't want him to, didn't want him to be any kind of brother, I fought with him, and in the process acted just like a younger brother. I tried to avoid playing this role, but the only way I could was to keep away from him and that seemed next to impossible. Somehow, wherever I went, Larry appeared—in the kitchen, in the living room, in the woods, at the cabin, out in the garage. He never sat still. I got so frustrated running smack into him every time I went out of my way to avoid him that I finally asked him if he were following me.

"No, you just happen to be where I need to go," he said.

"How could you need to go all over the house? You're everywhere. Can't you ever just sit?"

Larry sneered at me. "No, I guess not. Looks like you'll just have to live with it."

I also had to live with Larry's smoking. He had a cigarette bobbing between his lips all the time, while he talked, while he read, while he walked from place to place, even while he cooked. I'd watch him stirring some vegetarian glop in a bowl, or chopping vegetables, and he'd hold the cigarette in his mouth the whole time, letting the ash get longer and longer until I could see it about to drop off into the food, and I'd yell at him.

Larry would always say he was just about to deal with it, but I wondered if he just let the ash fall on the food and stirred it in with the rest of the mess when I wasn't there. How would we know the difference?

Larry kept a camera in the kitchen and took pictures of his creations, sometimes artistically arranging fresh vegetables around the dish to create a still life. At other times he'd ask me or Bobbi to hold up the dish and look as if we couldn't wait to eat it. This was true acting on our part. We knew that beneath the colorful beans and vegetables hid something dark and unidentifiable.

"Hey, it's good for you," Larry would say every time one of us rolled our eyes at the food he'd placed in the middle of the table. "It'll put hair on your chest, color in your cheeks, and pep in your step."

Bobbi would always say, "I don't need hair on my chest, what I need is a thick juicy hamburger with cheese and lots of ketchup."

Pap and I would agree, but Mam and Larry stuck to their seaweed.

Larry claimed these were healing foods that would repair the damage done to our bodies by the environment. This he said with the smoke from his cigarette billowing from his nostrils.

But as much as Larry irritated me, it was Bobbi who sent me over the edge. I wanted her out of our house. I spent every moment at home with my shoulders hiked, my eyes alert, my ears pricked, because I never knew what Bobbi would pull next. One moment she'd head off to school wearing my rain forest T-shirt, and the next she'd draw arrows on my globe with indelible ink, insisting that she'd thought the ink would come off!

She had picked the other attic room for her bedroom, and I felt certain she did it just to goad me, just to keep me from having the third floor to myself. At our old house we had one bathroom, and Mam, Pap, Grandma Mary, and I shared it with no problem. In the farmhouse just Bobbi and I shared the bathroom on the third floor, and we fought over it all the time. All I needed was ten to fifteen minutes a day in there, but they were impossible to get because Bobbi was always in it doing who-knew-what. When she came out she looked the same as when she went in, unless she went in to take a bath; then she came out all shriveled up from soaking for so long, gagging me with her overperfumed body.

We fought the most over the laundry, however. That was her job, and she felt it her duty and right to barge into my room without knocking and sweep my clothes off the floor even before my body heat had left them. I believed she watched me undress through the crack in the door and knew just when to come storming in. And I didn't like her looking at my underwear and my jock strap. I felt it gave her some unfair advantage over me.

Then I noticed one day that my jeans came back smelling unwashed. I banged into her room with the unfresh-smelling jeans in my hand and accused her of only doing half my laundry.

"You only wore those once," Bobbi said, lazing on her sleeping bag and flipping through a *People* magazine.

"Right, I wore them, now you wash them."

She sat up. "I'm not going to wash a pair of jeans that you wore only once. Who does that?"

"I do—Grandma Mary did."

"Why?"

Was she dim or was she trying to irritate me? "The same reason you wash my shirts and my—my other things."

Bobbi leaned back against the wall, picking up the magazine so it hid her face. "Bull. Nobody washes their jeans after one wearing. Next you'll be asking me to iron a crease down the middle. JP, you are so anal retentive."

"Okay," I said. "Okay, I'll wash my own clothes. From now on, just stay out of my stuff."

She shrugged. "Fine with me, no skin off my nose."

She lowered the magazine enough so I could see her eyes. "Wednesday is your day. Every other day is taken. Now get out of my room, your breath is making the paint peel."

I managed to do my laundry one time, but then I kept forgetting. After I had missed two Wednesdays in a row, I told her I wanted Thursdays.

"Forget it, JP. I've got a schedule to keep. How would you like it if I came along and stuck fresh grass in the lawn right after you cut it? Now, either do it on Wednesdays or let me do it."

I let her do it, swearing to myself that I'd find a way to get Mam to kick her out of our house.

Then one day I changed my mind.

It was a cold Saturday in October. Mam had gone out to lunch with Dr. Mike and afterward they were going to take in a few art galleries in town and across the bridge in Lambertville. When Mam announced this I didn't say anything; I just got up from the table and left. I went out to start work on the yard, and later Larry and Bobbi joined me.

"Slow down, JP," Larry had said to me, noticing the furious way I was attacking the leaves with my rake. Then after another minute, he added, "They're just friends."

"I know!" I said, shouting at him, still raking, catching bits of dirt and grass with the leaves. "You think I don't know?"

"Yeah, I think there's a lot you don't know."

"What's that supposed to mean?"

Larry didn't answer. He just raked at the leaves, working next to Bobbi and keeping his distance from me and my angry rake.

I worked over the yard until, breathless and exhausted and sweating in my T-shirt, I couldn't do any more. I stopped and took a look around. The brightness, the clear invigorating air, caught me by surprise. The leaves were at their peak, and we had reds and yellows and oranges fanning like flames above us in the sky and a sunset at our feet. Single leaves were floating down from branches, saucers of colored lights. I stood out on the lawn in the midst of this, rake in hand, dizzy with exertion and the swirl of brilliant colors around me. I had never seen an autumn so bright. In our old neighborhood the colors were muted, as if the dust and dirt of our lives settled in the trees there, coating the leaves.

The light, the colors, did something to me. They sent a shiver of peace down through my center, and I took a deep breath and let it out. I took another and let it out. The peace spread across my chest. I could smell burning leaves in the air.

"Feel better?" Larry paused and asked, taking in the trees and sky with his gaze.

"Some," I said.

Then we heard Pap singing, and the three of us looked at one another.

Mam had given Pap the job of dusting and vacuuming the house. It took forever because he couldn't help but stop in the parlor and play the piano. Larry had been half-right about Pap and that piano. He was drawn to it like it was chocolate ice cream on a cone. He'd sit down at the keyboard and announce to his imaginary audience, "Now I will play and sing for you. Please be quiet." Then he'd run his fingers all over the instrument, up and down the keyboard, banging and crashing out the notes, no tune, no rhythm, and on top of this racket, he would sing his favorite songs, songs Grandma Mary had taught him: "I've Been Working on the Railroad," "Found a Peanut," "My Darling Clementine," and a few others. If he couldn't remember the words, he made them up. Pap could carry a tune pretty well, and he never let the noise his hands were making throw him off.

On that day, we heard the vacuum, Pap, and the piano all going at once. We could tolerate it well enough from outside, but Mam didn't like the vacuum just running with the hose sucking up the same spot on the rug. "It could overheat," she said.

Bobbi, Larry, and I looked at one another as if to ask which one of us was going to go turn off the vacuum, when a familiar old Maverick rolled up our driveway and stopped when it hit the bottom porch step.

Bobbi dropped her rake. "Shit," she said.

Mr. Polanski got out of the car and stood a moment, looking out at us as if he were trying to determine who of us was his daughter.

He stood tall and broad, with one shoulder higher than the other. You wouldn't notice this except that Mr. Polanski always tried to even them out by jerking his higher shoulder down every now and then as if he were having a spasm. When I was younger, that movement alone used to send me racing to the safety of my house whenever I saw the man heading down our street toward the train station. He had small, deep-set eyes and a narrow jaw so that when you looked at his face what you saw was a big expanse of flesh going nowhere, turning into nothing smart like a well-defined nose or a decent pair of ears. To understand how he had managed to father someone as attractive as Bobbi required even more imagination than it did to figure out me and Pap.

Mr. Polanski dropped back a step, as if he had stumbled over a stone. He caught himself, jerked his shoulder down, and raised his arm, pointing his finger at Bobbi.

"Bobbi, girl, you come on home where you belong."

"No, Daddy," Bobbi said, folding her arms in front of her chest, her feet together, legs stiff. "I'm going to stay here."

"You ain't, neither. Now, come on, or you know what." He jerked his shoulder again and took a couple of steps onto the lawn.

Larry took a step closer to Bobbi. He stood with his legs apart, his fists clenched as if he was preparing to fight this hulking man. Larry was taller, but his body, fed on seaweed and algae, looked frail even standing beside Bobbi. He didn't have a prayer of defending her.

I moved in on her other side and tried to think what to do should the man make a move to take her away. I could feel my heart beating hard and it felt as if it were in my throat. I wanted to swallow but I couldn't. I couldn't even breathe. Bobbi's father had always scared me, and it wasn't just the jerking motions, either. His eyes, though small, held a wildness in them, a fierceness I didn't understand. It seemed to come from some hidden terror within.

"Come on, now. Come to me, now," Mr. Polanski said, holding out his hand, his fingers beckoning, twitching. His voice sounded so calm and steady, yet it was chilling. I could sense his rage seething behind each word.

Bobbi took a step backward, stumbling on her rake. "No, Daddy." She straightened up, tucked her shirt into her jeans, and tossed back her hair with her head. When she did that move with me, she did it with defiance, belligerence, but with her father, it was more as if she was steadying herself, clearing her mind of clutter, and focusing on her father. Larry and I stepped in closer.

"You better do as I say, girl, and youse"—he looked at Larry and me—"youse better get inside and stay out of what don't involve you."

His words didn't frighten me as much as his nervousness did, and the way his wild eyes kept shifting to me, then Bobbi, then Larry. I could see he wanted to attack us. I could almost see his mind working, trying to figure out his best advantage. Larry held out his arm in front of Bobbi and said, "No, Mr. Polanski. We're eyewitnesses. If you take Bobbi it will be against her will, on private property where you haven't been invited. And if you touch her, we'll be able to tell the authorities, and then maybe they'll put you where you belong."

Larry's words sounded tough, but his jaw quivered, making his words come out in sobs.

"No queer drug addict goin' to tell me what to do with my own girl. And it's my word against yours." Mr. Polanski stepped closer with each word, then he lunged forward, surprising us all. He went for Bobbi, grabbing her by her hair, and then by her arm, twisting it and pulling her forward.

Bobbi tried to hold back, but the grass and leaves made the ground too slippery and she slid onto her bottom.

Mr. Polanski kept on dragging her while Bobbi fought to get up again, and I jumped in trying to loosen the man's grip. I could smell liquor on his breath when he lunged at me, elbowing me in the ribs without skipping a beat with Bobbi. I fell on the ground with a grunt and looked for Larry to help me, but he was running away toward the house.

"Daddy, you're hurting me," Bobbi cried.

"Then stop fighting. Stop it!" He slapped at her face, still holding on with his other hand, still pulling her forward toward the car, dragging her body on the asphalt. "You're going with me, girl."

I had gotten to my feet again and tried to place myself between Bobbi and her father, but their arms were all over the place and Bobbi, breaking free for an instant with a sudden jerk of her arm, rammed it into my face and I reeled back, falling against Mr. Polanski's car.

Bobbi realized what she had done and stopped struggling to see if I was all right. She didn't say anything, it was just a look. But I understood.

Mr. Polanski took advantage of her hesitation and grabbed both her arms and pulled her to her feet, trying to throw her body toward the car.

I had just decided to ram my head into Mr. Polanski any way I could when Larry charged out of the house, camera in hand, and started taking pictures.

We all heard the sound of the film winding to the next frame and stopped fighting. Mr. Polanski let go of Bobbi, and she dropped back to the ground and stayed there, hunched over, hugging herself. I stood beside her, breathing hard now, my knees shaking, wanting to put my hand on her shoulder but unsure how she'd react.

"Now I got proof," Larry said, backing up yet still clicking away with the camera.

Mr. Polanski waved his hand in front of his face, squinting as if the camera were a spotlight.

"You give me that camera, Lawrence Seeley. I can tell the law a thing or two myself—damn fairy."

Larry looked up from the camera. "Like you said, my word against yours. Now leave us alone. Go on and leave us alone, or I'll turn these photos in to the police."

Mr. Polanski started forward after Larry, but Larry lifted the camera and started clicking again, so he backed up, gave Bobbi a nudge in the back with his knee, and said, "You're in big trouble now, girl."

He got into the car and began backing down the drive. Bobbi jumped up and ran after him, shouting, "Daddy, be careful. Drive careful, Daddy. Drive careful."

Chapter Eleven

★

DAYS PASSED AND Bobbi didn't say anything to me or Larry about the afternoon when Mr. Polanski came. She just acted as if nothing had happened, nothing had changed, but I knew it had, I knew *I* had changed. I couldn't hate her anymore, and I felt ashamed that I had attacked her that night in the Seeleys' yard. I wanted to apologize to her, to say I hadn't understood then, not about her father, not really, but I didn't know how. I didn't know how to act. I had known most of my life that Bobbi's father beat her—not that anyone could ever prove it, not when Bobbi herself always denied it. I'd heard the stories, seen a bruise or cut now and then, the sprained arm, but I'd never imagined her father actually hitting her. I never could have imagined it, what with a father like Pap as my frame of reference. That afternoon had been the ugliest, most intimate scene I'd ever witnessed. Until then, I had never really known what violence looked like.

I couldn't talk to Bobbi. She tried to pick fights with me and I couldn't respond. I let her win, have her way. I let her storm about the house, let her stay in the bathroom all night if she wanted to, let her sneak off with my microscope, and I never said a word, because now I understood that it was all just an act, that she wasn't as tough or as fierce as she pretended to be. And after the look that had passed between us when she'd accidentally hit me in the face, I knew, too, she had a heart.

Then one day she barged into my room and said, "I'm not made of eggshells, you know."

I looked up from my desk. Bobbi had on my Einstein T-shirt. She stood with her hands on her hips, her jaw jutting forward.

"I know," I said, and returned to my history.

"I liked it better when we fought," she said.

I twisted around in my seat, startled by her words. "That should tell you something," I said.

"You stink!" Bobbi marched off, slamming my door behind her, and I felt a sickening sadness rip through me. I turned again to my work and stared at the same words in front of me until they doubled and blurred, shifting first left, then right, like amoebas dying under the light of the microscope.

A few minutes later, Bobbi charged back in and stood over me, breathing hard and breaking my mood.

"Okay," she said, as though striking a bargain with me, "just don't keep tiptoeing around me all the time, you know? Say something once in a while. You make me feel like—like nothing."

"Me? I do that?" I pushed back from my desk, setting my pen down in my open history book.

"You're such a stiff, O'Brien. You really are anal retentive."

"I just don't know how to—what to say anymore." I reached out my hand, wanting to touch hers, then let it fall in my lap. "Bobbi, I'm sorry—I mean, how can you stand him? How can you let him—"

"I don't let him!" Bobbi shouted in my face. "I don't let him, he just does. He just does whatever he pleases."

I sat up straighter in my seat.

"See? Anything I say is going to be wrong," I said. "What is it you're trying to prove, anyway? I don't want to fight with you."

Bobbi leaned forward, placing her face in front of mine, and squinted at me. "You think I'm weak, don't you? You saw me with my father and you think I'm weak."

"N-no, I understand—"

"Well, James Patrick, I'm not weak! I'm not my mother! I can take it. I can take anything my father throws at me." She straightened her back and kicked at the seat of my chair, just missing my knee. The chair jerked backward, jolting my head back, too.

I stood up, backing toward my bookcases, brushing the wild strands of hair out of my eyes. "And your mother can't, so she's weak?"

"Never defends me or protects me. Teaches me how to lie. Says for me to tell the teachers I fell, or a dog bit me. What kind of mother is that?"

"I—I—"

Bobbi pointed at me. "I'll never be like her."

I looked straight at her. "So who are you like, then? Your father?"

"Go to hell, O'Brien!" Bobbi strode out again, slamming the door, and a few seconds later the door opened about a foot and my Einstein shirt went flying across the room. It hit one of the bookshelves, slapping the spot where my microscope used to be, and then dropped to the floor.

"And give me back my microscope!" I yelled, grabbing up my shirt. The shirt felt warm in my hands and smelled sweet and powdery. I tossed it on my bed, sat back down at my desk, and tried to concentrate on my schoolwork. I had exams in both history and French the next day. I wasn't worried about them; I knew I'd do well. I had no problems making As at the new high school, but I did have problems making friends, at home and at school. Keeping my face buried in books took my mind off of this fact and kept me from examining the problem too closely. I knew I wouldn't like what I found. Until the move, I had never realized how much I had depended on Tim Seeley, for his friendship, for the way he could tease me out of my moods, and for the way he'd let me know when I said or did something stupid.

His friends became my friends, and I'd never noticed until we moved that it had never been the other way around, it never could have been, because I had never made a friend that wasn't Tim's first. Without him I had no one to talk to here, and I found myself spending more and more time hanging out in the computer lab, talking to the teachers more than to any of my classmates, and when the lab teacher offered me a job as his assistant in the lab during my two free periods and the assistant principal offered me one in the office after school, I jumped at both offers. It meant less time sitting by myself, and the office paid me for my work. It wasn't much, but I wanted it so I could contribute to our house fund.

The house fund was my idea. We had money now. Mam had her job; we had Grandma Mary's insurance money and money from the sale of the house. But with Mam getting to work late half the time, I worried she'd get fired and we'd lose her good income. Mam had set aside the rest of Grandma Mary's insurance for Pap's future, in case anything should happen to her, she said, and the money from the house wouldn't last forever. Besides, I resented Bobbi and Larry's freeloading and taking everything for granted. Larry had even taken to bossing me out of the cabin anytime he found me in there, as if it were his property.

I held a meeting in the upstairs hall bathroom. It was a narrow room with a bathtub on legs, a large washbasin that took up most of the space, and your basic toilet in the corner. Larry and Bobbi grumbled and shuffled into the room, where Mam had already found her spot on the floor, sitting cross-legged with a slice of zucchini bread on a napkin in her lap. Larry and Bobbi sat down on the edge of the bathtub, stretched their legs out in front of them, and passed a cigarette back and forth.

I stood leaning against the wall, wedged between the sink and the entrance, and Pap sat on the closed toilet bowl. He thought sitting on the toilet in front of everyone was funny enough to mention every few minutes, and he giggled over it until Mam set her hand on his lap and he stopped.

"I called you into the bathroom," I said, once we were all settled, "because it's in need of the most work." I pointed at the ceiling.

"Plaster is falling everywhere, and this floor"—I pushed my weight forward into the floor and the wood gave under me, groaning and threatening to give way completely—"this floor's pretty much rotted out, and the toilet overflows."

"Like this!" Pap imitated flushing noises and tossed his arms up as if demonstrating an eruption.

I cleared my throat and continued, speaking over Pap's giggles. "We also have a couple of bedroom ceilings that look as if they're about to come crashing to the floor, a leaky roof around my chimney, some floors that need refinishing, and others, especially the parlor, that need shoring up from the basement before that piano we've got in there falls through. Also, several of the rooms could stand fresh paint. All of this costs money and, folks, the money's getting tight."

"But not too tight," Mam interjected.

"True," I said. "And if you're willing to shop at the grocery store instead of the health food store, we could really save a bundle."

"No way." Mam shook her head and Larry stubbed out his cigarette on the edge of the tub and stood up with his arms crossed in front of him.

"Well, then," I said, "we all need to pitch in. Get jobs, those of you who don't have one, and put a portion of your earnings into a house fund for repairs and groceries and stuff like that."

I waited for everyone to groan and grumble. Instead Larry suggested that we do the work ourselves.

"I know we don't have any experience, but there's this *Reader's Digest* do-it-yourself manual I saw at the bookstore we could use. I'll pay for the book. I get a discount," Larry said, glaring at me as if to say, *I already have a job, you stiff.*

He had gotten a job at Farley's Bookstore in town, but so far the store had profited more than he had, because he came home just about every day with a small stack of books, and always with one for Mam.

Mam and Bobbi thought Larry's idea was a good one and that maybe we could do half the work ourselves but leave some of the more difficult tasks to a professional.

"Either way," I said, interrupting their enthusiasm for the do-it-yourself idea, "it's going to cost us, and I think that each of us needs to contribute monthly to the house fund."

Everyone agreed and Pap said, "You know what this toilet does is just like the creek overflowing. Remember the creek all over our house, and Mrs. Jerico, she got snakes in her house and she rode away on her bike in the water with her cat on her shoulders? Remember funny Mrs. Jerico?"

Even I had to laugh at that memory, and instead of laughing to ourselves with our heads turned down the way we all usually did, we laughed looking at one another, nodding at the shared memory of the time the creek overflowed and we moved from house to house helping one another salvage furniture and bail out basements, making runs to the McDonald's and eating together at picnic tables set out in the street, then talking late into the night. Then this feeling ran through each of us. I felt it, and I could see it on the others' faces, in a look of recognition: We all came from the same place. It was almost as if another person had entered the room and passed his hand over each of us, baptizing us, five people, one memory, one household, one family.

Chapter Twelve

★

I SAW OUR new family as a ship. At first it had been a sinking ship, with a hole in its side so large that the best thing any of us could do was abandon it and swim to safety. Then as we tried to adjust to one another, it became a ship that needed constant bailing, first from one side, then from the other. It stayed afloat, but only as long as we kept bailing. Then after the meeting in the bathroom, the ship ran aground, and the five of us, stuck on our small island, could put down our bailing buckets and take a long deep breath. We could walk the length of the ship, and the ship, though tilted, wouldn't move. We could step outside the ship, explore the island, and know that when we turned back, there it would still be—until the tide came in, or a wave, or a storm, or some other turbulence came along to dislodge us and send our ship back into the cold dark waters.

Everyone acted as if running aground was the way it should be, as if this were the most stable condition, but I knew nothing had been fixed. We still had the hole in the side, we'd still have to bail like crazy when the tide came in, and I knew it would. I knew the only really safe place for us to be was anchored back in homeport, no holes and no added weight. I just didn't know how to steer us there, not when everyone was happy where they were and Mam was captain of the ship.

Larry had discovered that we had run aground in a town filled with artists—actors, potters, painters, musicians, and writers. This discovery changed Larry. He started seeing himself as a poet, and he invited other wannabe poets to the house at night to read and critique one another's work. When Larry read his poems to the group, his voice took on a haunted, moaning tone, and since he loved the English poets, he read with an English accent. After a while he started using the accent in his everyday speech, until, at last, it became his usual way of speaking. He began to use the word *bloody* a lot. He'd say, "It's bloody hot in here," or "I bloody well have a right to be in here, you swag." He started calling our meals *repasts,* and flashlights *torches,* the hood of the van a *bonnet,* and gas *petrol,* all words he'd picked up from the poetry and the Agatha Christie mystery novels Bobbi had been taking out of the library and Larry had been snitching from her.

Then I noticed Larry was wearing black turtlenecks all the time. He took out all his earrings except one, grew a goatee, and wore Mam's red plaid scarf around his neck, even indoors. He said the scarf was his signature. Every poet in the group had his or her own signature and own pose. Harold, the angry poet, wore his hair in a tangle of dreads and dressed in colorful African robes that came down to his ankles; Jerusha, a cellist and the most talented of the group, wore ties and men's suit pants; Leon, more interested in Jerusha than in poetry, wore tall L. L. Bean hunting boots with the laces wrapped around the boots like a ballerina's toe shoe; and Melanie, the nature poet, wore thin cashmere sweaters over long and lacy dresses she bought at the vintage clothing store in town.

The poetry sessions at our house became so successful that Larry and his friends gathered there every night. They'd talk all night long, drinking cheap gallons of wine or sipping herbal teas, and Mam didn't mind a bit. She loved all the comings and goings of Larry's friends. She loved the crowd they made in the kitchen, squeezing in with the rest of us for dinner at a table built for four.

"Now, isn't this cozy," she'd say, looking around the table at us and reaching out to squeeze someone's hand.

She loved their poetry. She loved their moody, over-emotional existence, and the group sought her advice on everything from poetry to love, and a lot of that love went on right under our own roof. Larry and his friends passed themselves around, hooking up with one person one week, then moving on to another the next. I never saw the same coupling two weeks in a row, which meant there were a lot of lovers' quarrels and hurt feelings and making up going on all over the house.

They argued about everything and Mam loved it. "I just love a fun fight," she'd say, after what she thought was an exhilarating argument over the looting of Egyptian pyramids, or euthanasia and living wills. Of course, most of the time they argued over poetry and poets, discussing the false lives and improper desires in T. S. Eliot's *Waste Land* for hours on end, the air thick with cigarette smoke.

Sometimes the discussions lasted so long the group would all stay the night, and I'd come down in the morning and find bodies scattered about the house, asleep in chairs, on the couch, on the floor, anywhere they happened to be when sleep overtook them. Sometimes I'd even find Mam asleep right alongside the others, covered in someone's old ratty coat. I'd stand and watch her and wonder who she had become. I didn't know her anymore, and I didn't know the others, either, Larry or Bobbi or even Pap. All of them had become different people from who they were back home.

Bobbi got a job at the veterinary clinic after school and became a foster parent to the stray cats, dogs, and ferrets she picked up at the SPCA once in a while. She and Pap loved the animals. They'd feed them, cuddle them, talk baby talk to them, and laugh together over the silly things the creatures did. Bobbi and Pap became close through the animals, and it changed both of them. Bobbi stopped yelling at everyone and even left me alone, for the most part. She made friends in school who didn't know about her past reputation, and she sang in the school chorus.

Pap didn't wander around the house looking for something or someone to entertain him. He didn't wander outside anymore, either. He had Bobbi now, and they did everything together. They would climb through the second-floor hall window out onto the porch roof and sit with the Nativity set. I could see their still, dark forms among all the lit bodies. They sat together, arms around each other, rarely speaking, as if they were waiting for something.

Mam looked at them through the window one evening

and said, nodding to herself, "Bobbi needs Pap. He's a good father to her."

I didn't say anything, but I looked out at the two of them and wondered. Could Pap ever be a father to someone?

Every morning, the two of them got up at five-thirty and slipped out to go to six o'clock mass. As far as I could tell, most of their conversations were about Jesus, and sometimes I'd see Bobbi reading to Pap from the Bible the same way Larry would read Tennyson's poetry to Mam, as if they were sharing something deep about themselves.

Pap still went to the Center every day with Mam, and he loved this. He took a gym class, an art class, a reading class, and then Mam's horticulture class, where he learned how to propagate, grow, and maintain flowers and vegetables and other plants. He worked in the greenhouse with his class-mates, and Mam said he was a natural at digging dirt. He loved his new job, as he called it. He'd come home with egg cartons filled with dirt and seeds, and he'd set them near the windows in the kitchen and talk to them. Sometimes he'd take the poor things into the parlor with him and play the piano and sing to them. We were amazed when the seeds started growing and he had to transfer the plants into pots, but no one was more amazed than Pap.

"I just love to grow seeds, now," he'd say, holding up his pots. "Look what I got, everybody, and we can eat these in our food when they're all grown up."

Mam gave Pap a patch of lawn to turn into a garden, but since it was autumn, and then winter, all he could do was rake leaves and scoop out the snow so he could talk to the frozen grass, promising it that he and Bobbi would someday turn it into a beautiful wildflower garden.

This was our new life. Everyone wandered off during the day to school, to jobs, but in the early evenings we'd gather again, five, seven, nine of us (not including Bobbi's critters), and the noise—piano music, readings, arguments, cooking—the chaos would begin.

I never knew what to expect. I never knew who I'd find in my bathroom when I came home in the afternoon, or who I'd find napping on my bed. I didn't know which of Larry's friends would help him with dinner, creating even more bizarre concoctions than before, or how many there'd be squeezed in at the table. I didn't know what kind of animal would sit on my feet while I ate or escape at night and crush my chest while I slept. If I wanted Mam, I never knew where I'd find her—listening to poetry, working out in the yard at midnight, on a date with Dr. Mike, asleep in a bathroom or on the living room floor or, sometimes, in her own bed with Pap.

While everyone around me seemed to have found themselves, I grew more and more lost. While everyone else could hear their own voice in the midst of the cacophony, I grew more and more silent. I spent my evenings up in my room, eating and studying with the radio on so I wouldn't hear the others below and have to think about how I didn't, couldn't, fit in. I wanted to tell Mam. I wanted her to know how I felt about our new life, and I wanted her to care. I wanted to say to her, "Okay, Mam, either I go or they do, you choose," but I was afraid she wouldn't choose me, and I had nowhere else to go.

Chapter Thirteen

⭐

ONE SATURDAY MORNING after the first snowfall of the year, I found Mam outside sweeping snow off the porch, and I asked her if she would go for a walk with me in the woods. We had lived in the house three months and yet we had never taken the time to explore the land beyond our front door. At our old house, when Grandma Mary was alive, we lived outdoors; we explored the creek and its wildlife on a daily basis, and I realized, looking back on those days, that there was a certain sanity in our lives there. Paying attention to the minute details of the life at the creek, the changing seasons, kept us sane, focused, centered even. Now we were all crazy, wild, out of control. We had no Grandma Mary, no creek, to keep us grounded. That was what I wanted to discuss with Mam.

Mam loaded up a pack with binoculars, camera, pita sandwiches, herb tea in a Thermos, cups, and a notebook for drawing. I carried it on my back, pleased to think that we'd be gone a long time. I needed that time to figure out how I would say what I wanted to say.

We found a path in the woods marked with deer prints in the snow. We followed them beneath a steeple of trees that Mrs. Levi had claimed were planted back in the days of William Penn. Most were tall, slender trees that bent easily with the wind, and the few birds left to sing in them sounded so far away in those high, high branches that only their echoes reached us.

Mam stopped and closed her eyes to listen to a cardinal. She had her hands stuffed in the pockets of a coat I'd never seen before. She held her face up to the sky, her back slightly arched, her eyes closed.

"Listen," she said, smiling to herself.

I didn't listen. I watched her instead. I wondered if by staring at her long enough I could figure her out, because I had a feeling words wouldn't work. She had on jeans and Larry's boots, which were at least three sizes too big for her. She wore her hair knotted up in some kind of mess held together with a plastic grabby thing that looked like a butterfly. I had seen the same hair holder in Melanie's hair the night before. She had on Bobbi's long Egyptian-style earrings, which were too large for her narrow face and looked out of place dangling next to all her freckles. They were meant for Bobbi, not her. I looked at Mam and thought that she had become, like the clothes she wore, a hodgepodge of different people. I missed the old Mam, the Mam who wore her own jeans and plaid shirts and her own boots and who spent hours exploring the creek with me. I missed being with her alone. I missed talking to her about nothing. We used to have so much time to talk that it never mattered that it was about nothing, because that nothing was everything. Now I had to think about what to say, plan it, make every word count, because I didn't know when I'd get another chance.

I tried to ease into the conversation by just getting her to talk.

"I'm glad you like living here, Mam," I said, looking up at the treetops so far away.

Mam opened her eyes and smiled at me. "I do," she said. "I love it. And I love the house and everyone in it." Mam ran her hand down the trunk of a tree and leaned forward to smell it. "Mmm, you can smell the sap already. Come on, smell."

I leaned forward. I couldn't smell anything.

"You know, I'm really good with people," Mam said, starting to walk again, leading me along the deer path. "I never knew that about myself, how good I am with people— outside my teaching, I mean—how much I love it." She turned back and grabbed my hand and pulled me forward.

"This trail's kind of narrow," I said, hanging back, not wanting to talk face-to-face or even side by side.

Mam pulled me along, talking all the while. "I thought I was an introvert," she said. "Imagine going all your life thinking of yourself as a loner, an introvert, telling yourself you don't need people and then discovering—well, life! I think I've been dead all these years. I've been hiding out in the woods, in the creek, in Grandma Mary's house. It never occurred to me to go out and get my own life. What a scary thought. That's what I used to think. I was so afraid of people."

"Some people, though, are natural introverts," I said, pulling my hand from her grasp. "Some people don't like crowds and groups all the time. Some people like it quiet, less chaotic."

Mam stopped walking and turned around. She blinked at me, her eyes a deep dark blue in the filtered light of the woods. "Might you be talking about yourself, JP?"

I leaned against a pine tree and kicked my heel into the snow. "I hate chaos," I said.

Mam nodded. "You like stasis."

I stopped kicking and looked at her, startled that she knew about chaos and stasis. I started walking and Mam walked beside me.

"What's wrong with stasis?" I asked, watching my feet make tracks in the snow.

"JP, you know better than I do that it's impossible. You read the book. It can't last, it can't be maintained. Things do change."

"That's not true," I said. "Not with everything. Not with water kept below thirty degrees, not with—"

Mam threw her arms up. "JP, we're not ice! Stasis is stagnation, and stagnation is death."

"So is chaos. Chaos is just as impossible, totally unpredictable. I never know if I'm going to be able to sit down at dinner and have my own space to myself or be sharing it with Jerusha, the she-man."

Mam laughed. "I think she likes you." She started walking again, and I followed.

"I hate the way she takes food off my plate. She just takes it! I hate them crowding in on our dinner. And I hate finding that Harold guy using my bathroom. He has to climb two flights to use it. Why can't he go downstairs?"

"Maybe he wants privacy. Maybe he's like you and needs to get away every now and then."

Mam waited for me to catch up, then she linked her arm in mine and said, "I spent so much of my life alone, JP. I was surrounded by my family and yet, except for your uncle John, no one paid any attention to me. Of course, I never made the effort to get to know anyone. I was shy and awkward. Like you, I spent so much of my life and my schooling in my bedroom. It was easier just to keep my head buried in my books. It's easier, JP, but not better. I agree chaos is no better than stasis, but there's got to be a middle ground, doesn't there?"

"Yeah," I said. "My book calls it complexity."

"Complexity." Mam nodded and considered the idea awhile, slowing her walk and staring at her feet.

"Complexity. That's perfect, isn't it? That's such a rich-sounding word. That's exactly what we are, isn't it? Complex." She squeezed my arm and shook it. "Tell me about it, scientifically, I mean."

This felt good, Mam asking me something, wanting me to teach her. "Well, to put it simply, complexity is that place where things aren't predictable but they aren't out of control, either."

"Exactly!" Mam said. "I like it, go on."

"Take for instance water. If you freeze it you've got stasis, if you boil it you've got chaos, but there's that point just before boiling where the molecules could go either way and—"

"That's perfect!" Mam interrupted. "That's what we'll work toward. How about it? Complexity." Mam nodded to herself as if she'd solved it all. As if just by saying this she could pull us back from the chaos.

"Mam, you didn't let me finish. You know where complexity exists?"

Mam nodded. "In just about everything, I'd guess. All of life is complex."

"No, Mam, I mean mathematically, scientifically."

"Tell me. Where does complexity exist?"

"At the edge. At the edge of chaos. That's what they call it, and the edge is too close to chaos for me."

"Well then, JP, you're stuck," Mam said, and then realizing the truth of her statement shook her head and added, "and you're lonely, and I can't seem to do anything about it, can I?"

I shrugged and pulled my arm away from her and walked a little faster. She kept up.

"What about Timmy? Why hasn't he come by for a visit? Why don't you go see him?"

"He's so different now," I said. "I talk to him on the phone and we've got nothing to say. I'm talking about the second law of thermodynamics and nonlinear equations, and he's talking about football and Laura Pentero and some party he went to. I don't know. He's gone wild."

Mam nodded. "He's changed, too. That's all it is, JP. Life just changes and you can either move along with it or stand there, but either way it's going to keep on moving."

I stopped. "It's the way it's changed. Look at you, Mam. Why do you have on Larry's boots?"

Mam looked down at the boots and laughed. "Is that what's bothering you?"

"And you have on Bobbi's earrings, and Bobbi keeps taking my Einstein shirt and most of Pap's shirts, and Larry wore and ripped my jeans."

Mam leaned back on her heels and clicked the toes of her boots together. "I've got on Larry's boots because they were right there by the back door and my boots are somewhere in Bobbi's room, two flights up."

"I could have gotten your boots for you. You just had to ask."

"These will do," Mam said, still staring at them.

"Why can't everybody just keep to their own stuff? I can't find anything anymore. It's a mess. I don't like it."

"You want us to leave your things alone?"

"Yes! I want everyone to leave my stuff alone. If they want something, they can ask first. Nobody asks, they just take. I hate it."

Mam started walking again, her hands in the pockets of her jacket. I followed her, keeping a couple of steps behind.

"Okay, JP. Tonight at dinner I'll tell everyone that your room is off-limits. Will that help?"

"Yes."

"Anything else?"

"Yes."

Mam turned around and waited for me to catch up to her. I didn't want to. I preferred talking to her back.

"What is it, then?" Mam looked wary, as if she knew what I was going to say.

"It's Dr. Mike."

Mam nodded and turned and started walking again. She didn't want to face me, either. I talked to her back.

"You said he'd stop coming around when we moved. Remember? You said it would all be over, but you still see him. Mam, you're going out on dates with him and you're married. What would Grandma Mary say?"

"I refuse to make predictions about what someone who died might have said. She's gone and I'm here, and I've got to live my life."

Mam sounded angry, but I wasn't sure if she was angry at me or Grandma Mary—maybe us both.

Mam ducked under some low-hanging branches and I followed her, holding my hand in front of my face in case she let a branch go too soon. She was moving fast, breathing hard, not looking to see how far behind her I was walking.

"I told you," she said, "I'm not going to be like Grandma Mary. I'm not even going to try." She stopped a second and thumped her chest with her fist. "This, JP, who you see now, this is me. This is who I am. I like people. I want to be around people. I don't want to hide away anymore. I want a family and good friends, and one of those good friends happens to be a man." She turned back around and continued along the trail. "I can talk about things with Mike I can't talk about with Pap or you or Larry or Bobbi. I can bring out this other side of me. I'm not all one thing. I don't love just one thing, or one person."

I stopped walking and pounded my fist against a tree. "So now you love him? First you say you're friends and now you love him?" I didn't know what to do. I wanted to run away. I wanted to stay and yell at her, demand that she stop dating Dr. Mike and kick everyone out of the house who wasn't family—real family. Instead I paced. I kept my head down, watching my feet, tramping down my old tracks again and again.

"JP, of course I love him, the way I love Larry or Bobbi or any of the others who come to our house, the way I try to love everybody. I'm not *in* love. I don't love him the way I love you or the way I love Pap. You two are special."

"You could have fooled me." I stopped pacing and looked at Mam in her big old coat and huge dangling earrings. "I never see you anymore." I pointed at her. "I never see *you*! Even when I do see you, it's not you. You're part Bobbi or Larry or Jerusha. Look, even your freckles have faded. You're someone else. You're not my mother. You're nobody's mother. You're acting like a teenager. It's embarrassing. Yeah, that's it. You embarrass me. I hate who you are! I hate this life!"

Mam let me have my say, and I could see tears in her eyes, but she held on. She kept her head up, her jaw forward, her hands buried in her coat pockets.

When I finished yelling I ran back toward the house, the pack filled with our day's supplies bouncing on my back.

Mam stayed in the woods. She stayed there all afternoon and on past dark. Everyone wanted to know where she had gone. I kept telling myself that she was fine, she knew how to get around in the woods. I told myself that I didn't care where she'd gone, but the longer she stayed away, the faster I found my heart beating, and I couldn't concentrate on my studies. I heard the others downstairs organizing a search party. I looked out my window when the porch light went on and saw them all gathered in the driveway, Pap and Bobbi and Larry, with his odd assortment of friends. I wondered why they just stood there. Why weren't they running out to the woods? They were so slow. I pounded my wall and yelled through the glass pane, "Get a move on!"

Then I saw Dr. Mike's BMW rolling into the drive and swerving onto the grass to avoid the junk heaps lined up near the porch. He drove right over to the group and stopped his car, and both doors opened. Dr. Mike got out of one side and Mam out of the other.

Pap ran to Mam and hugged her. The others crowded around and I could see Mam explaining herself, her hand pointing to the woods and then at Dr. Mike. I watched them all head back onto the porch and heard them come inside, their voices filling the halls, and then the whole house filled back up with voices and music and laughter. I turned on my radio and sat at my desk. I had a lot of work to do.

Chapter Fourteen

★

MAM TOLD EVERYONE that I wanted my belongings
and my room left alone. Late that night the household paraded in and dropped off my clothes, books, chess set, microscope, Swiss Army knife, a pair of shoes, a five-dollar bill,
and some change. Half the stuff I hadn't even known was
missing, and some of the shirts and books didn't belong
to me.

Jerusha came in last and handed me my book on biodiversity. She sat down on my bed, making herself at home by
drawing her knees up under her chin, the heels of her boots
digging into the edge of the mattress. She looked at me with
her protruding eyes and said, "I'm interested in science, too.
I'm not just into poetry. It's neat how species change, isn't it?
I mean, just by living in a different climate a finch can take on
a whole different set of characteristics and needs from his fel-
low finches in another climate."

I sat at my desk and nodded, waiting for her to leave.

Jerusha made me uncomfortable. She seemed too intense, with her large staring eyes and the veins in her neck that bulged anytime she spoke. Her voice sounded hoarse and raspy. She was stick thin and never seemed to eat except to pick a bit of food off of my plate. She wore her dark brown hair straight, cut just above the shoulders, with bangs that came exactly to the top of her brows, and she had on a man's pinstriped suit with a superwide Minnie Mouse tie.

"I'm sorry I took your book." She sighed. "I'm sorry, you know, everybody's been getting into your stuff and you don't like it. You should have said something sooner. No one was doing it to steal from you or anything."

All evening, as each person had come in with my things and apologized, I had felt like a cranky old man. They all made me feel as if I were being selfish to want to keep track of my things, to want to hold on to it all, but it did belong to me, and it was all I had.

"If you'd just ask first, maybe I'd let you borrow my books," I said to Jerusha. "I hate people just taking stuff. It doesn't seem to occur to anyone that I might want to read that book or wear my own shirts or use my microscope. My grandmother gave me that microscope."

Jerusha shrugged, hugging her knees. "Sorry," she said.

"Yeah, well."

She sat on the bed, nodding at me as if she wanted me to say something more, but I couldn't think of anything else to say so I told her I needed to get back to work.

"You work a lot."

"Yeah," I said, turning back to my desk and my books and pretending to get interested in my studies.

"I graduated from high school when I was sixteen," she said.

"Mmm," I said, a surge of jealousy rising up in me. I, too, would be graduating at sixteen, and I had been proud of that—well, stuck up about it, really. I had skipped the fourth grade. Back then, the whole school, the whole neighborhood knew it. I'd made sure of that, and I loved hearing people say things like, "That smart O'Brien kid with the retarded father. Looks like he got all the brains."

I didn't mean to be cruel to Pap; I just knew how people saw things, and I wanted to make sure they understood that just because Pap had brain damage didn't mean I did.

"I'm taking this year off, though—from college, I mean," Jerusha said, and I looked up.

"I didn't know you went to college. How come you just— well, why don't you have a decent— How—"

Jerusha laughed, nodding. "What am I doing waitressing for a living? That's what my parents want to know. They want me to finish college and go to med school."

I turned around in my chair to face her. "Well, if you've got the brains, why not?"

"I'm not sure I'd love medicine enough. I don't know what I want to do. I love music and poetry, I'm interested in science, but then I'd like to do something—I don't know, maybe join the Peace Corps or something." She raised her brows, closing her eyes, and grabbed the toes of her boots. "I've had several pieces of poetry published and I've got a manuscript out, so maybe I'll be a poet."

"If you're serious, why do you hang out with those pretentious lunatics?"

Jerusha unfolded herself and stood up. "Because they're fun. So I'll see you, then," she said, giving me a half wave before leaving.

Maybe Jerusha and I could have been friends, but like Mam, she always hung out with the group. Once I tried to bring up biodiversity with her at the dinner table and the whole conversation around us stopped. Jerusha looked at me, then at the rest of the table, and broke into laughter, resting her head on my shoulder a second as if she thought I was just the silliest, most pitiful person she'd ever met. I tried to laugh it off, too, but after another five minutes, when the conversation got rolling again, I got up, leaving my plate for Jerusha, and slipped back up to my room, where I belonged.

★

CHRISTMASTIME HAD ALWAYS been a big deal at our house when Grandma Mary was alive. She had been born on December eleventh and Pap on Christmas Day. The whole month had been a time of mounting excitement for all of us, but that year as the days drew closer to her birthday, my heart, my whole body seemed to get heavier and heavier. When I awoke each day I felt as if I were getting up to go to her funeral all over again.

Pap, however, was his usual excited self. He had always been possessive about the month of December. This was his special month, the month he shared with Jesus, and when in church the priests talked about Christmas Day and Jesus's birth, I think Pap believed they were talking about his birth, also, as if he, too, were born in a manger.

He loved Christmas carols and sang them as if they belonged to him, his own birthday songs. When others sang them with him, he'd blush and hang his head and sing quieter, finishing with a shy smile.

That December, Mam and I had purchased several gallons of paint and we were all working to get the downstairs rooms painted before Christmas Day.

One late afternoon when Mam and Pap had not yet returned from work, the rest of us got busy painting the woodwork in our dining room a color called Soldier Blue. Larry, Harold, Leon, and new guy Ben, all in their jewelry, scarves, and boots, worked on the molding around the ceiling and floor, while Melanie, bending and dipping as if she were at a ladies' tea, Jerusha, with her Winnie-the-Pooh tie tied around her head, and another new addition named Susan, a guitar player, did the windows and doors. Bobbi and I painted the mantel and shelves around the fireplace.

While we were working, Bobbi turned the radio down and brought up the subject of Pap's birthday, and said that Pap didn't want tofu and seaweed for his birthday dinner.

I told them that we always had a special dinner for Pap on Christmas Eve and suggested having roast beef and chocolate cake, which was what Grandma Mary had always prepared for him.

Bobbi dipped her brush into the bucket of paint she and I shared and said, "No, he told me he wanted hamburgers and hot dogs and potato chips."

Larry and Jerusha gagged.

"Why don't we just inject ourselves with lard, it's a lot faster," Larry said.

Harold said, "Not half so tasty, though."

"Maybe you're the one who wants the burgers," I said to Bobbi, and she sneered at me.

"Ask him yourself, then, if you don't believe me. He also said he wanted to toast marshmallows."

We all laughed, but then Susan, who was a lot like Mam and game for anything, said, "Well, why not? We could light a fire in one of these fireplaces and toast them inside."

Bobbi shook her head. "No, he wants it outside, at night, so he can see the Nativity."

"Well, that's impossible," I said, painting across the top of the mantel and getting Bobbi's hand by accident.

"Hey! You did that on purpose."

I held up my hands. "I swear I didn't."

"Yeah, well, watch it."

Susan said, "Why is it impossible? We could make a pit in the ground, or build one if the ground's too frozen, and do the hot dogs and hamburgers and toast the marshmallows all outside. It would be great. We'd just need a lot of blankets and stuff."

Leon said, "I've got some old wool army blankets we could use, and a grill we could set over the pit. Yeah, it would work."

Then everyone started talking, making suggestions, each one more ridiculous than the next, and I said so.

"You guys are crazy. We're not about to have a weenie roast in the middle of December—give me a break. The least we could do is give Pap a decent roast beef and chocolate cake dinner like he's always had."

Susan turned around to face me, her whole body covered in more paint than she was putting on the door, and said, "You're a real killjoy, JP, you know that?"

"Lighten up, JP," Harold said, and Ben and Leon agreed.

Larry said, "Leave him alone," and Bobbi said, "Why? He's always acting so superior. Mr. Know-It-All. 'You! Paint the doors, and you, paint the windows,'" she added, imitating me. "Mr. Boss Man, telling us all how to paint. 'Even strokes, even strokes'—give it up, JP."

"Mam put me in charge," I said, my voice cracking.

"That's 'cause she's trying to get you to participate, fit in, but all you do is drag everybody down." Bobbi ran her paintbrush across the mantel where I had already painted.

I slapped my brush down on the mantel, not caring where the paint landed, and said, "Fine, all of you do what you want. You can toast marshmallows in a snowman's mouth for all I care. Nothing I say matters, anyway." I marched out of the room and headed for the stairs. I heard Susan say, "Spoiled baby."

Then Larry said, "That's enough. Leave him alone. He's allowed to have his opinion," and it occurred to me then that I had become Larry, the old Larry, always on the outside, unable to fit in at school or at home. I thought about this, climbing up the two flights of stairs to my room. He had come into our home and taken over my position in the family. He played the role of the oldest child now, and he had collected about him all the people he could find who were enough like him to make him feel good and right, while at the same time managing to shove me off balance and out in the cold.

On Christmas Eve we celebrated Pap's birthday just the way everyone wanted it. I knew Mam was pleased; she liked anything that was held outdoors. And Pap was so excited he couldn't do anything right and went around all day with his shoes on the wrong feet, refusing to change them. Late in the afternoon Mam hauled out the wool blankets Leon had brought us and spread them out on the lawn, while Larry and I dug through the semifrozen ground to build a pit and light a fire. Then we all sat out on the blankets, wrapped in everything warm we owned, and grilled hot dogs and hamburgers. We toasted marshmallows and watched the glow from the campfire, the lighted Nativity set looming above us.

Pap stuffed two wrinkled hot dogs in his mouth, no bun or condiments, then jammed several puffy-skinned brown-black marshmallows down his throat and said through the sticky wad in his mouth, "Okay, let's stop now and open my presents already."

Bobbi, who had been stuffing down just as many hot dogs and marshmallows as Pap, jumped up and ran to the porch for her gift. We knew she had been excited about what she had bought Pap. She had bustled around the house all day, teasing Pap and trying to get him to guess what she had bought him.

Bobbi handed Pap his present and Pap tore off the wrapping paper without even looking at it. He opened up the box in his hands and found a set of gardening tools, silver with red handles. Beneath the tools were packets of wildflower seeds and a booklet with colored photographs of flowers. Pap drew in his breath with delighted surprise. But you could hand him a bar of soap wrapped with a bow and he'd be pleased.

Bobbi knelt down beside him. "Your very own garden set, Pap. Take good care of them."

Pap hugged the box of tools, and then Bobbi. "Yes, I love these all, and I love myself gardening. Don't you just love me gardening? Don't you love it's my birthday? What else did I get?"

We all gave Pap something for gardening—pots, a kneeling pad, a pair of gloves, and then because we still had two more hours until we all piled into Larry's van and went to midnight mass, we decided to give out all the presents. I gave Mam and Pap my school picture in a frame I bought at a boutique downtown. I gave Larry a bunch of recipes I'd copied out of the *Vegetarian Times* magazine. Mrs. Pallo, who worked with me in the school office, had tons of back copies of the magazine in her home, and she brought them in and I copied a bunch of the recipes out on index cards and bought a fancy recipe file, also at the boutique store. I gave Bobbi my Einstein T-shirt and she hugged me. Mam saw us and wiped her eyes as if she had tears in them. I gave Larry's poet friends each a copy of the poem "Howl" by Allen Ginsberg, the group's favorite poem. I'd typed it into the computer at school, created a design around the edges, and printed it off on gold paper.

Mam gave everyone books, except for me and Pap. I had been hoping for a computer. I had imagined it every night before falling off to sleep. Mam knew I wanted it, and I felt sure she'd get me one this year. She had said that all of Grandma Mary's insurance money was for Pap, but I knew she had set some aside for me, since I had put all my money into the house fund. I couldn't wait to get the computer. I imagined all the work I could do right in my own home, up in my own room. Then, when she brought out our gifts, mine and Pap's, I saw right away that it wasn't a computer. She could hold the gift easily in one hand. I felt betrayed. She handed me the wrapped present with eagerness and joy in her eyes, and all I could do was look back at her dumbstruck. She gave us the exact same thing, as if we were brothers, as if we were just alike. We both got cameras. Nice ones—both of us. I thanked Mam and set the box by my side, but Pap put the strap around his neck as Larry instructed and began taking pictures, with everyone giving him advice on how to get a good shot.

I caught Mam looking across the flames at me, and I could tell by her expression that she knew I felt insulted. I tried to smile. It was a great camera, after all, but I could feel my smile turning into something more like a grimace and I looked away.

Then Larry announced that he had a special gift for all of us. He asked Ben to give him a hand and they left us by the pit and ran down toward the cabin. Pap took a picture of their backs.

We knew Larry had wanted to fix up the cabin in the woods and live out there, so we all guessed he had finished working on the floor, but why, we wondered, didn't he ask us to follow him?

A minute later Pap jumped up and got a picture of Larry and Ben struggling up the slope of the lawn carrying something big, something wooden, between them. We couldn't make out what they had until they got within range of the campfire and set the object down before us.

Larry stepped back and said, "*Voilà!*" Pap snapped another picture, this time of a long wooden table. It had been made in the style of a trestle table, only Larry had used old wood he'd found out in the garage so that it looked like an antique.

"Feel it," he said when everyone crowded in to get a better look. "Run your hand over it. Go ahead, you won't get a single splinter." We all ran our hands over the surface and agreed on how smooth it felt. Then, instead of carrying it into the kitchen, we brought the chairs out to the table and stayed outside.

Mam shook her head, ran her hand over the table again, and said, "I never knew you were so skilled, Larry. This is really a beautiful job. You're an artist."

Larry took the cigarette out of his mouth and grinned. "I never knew it, either. You think it's good? Did you notice I used old nails? I got them at the junk shop on the road to Lahaska. They've got all sorts of old junk from houses, windows and doors and things. I was thinking of maybe making my family one. You think they'd like one?"

Everyone said yes except me. I hated the table. It was perfect, the perfect gift, and it made my stupid picture in a frame appear childish and unimaginative.

Larry said, "I like this because it looks antique. I like that part of it. But my father, I think he likes things to look new. Maybe he wouldn't like it." He shook his head. "No, he wouldn't like it."

We all sat there a moment thinking our own thoughts. I thought about families and wondered if the whole crew would be staying over that night for Christmas or if they'd go home to their own families.

Then Pap started singing "We Three Kings," holding his

camera out at arm's length and taking pictures of himself with his mouth wide open. Then everyone joined in, huddled beneath the wool blankets, their bodies swaying shoulder to shoulder. I was the only one not singing, not swaying. I stared out beyond the table, looking up at the Nativity, and I thought it looked beautiful that night, the lighted figures shining in the darkness. The thought surprised me, and I sat staring at the Nativity a long time while the others ran through a round of Christmas carols.

Then I noticed Bobbi sitting next to me. I heard her voice above all the others and was startled by how beautiful it sounded, how rich and strong and pure. I turned toward her and held my breath, listening. I wanted everyone else to stop singing and sit silent while she filled us with her voice, her music. Then they sang "Angels We Have Heard on High," and I thought, *Here it is. Here is order, here is beauty, here is perfection.* Her music, the music from her own throat, made my throat knot up, and I felt as if I wanted to cry, or cry out. I searched my mind for something sad, and found Grandma Mary waiting for me to mourn her passing, to finally cry for her. I turned away from the others. I closed my eyes and remembered Grandma Mary.

Chapter Fifteen

★

WE DRAGGED HOME exhausted after the party and mid-night mass, and by two in the morning the household had settled down; everyone had found a place to sleep for the night—in sleeping bag, bed, or sofa—and had gone to sleep.

At a little after two-thirty I heard a knock on my door. I sat up and before I could say anything, I heard, "It's Bobbi. Can I come in?"

I paused a moment, not to consider her question but to wonder if I weren't dreaming. I had been lying awake thinking about her—or I thought I had been awake. In my mind I could still hear her singing, and I'd decided I wanted to hear her voice in my head the rest of my life.

I saw the door open and Bobbi stuck her head in.

"JP?" she whispered.

"Yeah, come in, sorry."

Bobbi entered kicking the swimming raft she slept on, and her sleeping bag, into the room ahead of her. Behind her came Parakeet, a ten-year-old golden retriever who had lived in our house for the past week.

"Mind if we sleep on your floor?"

I *was* dreaming!

"No, uh—yeah, okay, sure."

Bobbi dropped her raft on the floor and spread her sleeping bag on top.

"Don't get any ideas," she said, slipping her pillow out from within her bag.

"What ideas?"

"It's just Christmas Eve's never been a good night for me, with my father and all. I just thought I'd feel better with some company." She climbed into her sleeping bag and squiggled down inside it. Parakeet waited for her to get comfortable, then she climbed aboard, circling this way and that before settling halfway on the foot of the raft and halfway on the floor. Bobbi said, "Good girl," then to me, "You don't have to talk to me or anything."

I lay back down in my own bed and stared up at the ceiling. "No, it's okay. Whatever."

We stayed quiet a few minutes and then Bobbi said, "Nice service, huh?"

I thought of Bobbi singing next to me in the pew, incense and candle-wax smells swirling around us. "Yeah, really nice."

"Pap sure got excited."

"Yeah, he gets like that—his birthday and all."

We stopped talking again and I thought how nice it was to have Bobbi in my room, how I wished I had the guts to invite her into my bed.

Then Bobbi asked, "You ever wonder what it's like to be someone else?"

"Like who?" I asked.

"I don't know, anybody. What's it like to be you, JP?"

I sat up on one elbow and looked down on her. I shrugged. "I don't know. Quiet, I guess."

"Peaceful, huh?"

"No, just quiet." I felt uncomfortable talking about myself this way. I asked her, "So what's it like to be you?" just to change the subject, and then I realized, as she started to answer, that I wanted to really know.

"Scary."

I nodded. "Your father."

"No," Bobbi said. "Me. *I'm* scary. I don't know who I am, what I want. I never know what I'll do next." She stretched her arm down and reached for Parakeet's head. Parakeet inched her way forward and allowed Bobbi to play with her ears. "It's funny, but with Daddy the scary thing is you never know what's going to trigger one of his fits, but then when he's hitting me, there's this peace that comes. It's the only time I ever feel it. It's like I'm so scared, every day, all the time, I'm so afraid, and then Daddy beats me and I don't know when he'll stop or what he'll do next, and it's too much. It's too much, and then there it is, this quiet. It just comes over me. It's like one second I'm burning, I'm on fire, and then the next I'm floating in a boat down the river. I'm not there when he's beating me anymore, and I think he knows it, that's why he keeps hitting and hitting. He knows I'm not there. I'm in my boat. I'm floating down the river."

Bobbi's voice sounded trancelike when she spoke, as if

123

she were in the boat while talking to me, and I floated along with her. When she stopped speaking I didn't know what to say, and we fell silent again.

Then Bobbi said, "You know, I go to mass and I say the 'Our Father' and all I can think of is my own father. I wish I could think of God as being more like Pap."

"Pap? Now there's a scary thought." I rolled onto my back and laughed.

Bobbi sat up and faced me. "What is it with you? I mean, you have the greatest parents in the world. You've had all this love surrounding you all your life, and yet you've never loved anyone back. You're pathetic, you know that?"

I stared at the ceiling. "Thanks."

She slid back inside her sleeping bag. "Well, it's true."

I didn't say anything.

"JP?"

I let the silence hang between us for a while, and then I said, slowly, my voice sounding lifeless even to me, "So why did you come in here to sleep tonight? Why not spend the night with the others downstairs?"

"That's easy. You're the safest person I know."

"Safe?" I said. That was a new one.

"You're stable. You know? You got your feet on the ground. Actually, they're downright stuck in the mud"— Bobbi chuckled—"but it's comforting somehow. I mean, you'd never do anything unexpected. You're predictable and straight as an arrow."

"Sounds boring," I said.

"I don't know. You tell me, are you bored?"

I thought about it. I couldn't remember ever being bored. I had too many books I wanted to read, too many thoughts circling my head.

"No," I said. "I guess I'm just boring, but I'm not bored." I sat up. "Like, take for instance the other day when it rained so hard and everybody was complaining."

"Yeah, I just about froze to death," Bobbi said. "I got soaked."

"But you see, I thought it was cool. I sat up here in my room looking out the window, and I guess our gutters are stopped up because the rainwater was spilling over the sides and running in streams past my window. Now, each stream had its own flow and each flow was sporadic—unpredictable, sometimes pouring out a little to the left then shifting to the right, then stopping, then on the right again, or maybe left—totally unpredictable. I had before me the perfect example of chaos."

Bobbi groaned. "Chaos!"

"Wait a minute. See, what was neat about it was that even though you had all this random spilling out of water, if you closed your eyes and just listened you heard a rhythm, a unified sound. So, like, there's this pattern that emerges, this stability in the midst of chaos. I'd read about it, worked it out on the computer even, but there it was in front of me, this steady state! That's what I'm looking for and there it was, right in front of me."

I'd gotten myself all worked up. The discovery had been so exciting, so perfect, and it was my own, not something I picked up in a book. I wanted to record the sound and chart it on a graph and see what kind of pattern I'd come up with on the computer at school. That was my latest idea, but Bobbi didn't seem interested.

"You're right," she said. "You may not be bored, but you sure are boring. 'Night."

"'Night," I said, deflated. Then I added, "You sounded great tonight. Uh—I mean, singing. You have the most— you have a beautiful voice." I said these last few words and my own voice choked on me. I lay back down and told myself to just shut up.

Then Bobbi's face appeared in front of me. "You're not always boring. Somewhere you've got heart, huh?" Then she kissed me. It was brief, but it was on the lips and I went to sleep a happy man.

Chapter Sixteen

⋆

I WOKE UP Christmas morning knowing I'd fallen in love with Bobbi. She and Parakeet had already left, but her sleeping bag still lay spread out on the raft beside me. I reached down and touched her pillow. The pillowcase had a print of buttercups all over it, and it reminded me of Bobbi, the new Bobbi, the Bobbi from last night. I'd never seen that side of her before. I'd never known it existed, and I wondered how this angel with the sheening voice had slipped in and taken her place without anyone noticing. I sat up in bed and laughed, tossing her pillow up and grabbing it.

I saw the camera Mam had given me sitting on my shelf, and it no longer angered me. I would take pictures of Bobbi, lots and lots of pictures.

I headed downstairs with my camera and heard the *Messiah* playing on the radio. I hummed along, thinking that maybe Christmas would turn out to be all right, even if Larry did prepare the dinner vegetarian style. I had Bobbi to think about, Bobbi to follow around, to listen to, to take photographs of; I had Bobbi. I found her with Mam and Jerusha practicing yoga poses on the floor of the living room, and I took a picture of her attempting to twist her torso around one way while her legs were crossed and twisting the other. She couldn't do it as well as Mam and Jerusha, and the effort showed in her red, tensed face and her hiked shoulders. Her body wasn't long and lean the way theirs were. She was more compact in size and broader in the shoulders, like a swimmer. Yes, she had a swimmer's body. She was a swimmer. A swimmer. I imagined her in a bathing suit, swimming in the cool clear water, swimming toward me, wanting me. I imagined myself diving in above her and coming up behind her underwater.

"What's that stupid look supposed to mean, O'Brien?" Bobbi broke into my fantasy. "Stop staring at me and get your camera out of here. Mam"—she twisted around the other way to face Mam—"tell him to stop. I don't want him in here taking pictures." She looked at Jerusha, who had moved into the next twisting pose, her face hidden by her legs.

"Doesn't matter to me," Jerusha said. "He's not taking my picture, just yours."

Before Bobbi could say anything else, Mam cut in and said, "JP, why don't you see if Larry needs any help in the kitchen? The men are all in there, I believe. And see if Pap's doing all right."

I left them alone, but I didn't join the guys in the kitchen. I knew they didn't want me around—the killjoy. I went to my room, only this time I didn't read or study, I simply replayed the night before in my head and waited for my next opportunity to spend time with Bobbi.

Later that morning I heard Bobbi and Parakeet coming up the stairs and I dashed out of my room, camera in hand, and took her picture in the stairwell.

"Smile," I said, and Bobbi stuck her tongue out at me.

"That should be a good shot," I said. "So, you want to take a walk later?"

Bobbi looked at me and I couldn't read her expression. Was she disgusted or perplexed?

"A walk?"

"Yeah. It's such a nice day out, and—"

"What window you been looking out? It's pouring rain."

"I mean inside. It's a nice day inside. I thought we could take a walk around the house, you know, stroll around Larry's table, take in the living room, the dining room..."

"Strange, O'Brien, very strange," Bobbi said, continuing up the narrow steps, pressing her back against the wall to avoid touching me as she did so. Parakeet trotted up after her, also avoiding me.

"Is that a no?" I asked.

She waved her hand above her head, not looking back. "You got it."

I didn't know what I was doing. I knew I was acting obnoxious, but I couldn't help myself. I'd never felt this way before. I felt stupid and goofy and drunk.

I searched for her again later and found her out on the glassed-in porch, singing "What Child Is This?" to Susan's guitar playing. I stood in the living room and listened through the glass door that separated the two rooms. I drew in my breath and closed my eyes and felt her song fill me and drain me at the same time. So many emotions ran through me: joy, despair, love, longing, peace, anxiety. My body went limp; my arms, which I'd been holding up with the camera in my hands, ready to catch a quick shot when Bobbi and Susan happened through the door, dropped to my sides, and the camera fell to the floor. I thought it was my heart. The singing stopped and I stopped breathing. And I thought, *Her singing breathes life into me. I cannot live without her voice.*

Then Bobbi came to the door and looked at me through the glass. She looked cross. She opened the door a crack and stuck her head out. "What are you doing now, O'Brien?"

My mouth opened and shut a couple of times, and then I said, "You two should sing that song for us after dinner. You could put on a show."

"Maybe if you'd give us a little peace instead of tossing your camera on the floor to get attention, we could practice enough so we could do that." She looked down at the camera a second and then back at me. "Scram!" she said.

I picked up the camera and took her picture. She gave me a disgusted look and closed the door.

Christmas dinner was the usual—noise, laughter, arguing—chaos. Mam, Melanie, and Susan had moved the large Christmas tree with everybody's homemade ornaments and popcorn and cranberries draped in its branches over to the corner of the dining room, to clear a space for Larry's table. Up to that point the dining room had had no furniture in it at all, just a lot of Pap's plants and everyone else's junk brought from the backs of their cars and dumped on the floors.

I had planned to sit next to Bobbi at dinner, but Ben had set out place cards and I ended up between Pap, who sat at the head of the table, and Larry. I couldn't even pay much attention to Bobbi, because loudmouth Larry dominated the conversation. He acted as if he were the star of the show, with his perfect antique table, his Christmas dinner, and all his friends gathered around him. He acted as if he, instead of Pap, sat at the head of the table. He played the great host, talking too loudly and trying to entertain us and make everyone laugh. He and Ben had put on mime costumes, black stretchy pants and black-and-white-striped shirts. I couldn't tell if the costumes were all one piece, but I knew I wouldn't be caught dead wearing one. They clung to Larry's and Ben's bodies like Saran Wrap, and Ben, still built like the football player he used to be, looked like a huge piece of furniture, an armoire or a grand piano. They weren't in white face, but Larry had shaved off his goatee and had pulled his hair back and tucked it under the hat. I didn't know what the two of them were up to, but their miming at the table had everyone howling with laughter except me. I'd never seen Mam enjoy herself more, or Bobbi laugh so much.

I watched her laughing. The sun had come out. Its light streamed through the window behind me and lit up her face. And I looked at the others seated around the table and said in my head, *You want poetry? Bobbi's poetry. Look at her face, her eyes are blue poems, her lips red and small like a haiku, her skin buttery smooth and glowing—a sonnet. She's in your midst every day and you don't even see it. You can't even recognize true poetry when you see it, because you're all phonies.*

I wanted to say all this to Bobbi, I wanted to catch her eye

131

across the table and let her read my mind, but she was still laughing, watching Larry and Ben drinking from invisible dribble glasses, and I wished she were enjoying me, laughing with me, and I wished I thought the pantomime were funny instead of stupid. But all I could do was sit tongue-tied, unable to find any way to contribute to the nonsensical conversations and chaos.

After dinner we all cleaned up and the household exploded in rowdiness, with everyone, except me, snapping dish towels at each other and chasing one another around the house. I stayed at the sink and scrubbed pots and pans caked with dried-out sticky stuff and charcoal, and thought how it might help if Larry could ever think to use a bit of oil or butter in his cookware.

Hours after the meal had begun, we finished cleaning up and gathered in the parlor for the big show. I was the only one who didn't have an act. I hadn't known there was even going to be a show except for Bobbi and Susan's duet, but somehow, without clueing me in, everyone had planned to perform something after the Christmas dinner. Pap insisted on going first. He sat down at the piano and sang "I've Been Working on the Railroad," "O Christmas Tree," and "We Three Kings."

Mam showed us her winter drawings of the pear trees that stood barren in the backyard, the holly bush by the porch, and the cabin in the woods.

I kept eyeing Bobbi, looking for a sign that she would be next. That's all I wanted, to hear her sing again, but then we had poetry-reading time and Bobbi sat still, on the floor, her legs stretched out in front of her and her hands propping her up behind. Every once in a while she'd let her head fall back and she'd tilt it side to side so her hair would swing left and right, brushing the backs of her arms. The whole motion seemed seductive to me, sexy and private and exciting.

She caught me staring at her and I felt myself blush. I turned my attention back to the poetry.

Larry read a poem he had named "Survivors of the Waste Land," alluding to T. S. Eliot's poem *Waste Land,* and later to John Donne's line about no man being an island.

It was hard for me to follow. He asked the question, Who are the survivors of the Waste Land? But then I couldn't tell what he thought the Waste Land was. In Eliot's poem, which I had studied in school, the Waste Land was pretense, meaningless, dead lives. Larry's Waste Land seemed to be disease. Diseases of the body, AIDS and cancer; disease of the earth and sky and sea. Then he brought it closer to home and it was the deterioration of neighborhoods and the family, and then the Waste Land was the internet and television and the media, and he claimed we were all islands now, broken off from one another, isolated, nothing connecting us but wires and electromagnetic fields.

I had sat still during the dinner conversation, but this time I couldn't keep quiet.

"Are you saying you think the computer and the internet are waste lands?" I began.

"Waste lands. Yes." Larry nodded, and his hat fell forward. Pap laughed and knocked on the top of his hat. "They're supposed to be time-savers, connecting us to the rest of the world, but it's all so cold and remote, isn't it? And all that time we save, we spend doing even more work, faster. It's all

'Faster, faster, hurry up, faster.'" Larry used a lot of hand motions with his explanation and Pap imitated him.

Ben said, "We should let him wear a mime costume. Pap, I bet you'd be great."

I eyed Ben. I didn't want him changing the subject when I had something to say.

"You sound as if computers were singlehandedly destroying life, when in reality computers show us life, how it all works," I said. "We know more about life now and the way the mind works than we ever did, because of computers. Have you ever played the Game of Life on a computer?"

"Who needs the game when the real thing is tough enough?" Larry said, laughing. "Really, JP—play the Game of Life, maybe that's your problem. You play the Game of Life so much you don't have a clue—"

"All right!" Mam cut in before Larry could finish. "You both just have a difference of opinion, don't make it personal."

"It's okay," I said to her. "No, the Game of Life is no substitute and it's not meant to be, but what's so fascinating, if you'd ever played it, is that it's made up of just the simplest rules, and yet the patterns, the beauty that's created—it—it's like life. The rich complexity of life is just made up of a few simple rules. I mean, it's like the pattern in a fern leaf or a snowflake or..." I'd gotten excited, thinking of all the possibilities, remembering working on equations with Mr. Commer, the lab teacher, anxious to explain it all to everyone. I looked at them all watching me, listening to me. "I could show you, I could get some paper and I could show you. It's better on a computer, but the idea works on plain paper." I stood up and started out of the room to fetch a piece of paper, but then Ben, who lately had taken it upon himself to become Larry's most devoted fan, said, "You know, Larry, you should enter that poem in the poetry slam. What's the place where they hold the slam every week?"

"You think so? I don't know. I entered one once and really got slammed."

Everyone encouraged him to enter and Mam asked him to read the poem again. "Only slower, this time," she said. "You've got a lot of images there, let them each sink in. You're reading too fast and it really is good."

I looked down at Mam sitting on the floor, with Susan sitting between her legs and leaning against Mam's chest, and Mam pulling her hair back off her face and holding it back in a ponytail. I looked at Bobbi sitting with Harold and Leon, and the three of them were saying, "Yeah, come on, read it again." I looked for Jerusha and found her next to Pap with her knees drawn up under her chin and biting on a nail. She shrugged at me, as if to say, *Sorry, you lose.*

Nobody was interested in the Game of Life, or me. I turned to leave and the doorbell rang.

"Get it, would you, JP?" Mam said, talking over Susan's head.

Pap jumped up. "It's company!"

He joined me at the door, ready to hug whoever stood on the other side of it, but it was Mr. Polanski. Pap stood back from the door and hung his head.

Mr. Polanski cleared his throat. "I come to fetch Bobbi home for Christmas dinner. She should be with her family— her—uh—her mother misses her."

"Bobbi already ate," I said, grabbing the doorknob and attempting to close the door in his face.

Mr. Polanski stuck his body in and called out, "Bobbi? You in there?"

"Daddy?" Bobbi called from the parlor. She and Parakeet came out into the hallway. Bobbi smoothed down her hair as she hurried toward us.

"Daddy?"

"Hey, baby. Look at your old man, all cleaned up." He pushed the rest of the way through the door and shrugged his lopsided shoulders, then he kneed Parakeet in the chest to keep her from jumping up on him.

Bobbi reached for Parakeet's collar and held her back.

"Look at you, Daddy. You're wearing a suit."

Mr. Polanski shrugged again and cleared his throat. "I'm all clean now, and—" He cleared his throat again. "We'd like you home for a while, so how 'bout it?"

Bobbi didn't answer right away and he added, "Just for the rest of vacation, maybe."

Bobbi looked back toward the parlor. We could hear Larry reciting his poem again. She turned back to her father. "Yeah, all right. Let me get some of my things and I'll be right back." Then she hesitated, took a step toward him, and gave him a peck on the cheek.

Mr. Polanski broke into a smile and nodded. "Okay, then, I'll be waitin' in the car."

Bobbi left him and dashed up the stairs. Parakeet and I ran up after her, and I caught up with her on the third-floor steps.

"You're not really leaving, are you?" I asked.

Bobbi continued on up the steps. I followed behind.

"Don't say anything, JP, okay? I'm just going home for a couple of days. Just for the holidays, and then I'll be back." She had grabbed a grocery bag and was stuffing her clothes into it.

"But how could you—"

"I said, lay off!" She glared at me. "I swear, what is it with you?"

I shrugged. "I—I've decided—it's just that I like you—I guess."

Bobbi hoisted her bag onto her left hip and reached her free hand out toward me. She grabbed my hand and squeezed it.

"Thanks. I'll see you in a few days." She let go and knelt down to give Parakeet a hug. Then she looked up at me. "Look after her while I'm gone, will you?" She hugged her again, kissed her on her muzzle, and stood up. She started toward the door and then turned around. "So aren't you going to take my picture?"

"What? Oh yeah, sure." I fumbled with the camera hanging from my neck. She lowered her bag and smiled for me, and it was a smile full of hope and good memories, and friendship. Her smile, her singing, and her kiss were the nicest presents I'd received that Christmas.

Chapter Seventeen

★

BOBBI LEFT, YET I couldn't stop thinking, or dreaming, or fantasizing about her. I thought about her all the time, especially at night. I imagined us together in my room again, whispering about life and chaos. I imagined her kissing me, and better yet, me kissing her, the real thing this time.

Mam asked me one morning when she caught me staring into my bowl of cereal for too long, "JP, are you feeling all right?"

I felt surprised, even nervous, that she had caught me. Did she know I turned out my lights early in the evenings and climbed under the covers and fantasized about Bobbi? Did she know how long I stayed in bed in the mornings, how long my showers now took?

I told her I felt tired from so much studying. I said I'd be fine by the time vacation ended, and in my mind added, *when Bobbi gets back.*

I decided I would invite her to stay in my room again when she returned. I bought boxes of strawberry Pop-Tarts without the frosting, her favorite food in all the world, she once declared. I stacked them on my bookshelf so she'd see them when she first entered the room. I bought a case of Dr. Pepper, her favorite drink, and set it on the floor beneath the Pop-Tarts. I had walked through the woods and gathered pinecones and dry leaves and stones. I stashed my schoolbooks under my bed and created a nature display on my desk, imagining Bobbi glancing over it, picking up a stone to feel its heft, rubbing her thumb across its uneven surface, touching a pinecone and pricking her finger, twirling a leaf and smelling its brown earthiness, all while she talked to me, told me her fears and dreams. I would listen to her, and then I'd say what I should have said that Christmas Eve when she told me about her father. I'd tell her that I would take care of her, that I'd always treat her right.

I brought Mam and Pap's five poinsettia plants up from the parlor and set them about the room to add a touch of cheer and warmth, and I had my film from Christmas Day developed. I glued all my pictures of Bobbi on the sheet of posterboard I had left over from one of my science projects and taped the poster to the slanting part of my ceiling, above my bed. Then I sat back and surveyed the room and the photographs with satisfaction. All it needed was Bobbi.

The others were worried about her. We hadn't heard a word from her since she'd left, but I knew she was all right. I felt certain her father hadn't hurt her and everything was going well; she'd be back at the end of vacation. I figured my will alone would bring her safely home again. She had had on the Einstein T-shirt I had given her for Christmas when she left, and I imagined her wearing it every day and thinking of me as I thought of her. We were connected. I knew she'd come back.

Mam wished she would call. She said she'd feel better if Bobbi would call. I didn't want to hear her voice over the telephone. I was happy to have the time to plan, to prepare for her homecoming, to set it up just right. Speaking to her then, over the phone, would break the spell. We would not speak until we were alone in my room. It had to be just right, just perfect.

Larry suggested we all drive over to the old neighborhood and check up on her, but before we could do it, before I could object, Bobbi showed up, a grocery bag filled with clothes in one arm and a new boyfriend linked in the other.

His name was Don Delveccio, a twenty-eight-year-old whom Larry, Mam, and I recognized as the guy who used to go door-to-door offering to paint the houses in our old neighborhood or fix the plumbing or tune the car. Word got around that he didn't know what he was doing and no one would hire him anymore, and we figured he had moved on, but there he stood in our entrance, arm in arm with Bobbi, while she introduced him, her face glowing.

I watched her set her bag down on the dining room table. I saw her take her free hand and, together with the one holding on to Don, use it to squeeze Don's biceps, biceps about four times as big as mine. He smiled at her, cocky and proud, and Bobbi glowed. She glowed as though all of heaven's light shone on her. I stood in the shadows behind the others and tried to swallow, to breathe, but something, some invisible hand, was pressing on my Adam's apple.

No one else minded Don, not his age, not his reputation, not his looks. Those looks. He was good-looking to the point of being too good-looking, as if his looks were a mask, as if there were some ugliness hidden beneath that smooth tanned skin of his, behind his deep, blue-eyed stare, his firm jaw. He moved as if he were watching himself, noting his own every gesture, calculating, timing every action, every sentence he uttered. He was just too careful with himself, as though holding himself in check, guarding himself. I knew he was trouble, but Bobbi believed she'd found everything she had been looking for, in him. Even Bobbi's father feared Don, and that's what she wanted, she told me later, after Don had left and she had come to my room to retrieve her sleeping bag and raft, which still lay on the floor next to my bed.

We stood alone in the room, we talked, but our words were the wrong words, we said all the wrong things, and she didn't notice the gifts, the treasures I had placed about the room.

She told me, in a voice that grated against the voice I had given her in my fantasies, that she was in control at home now, and her father knew it. She laughed, and it didn't sound like music, like the tinkling bells of my fantasies, but like a dog's bark.

"He knows he's been replaced," she said. "Don is taller, bigger, stronger, younger, and better looking, and he made it real clear to Daddy, without actually saying anything, that I'm his now and Daddy had better not lay a hand on me."

What I had noticed when I'd watched her with Don that first day was the way Bobbi acted around him. She took smaller steps when she walked, made smaller hand gestures, even kept her voice small, timid, when she spoke around him. She looked at him after everything she said, as if checking to see if he approved. She moved and spoke as if she were in a box with a lid on it, and it reminded me of the pantomime Larry and Ben had done on Christmas Day, where they felt their way around an imaginary box, placing one hand at a time in front of them, then hands to either side, then turning around and feeling the invisible wall behind them.

Bobbi told me she had never felt so free, but I thought she had just leaped from one box to another, and when she left my room that afternoon, I reached up to the posterboard covered with her pictures and tore it down.

No one said much to Bobbi about her new boyfriend. I wanted to say something, to protest, but I couldn't put into words what I felt. I couldn't quite put my finger on what was wrong with Don, not in any way that would get rid of him. Since he lived some twenty-five miles away and Bobbi went to school during the week, he only came by on weekends, at first, always with some gift in his hands, flowers or jewelry; and he stayed only long enough to make polite conversation and pat Parakeet, pretending to like her, before whisking Bobbi away for the evening.

I tried to let go of my fantasy, to ignore Bobbi's presence down the hall and her face across from mine at the dinner table. I tried to bury myself in my schoolwork, in the neat stuff I was working on in the computer lab, only it didn't seem so neat anymore and the schoolwork felt tedious. I couldn't focus on anything. I felt as if I were treading on something slippery and treacherous somehow, and yet I didn't know where the feeling was coming from. I couldn't sleep at night. I felt restless, and then I noticed the whole household seemed restless, too. I could hear people all night long, getting up, walking around, the refrigerator door opening and closing, toilets flushing, voices whispering, laughter, tears, all of life, all night long. I thought how the chaos never rested, never slept. It boiled all day, all night, downstairs, upstairs, in each body, in each mind, even in my mind. I knew that, yet I could make sense of none of it.

I ate Bobbi's Pop-Tarts, drank her Dr. Pepper, let the poinsettias go without water, brushed my nature display onto my floor and never noticed when I walked on it, never heard the crunching sounds beneath my feet. I felt like a mess, a wreck. I believed the whole household was falling apart, that the house itself would come tumbling down any second and we'd all be buried in the rubble. For some reason our ship had at last dislodged from the shore and was setting out to sea, gaping hole in the side and all.

But for all the gloom and doom I felt, I didn't see it coming: Mam's little bomb.

She dropped it one night when we were all seated around the dinner table: Bobbi, Jerusha, Susan, Melanie, Ben, Harold, Leon, Larry, Mam, Pap, and me. Everyone was talking at once, as usual. We had finished eating but no one wanted to make the move to start cleaning the dishes, so we were all sitting and talking. I had just decided to excuse myself, which I usually did after Jerusha and I finished my dinner, and return to my room, claiming I had to study for a history test, when Mam banged her knife on the side of her glass and everyone stopped talking and turned to her.

Mam stood up, her face bright, excited, her eyes dancing. "I have some really exciting news to tell you all...," she began.

Pap bopped up and down in his seat. "And I know what

it is, and I'm not saying 'cause it's a secret about a Switzerland place."

"Patrick, let me speak."

Pap sat back and said, "I know, but I know what it is. I was just saying that, but I won't tell it."

I could tell Mam was bursting with some kind of news and I wondered if somehow she had entered and won another contest, this time a trip to Switzerland. I didn't have more than a second to wonder, because Mam blurted out, "I'm going to Switzerland!"

Pap clapped his hands and shouted, "Switzerland, yea!"

Mam nodded, tears filling her eyes with excitement. "Mike has invited me to go with him. He has a medical convention to attend there and I'm going. I'm going to Switzerland!"

Mam sat down and put her face in her hands and cried. "I can't believe it." She shook her head, her face still buried. "I'm going to see the Alps. I never thought..."

She didn't finish her sentence but burst into heavy sobbing and everyone gathered around to hug her, and she told them of her lifelong dream of traveling, and Pap wanted to know if Mam was happy or sad.

I left the table and went outside to stand on the porch, to breathe fresh air, to think a single, clear thought instead of the ones that were racing through my head like so many molecules unleashed and untamed, heated to the boiling point.

At last one clear thought did emerge: Mam could not go off with Dr. Mike. Whatever it took, I would stop her. I would kill Dr. Mike if I had to. It was as clear and simple as that.

Chapter Eighteen

★

I KNEW I needed a plan, but I couldn't come up with one. My mind kept imagining ridiculous or dramatic solutions like locking Mam in a closet and blasting away at Dr. Mike with a machine gun from my attic-room window, or standing on the runway, again with the machine gun, and forbidding the plane to take off with Mam on it. I had simpler ideas such as stealing her passport, which, I discovered, she'd gotten weeks earlier, meaning she'd been planning this trip with Dr. Mike a long time. I also thought about calling the travel agent, pretending to be Dr. Mike, and canceling the reservations, but I knew neither of these would be permanent solutions to my problem. The machine gun looked to be my best bet, but I couldn't begin to figure out how I'd go about getting hold of one or, once I did, how I'd actually use it. Still, in my daydreams, I shot down Dr. Mike all over town, at the hospital where he worked, at his and Mam's favorite restaurant, in the middle of an opera, at an art gallery, and the best one, as he was driving up the drive in his slick BMW.

I wanted to talk to Mam, but every time I thought of something to say to her I found I couldn't say it. I wanted to say, *I refuse to let you go!* I wanted to tell her what she was doing was morally wrong; she had a husband. She had me. I wanted to ask, *Are you sharing a hotel room? Are you sharing a bed?* Just the thought of asking, and worse, the thought of what her answers would be, kept me silent. I wanted to appeal to her practical side or maybe make her feel guilty by asking, *What will Pap do all day while you're gone?* But she had arranged for Aunt Colleen to take Pap to the Center for his classes. She had everything arranged.

Melanie and Jerusha brought hangers of dress clothes to the house for Mam to try on, clothes from their own homes. Susan lent her a pair of never-worn hiking boots that she claimed pinched her heel, yet she'd never bothered to take them back. Mam said they fit perfectly. She had everything going for her, and I could think of nothing realistic to stop her.

I noticed Mam was avoiding me. I'd try to catch her eye across the table at dinner, but she was too busy passing around books and pamphlets about Switzerland, telling everyone of her plans, and describing the fancy hotel where she'd be staying. She talked fast, hardly taking a breath, not letting anyone get a word in, especially me. The atmosphere in the house had turned festive, more so as the time drew near for her to leave.

All I seemed to be able to do was watch and hover. I found myself following her around when she was home, hoping for a moment alone with her and dreading it at the same time. I hung around outside her bedroom door, my head resting on the side of the door frame while Mam reviewed some of her high school French with Jerusha and Melanie. Both of them, I found out, had traveled all over Europe with their families. In between French dialogues, Mam would go into the bathroom, change into one of Melanie's outfits, and then come out saying *"Voilà!"* and walking as if she were on a runway. She wore her hair up in what Jerusha called a French twist, and her neck looked long and white, whiter than her face, which had the freckles to give it color. Melanie and Jerusha lounged on Mam and Pap's bed and gave Mam a thumbs-up or -down on each outfit.

I knew Mam saw me standing outside the door, but for the longest time she ignored me. Then she came out in a dark green suit and Jerusha and Melanie applauded and Mam turned this way and that like a model, and looking all proud of herself, she asked me, "JP, what do you think of your mother?" She smiled and held out her arms, still looking not at me but down at the sleeve of her jacket, admiring herself.

I said, "That's a loaded question," and Mam's smile faded. She flashed me a nervous glance, a flush rising up her neck to her face. Then she turned away from me and grabbed another dress. She said to the others, "Let's see if this dazzles." Her smile had returned, and she scurried back into the bathroom.

When Mam had closed the door, Melanie turned her head and said to me, "Can't you ever be happy for anyone? Give your mother a break, JP."

"Hey, why don't you give me a break and go live in your own home for a change?" I said, shifting so I stood in the doorway instead of leaning against it. "You must have the perfect relationship with your parents, right? That's why you stay here all the time."

Jerusha said, "He's right. We can't judge—"

"And I don't need you defending me," I said, cutting her off. "Don't act like you get it. You wouldn't be encouraging her if you understood anything. But nobody here gets it. You're all this kind of free-love, free-living, what's-mine-is-yours people. You wouldn't encourage her if you got it, so spare me, okay?"

I backed away, then turned and headed off to my own room. On the way up the stairs I heard Mam come out and say, "This knit dress shows my tummy bulge. I haven't had a tummy bulge in years. Not since ..."

She didn't finish. Jerusha and Melanie were insisting the dress looked great on her, and Mam, encouraged, said, "Yeah? You think so?" And I could hear the delight in her voice.

★

As the days passed and it got closer to the time for her to leave I realized I'd never say anything to Mam, never do anything but watch her leave. I stopped trying to seek her out, stopped trying to catch her eye, but sometimes I'd look up and catch her watching me, looking almost sad, or maybe just thoughtful, as if she were wanting to talk to me now. I heard her come up to the third floor once. I recognized her footsteps as she walked halfway down the hallway toward my room, paused, then turned around and went back downstairs.

The day before she was to leave she'd gotten out of work early and sat out on the porch alone, as if she were waiting for me to get home from school. I walked up the driveway, back-

148

pack hoisted onto one shoulder, and kept my glance downward, pretending I didn't see her rocking on the porch. As I approached the steps, Mam stood up. I didn't look at her but kept moving up the steps.

"JP, can we talk?"

I stopped, and still looking down, shrugged. "What's the use? Will our talking keep you from going to Switzerland with that doctor?"

"No, JP, but I think—"

"Then what's the use?" I adjusted my pack on my shoulder and headed for the door. I thought Mam might stop me, but she let me go. I dragged up the stairs, up to the third floor, and saw Bobbi coming out of the bathroom wrapped in a towel. I looked back toward her room and saw Don sitting on the floor, flipping through a magazine. *Was he living here, too, now?*

I shook my head and Bobbi asked, "What's the matter with you?"

I walked past her into the steaming bathroom and shut the door.

Mam left for Switzerland the next morning. I watched from my bedroom window. Dr. Mike picked her up. Larry and Ben brought out Mam's luggage. The rest of them flocked around Mam, all still in the clothes they'd slept in—none could be called pajamas. I saw Pap hugging Dr. Mike, then hugging Mam, then Harold, then Mam again. He started for Dr. Mike one more time, but Dr. Mike hurried around to the trunk of his car and loaded Mam's luggage into it.

Mam hugged everybody good-bye while Melanie kept adjusting Mam's coat and sweeping her hand across the back of it as if trying to brush something off of Mam's back. Susan handed Mam her purse and opened the car door for her. I felt something lurch inside me and I let out a sound like a sob, or like some wounded animal would make, and I saw Mam stop and look up at my window. I backed away, holding myself against my wall, stiff, not breathing, waiting, and then when I looked again the car was rolling down the drive and everyone was waving good-bye. Pap ran after the car, blowing kisses and following it to the end of the driveway.

Later that day, in school, I got my first B ever on an exam. I looked at it and felt nothing, no panic, no loss, no feeling that my brain was deteriorating. I said to myself, *Here it is, this is my life now.* I folded the test paper in half and slipped it into my notebook and got up and left the class. The class hadn't ended and the teacher called me back, but I kept walking.

I'd seen other kids walk out in the middle of class over the years and I'd thought they were jerks, losers. I did it and I felt a surge of power, of some kind of freedom I'd never experienced before. I kept walking. It felt good. I walked faster, my eyes fastened on the exit. I reached the doors to the outside and banged through them and walked faster, jogging down the steps, hurrying along the sidewalk, faster, until I was running. I felt my backpack slamming against my back, books jabbing at my spine, and I laughed. My mind had cleared. I understood those kids, those students who had gone before me over the years, who had stood up and walked out the door, slamming it behind them. They weren't losers. They were just taking back what belonged to them. They were taking back control, and that control gave them their freedom. Walking out, running out, felt so good, so free.

I shouted out loud, "I got a B!" And I laughed at the sound of my voice and shouted it again. "I got a B!" I kept running, shouting out words, sentences as I ran. "My mother's in Switzerland, everyone! She's sleeping with the great Dr. Wonderful! Dr. Great! Dr. BMW! Come to my house! Follow me and I'll set you free!" I ran toward home, shouting out anything that came to me. I was in control. I could do whatever I pleased, whatever, whenever, however. I could get Bs on tests, I could get Ds, Fs even. I could skip the tests altogether. I ran through town, past restaurants and Farley's Bookstore, all the way down the road past the playhouse, dodging tourists, shoppers, bums. I ran up and up the steep hill toward our house and I didn't feel tired, just exhilarated. *Follow me to my house, where love is free! Sex is free! We're all free!*

I stopped when I reached the driveway and stood panting, my arms dangling by my sides, my leg muscles quivering, wasted by the charge up the hill. A picture of the scene with Mam and Dr. Mike riding off in his car flashed through my mind. I shook the thought away and slouched toward the house, dragging up the porch steps and on inside. I could feel the quiet, the stillness, like a presence. I recalled the feeling I had the first time I had been alone in our old house after Grandma Mary died, that empty, desolate feeling. It all came back to me. I crept along the hallway and into the kitchen, half expecting someone to jump out at me from behind a door. I slammed my pack and my notebook down on the kitchen counter, relieved by the noise. I opened and closed a few cabinet doors and swiped at the dish towel hanging from one of the cabinet knobs.

I turned around to face the room, the mess, and remembered the way it had looked the first day we saw it. Then it had been neat and spare, and the wood floors shone and the kitchen fireplace had dried herbs hanging down. Now wet clothes hung in front of the fireplace. Dishes were stacked up on the countertops, cereal boxes left out on the table, the Mr. Coffee had been left on with half a pot of coffee still in the pot, and coffee stains covered the counter around it like outlines of foreign countries.

I left the kitchen and wandered through the other rooms and found the same mess—clothes strewn about, paint cans with colors drip-dried on their sides, paintbrushes stuck hard to the paper bags they were set on, books, musical instruments—cello, flute, guitar, harmonica, and ukulele—plants of every kind and variety, bottles of wine, beer cans, soda cans, potato-chip bags—some empty, some not—and shoes. Everywhere I went I found shoes. We had beanbag chairs in every color of the rainbow and one huge plaid one that Ben always sat in, and in the living room our latest addition, Ben's huge fish tank. I tapped the side of the tank when I walked past, and smiled. Ben had warned us all not to tap the side of the tank. I tapped it again.

I wondered where Parakeet had gone. I called her, but she didn't come. Then I remembered, Delveccio had convinced Bobbi to return her to the SPCA. Bobbi returned her on the sly so the rest of us couldn't complain. What Delveccio wanted, Delveccio got.

I stepped outside and stood on the porch, wondering what kind of free thing I could do next. Running out of school had felt so good, but coming home and touring the house, I had allowed my old self, my old mood, to creep back. I looked at the cabin at the edge of the woods. Everyone had started calling it Larry's cabin. Jerusha had brought over a box of tools one day and said, "I'll just go put it in Larry's cabin and surprise him." That was it. Everyone called it Larry's cabin after that. "I think they're all at Larry's cabin." "Would you go ask Harold if he wants to go to the concert with us? I think he's at Larry's."

I jumped off the porch and jogged out to the cabin. "My cabin," I said. I opened the door, expecting to see more mess, mess that had spilled over from the house—tools everywhere, maybe planks set over the missing floorboards—but the room stood neat and tidy. Larry had repaired the floor and kept it swept clean. I found the broom leaning against the wall beside one of the two windows. He had two boxes of tools set on the floor in the corner and a board he'd attached to the far wall where he hung still more tools. Newspaper had been laid out on the floor beneath this and on top stood another table, this one with a round top, freshly stained, giving the cabin its wood-and-chemicals smell. I ran my hand over the table. The stain had dried. I felt the side rubbed smooth by Larry's sanding, and circled my hand all around the rim. I remember he had bragged about using almost nothing but hand tools to make his table. He went into a long explanation of how he might set up a business creating colonial furniture using only hand tools, and wondering if he should apprentice under someone or just keep teaching himself.

"I was thinking," he said, dropping the English accent and developing a tougher, furniture maker's voice, "that I might just do it myself, go about it slowly. I'll take my time and learn it right. Start with tables and just keep experimenting. Then when I feel I know tables, I'll move on to chairs and beds. Yeah, I do better working on my own. It'd be too much like my old man standing over me if I worked under someone."

Another time he came in after cutting his hand on one of the tools, dripping blood in the hallway, and said, "I might just do tables the rest of my life. I don't think there's an end to what they can teach me."

I didn't know a table could teach anything at all, but I knew that the one I had my hand on was a piece of art. It was simple and sleek and stained in walnut. I saw the can of stain and a rag sitting on the newspaper beneath the table. I ran my hand over the top of the table and then backed away. I backed out the door and closed it.

"James Patrick, it is. See, Colleen, it's not a burglar, it's just me boy, James Patrick."

Pap ran down the slope toward me, his arms wide, while Aunt Colleen stood next to her car with her arms folded, watching. I hadn't heard them drive up.

Pap grabbed me in a bear hug and said, "You beat me home today. How come you're in Larry's cabin? Is Erin there, too? Is yer Mam in there?"

I pushed away from Pap. "No, Pap, remember? Mam left for Switzerland this morning."

"I know that already, James Patrick. I know it."

"I thought you were a burglar," Aunt Colleen called to me. "What are you doing home so early? Erin said you didn't get home till five or five-thirty."

Pap and I walked up the slope to where Aunt Colleen stood waiting for me, a bright green purse dangling from her folded arms. She looked majestic somehow, standing at the top of the lawn with the house looming in the background. She looked as if the house were hers and she was guarding it against the likes of me. I wasn't too far from the truth.

"James Patrick," she said, when we had gotten within closer hearing range, "I can't believe you and that sister of mine could allow such havoc. The house is a disaster area, and who in heaven's name were all those people I found lounging and scrounging about this morning? I thought I'd walked into the wrong house."

"That's the way Mam likes it." I shrugged, enjoying the indignant look she gave me.

"Well, she has gone clear out of her mind. I always thought there was something wrong—" She caught herself and, looking at us, said, "Never mind. I'm going to wait around until those others get here. Patrick says they live with you."

"Yup, I told you that already," Pap said. "They live here all the time and they eat with us even and they call me Pap 'cause they think I'm their Pap, I think. But I'm not really, am I, James Patrick?" Pap turned to me, but I didn't answer. I was eyeing Aunt Colleen.

"What are you going to do? Kick them out?" I asked.

"No. But I can make them clean up. I thought Erin said you had a schedule for cleaning."

I nodded. "Yeah, we did once, but there's just too many people now, and too much junk."

"Well, we can just get rid of all that junk. We can haul up a big trash canister if we have to, and load it all in. And we'd better do something about the ceiling in that parlor or you'll be having it in your laps. And the living room—we need a professional painter in there."

I felt a charge run through me. This was my day.

I said, "I've drawn up a plan of all the work that needs to be done. Want to see it?"

Aunt Colleen uncrossed her arms and stood taller. "Yes, yes I do, but you bring it out here. I don't think I could bear to go back in that house."

I ran up to my room and rifled through my desk drawer, hunting for the plans. The thin drawer overflowed with the torn photographs of Bobbi I had stashed there one furious afternoon, and I had to dig beneath flashes of her eyes, her hands, her hair, still feeling the pangs of hurt and envy, to find those plans.

I heard a car roll into the driveway and glanced out the window to see—who else but Don and Bobbi rolling into the drive in Don's pickup.

I found the plans underneath the one photograph I'd had blown up and didn't have the heart to destroy, even in my fury. It was the picture I had taken of Bobbi just before she left with her father that Christmas Day. I remembered how I had thought her smile held such hope, showed such good feelings between us, and how it was a shock to see it later when I got the prints back and find that her smile held fear and doubt, not friendship. Her mind was already on her father and leaving, and not bound up with mine at all. I had been the one full of hope and love. I had given her my feelings, believing they were hers, too, but the photograph told me the truth.

Don was standing with his arm around Bobbi and saying something to Aunt Colleen and Pap when I returned with my plans.

They all looked at me, and I held up my sheet of paper, avoiding Bobbi's eyes. I said, "Found them!" hoping I sounded more cheerful than I felt, and then Don said, "Well, look here, it's Little Pap," and he laughed at his own joke. Bobbi laughed, too, and then so did Pap.

I replied, "It's Dumb Don," and laughed back, and I saw his jaw tighten, the muscles in his face bulge out.

Pap laughed and repeated. "Dumb Don. I like that. Dumb Don."

I handed Aunt Colleen the plans and Pap repeated, "Dumb Don."

Then Dumb Don said to Bobbi, "Come on, let's grab some of my things and take them on up to our room."

Aunt Colleen looked up from the plans. "You live here, too?"

Pap chuckled. "Dumb Don."

Don squeezed Bobbi closer to him and, lifting his head, said, "I do now."

"All right," Aunt Colleen said in a let's-get-down-to-business tone. "We've got the four of you. You all can get started cleaning up the junk off the floors downstairs. Pick up the garbage, fold the clothes. Don, you haul the paint out to the garage."

Don eyed Aunt Colleen a moment, as if he were trying to decide whether he was going to belt her or not, then he backed up toward his truck. He reached into the bay and pulled out a duffel bag, hefted it onto his shoulders, and headed for the house.

Bobbi trotted after him and Aunt Colleen said, raising her voice, "I should imagine you'd have the downstairs cleaned up by dinnertime."

Don turned around and, walking backward toward the front door, said, "Lady, I don't do women's work."

Pap chuckled and said, "Dumb Don."

Chapter Nineteen

★

OVER THE WEEKEND Aunt Colleen had us all cleaning
and scrubbing, everyone except Don. She could never tolerate a messy home. She had even hired a painter and a work
crew to come, starting on that Monday, to fix up the place. To
make sure the workers kept up to the mark, she stood over
them all afternoon. One day I came home from school and
found her down in the basement holding electrical wires in
her outstretched hand, keeping them a safe distance from her
silk blouse and talking about red and blue wires to the elec-
trician. Another time I found her in my room, watching a
woman stirring paste in a bucket and asking her about water
stains on a white ceiling.

She strode about the house each day in her ramrod,
there's-business-to-be-done way, but then she met Mr. Fitzgerald, the painter, and something in her changed. Overnight
she became a different person. She stopped following the
other workers around and just stood talking to Fitzgerald,
who, she later told us, claimed to be a leprechaun. He was a

small, wrinkled man with a squeaky-sounding Irish brogue and a dark complexion. He chewed on the end of an unlit cigar and sang "When Irish Eyes Are Smiling" with Pap, who didn't know the words but sang anyway.

One day I overheard Aunt Colleen quizzing him, asking him leprechaun questions, such as, "Where do you live? How do you make yourself disappear? Let me see you do it. Where's your pot of gold?" And she laughed at all of his answers. I had never heard Aunt Colleen laugh before, and I thought maybe it was a first for her because the laugh sounded like a rusty hinge swinging back and forth.

Another time I overheard her talking to him in a more serious tone, saying, "I just told him to put on a little bit of foundation and blush. He's so pale in the winter, you know. I didn't want him operating on his patients looking like death himself. How would that be?"

Mr. Fitzgerald drew in his breath and said, "Indeed."

"But my husband has his pride. One of the other surgeons noticed the makeup and they made fun of him."

"Ach no! Pity, that."

"He wouldn't speak to me for a long time after that. Actually"—Aunt Colleen lowered her voice, but I could still hear her—"he moved out and lived at the club for a couple of weeks. And I don't mind telling you, I don't like staying in that big house all by myself, not at night."

"No. No, that ain't right, for sure. But he has his pride, ya see."

"Yes, but he is so pale. He doesn't have your fine dark complexion."

"I thank you fer that, missus," said the leprechaun, and then he added, "You missed a wee spot there, I think."

I couldn't resist, I had to peek in the room, and what did I see but Aunt Colleen dressed in a pair of overalls, with gloves on her hands and a bandanna wrapped around her head, painting right alongside Mr. Fitzgerald. I darted away again before they heard me gasp, and I decided that this ugly man had to be a leprechaun; there could be no other explanation for the sudden change in my aunt.

With all these changes going on I decided to try a change of my own. I wanted to create a Grandma Mary meal. I figured I didn't have to put up with Larry's or Mam's vegetarian glop anymore. I could make my own meal. I stopped at the grocer's after school one afternoon and purchased some hamburger meat and a few other ingredients. When I got home I went in search of Grandma Mary's recipe file, to check on the exact measurements for each ingredient. I went to Pap first. I'd seen him sitting up on the roof when I came home.

"Pap," I called out the window, "do you know where Grandma Mary's recipe file is? I need it."

Pap sat still as if he hadn't heard. He stared up at the sky. "Pap?"

"Yup, I have it, James Patrick."

"Can I borrow it, then?"

"Okay." Pap inched his way on his bottom toward the Nativity set and reached out for one of the Three Wise Men. He lifted up the base and felt around a second and then withdrew the file. He slid himself back and handed me the rusted file without looking at me. Then he returned to his watch of the sky.

"Thanks. Pap? Did you go to the Center today?"

"Nope."

"How come?"

"'Cause I need to stay up here."

I leaned farther out the window. "You been up here all day?"

"Yup."

"Well, Pap, when you coming in? It will be dinnertime soon."

"No, I'm not coming in now, 'cause I got to wait, is why."

I set the recipe file box down on the window ledge and climbed out on the roof. I sat down next to Pap.

"Hey, Pap," I said.

"I got to stop talking now." Pap sniffed up the snot running out of his nose and shoved his hair out of his eyes. His lips had a blue tinge to them.

"It's cold up here, Pap. Why can't you talk? What are you waiting for?"

"I'm waiting to see her."

"Who? Aunt Colleen?"

"You know, 'cause I can see her, but not *her*."

I took an exasperated breath. "Pap, that made no sense at all. Who can you see, who can't you see?"

Pap raised his chapped hand up in the air as though he were feeling something in front of him. "Me mam is here, of course."

"You can see Grandma Mary?"

"Yup."

"Where? What does she look like?" I tilted my head so it almost touched his, and gazed up in the sky.

Pap held up his other hand so that both arms were outstretched, and he looked like a person who couldn't see, who needed to find his way in the dark. "She's here. She's everywhere when I come up here." He smiled and gave a satisfied sigh and lowered his arms.

I tried to follow his gaze, to see what he saw. I couldn't see anything. I shook my head. *Of course I don't see anything. Have I gone crazy looking for Grandma Mary in the clouds?*

"What are you waiting for up here, then?" I asked Pap.

"Me wife." Pap turned to me. "Do you see her, James Patrick?"

"No. Do you?"

"No, I can't see me wife at all up here."

"That's probably because she's not dead, Pap. Don't you think? She'll be home before you know it. Then you'll see her every day."

"But I need to see her now. Do you see her, James Patrick?" Pap stared back into the sky.

"Are you going to stay here until you see her?"

"Yup."

"What if you never see her? What if you can't see her until she gets back from Switzerland? You can't stay up here all night long."

"Yup, I can, too, if I want."

I stood up. "Pap, come in now, okay? It's cold. You can look for her again tomorrow after your classes."

"No, I'll just stay here, and yer not me mam, yer me little boy, I think."

"Great," I said. "That old song again."

I left him on the roof and took my recipe file box down to the kitchen. I dug out Grandma Mary's recipe for chili con carne with pasta and began cooking. I was deep into it when some of the others came home and wandered into the kitchen.

"Smells good," Harold said, standing behind me and drawing in his breath through his nose. "What is it?"

"Nothing. It's for me," I said.

Jerusha and Melanie came in and asked the same question. "It's just a chili recipe."

"It's just for him," Harold added.

"Well, you are all vegetarians, remember?"

Then a few minutes later Ben and Susan came into the kitchen, and I knew Larry wouldn't be far behind.

Susan started to speak, but Harold and Melanie spoke up at the same time and said, "It's chili, but it's just for him."

Susan looked in the skillet. "You've got enough to feed an army."

"I'm hungry, and it's for more than one day." I inched closer to the stove, bending over the skillet and stirring the contents.

"Geez, you act as if you think I'm going to cheat off your test paper or something," Susan said, backing away.

Then Larry came in and everyone said, "It's chili but it's just for him." And Ben added in a squeaky voice, "You can't have any, it's mine, it's mine!"

Larry walked over to the stove. He picked up the container of cumin off the counter and examined it. I grabbed it away from him. "Just lay off, Larry. I'll be done in a few minutes and then you can have the kitchen."

Larry backed away and watched me pour the chili con carne over the noodles I had sitting in a casserole dish. Then I sprinkled shredded cheddar cheese over it and placed it in the oven.

"You know, that's my skillet you're cooking with," Larry said. "I don't recall you asking to borrow it."

"It is not," I said, moving to the sink with it so I could wash it out. Larry came up behind me.

"That's my sponge, too. I bought that sponge myself the last time I went shopping for groceries for everybody. When's the last time you went shopping for groceries?"

"This afternoon," I said, hunkering down over the pan and rinsing it out.

"Cute, O'Brien."

"And that's Larry's dish towel, so don't think of using it to dry dishes," Ben said.

"And that's Larry's mat you're standing on," Harold added, standing up and drawing closer to me.

"And Larry's sink." Susan got up and began moving toward me, too. I had turned around so my back was to the counter. I held the dripping pan in my hand.

Melanie laughed and stood up to join them and said, "This is Larry's kitchen. You have to pay a fine to use Larry's kitchen."

"Yeah, you have to pay a fine," Harold said, and then they all said it, chanted it at me. "You have to pay a fine. You have to pay a fine."

I pushed through them, slammed the skillet back down on the stove, grabbed a pot holder, and pulled my casserole back out of the oven.

"No, no," Ben said. "That's Larry's oven mitt."

I set the dish on the table, where only Jerusha sat, and I said, "Here, you skinny, bug-eyed bug. Eat this!"

Then I strode out of the kitchen and up the stairs with the group of them laughing and applauding.

"Larry's kitchen, my ass," I muttered. "You want to play games, I'll give you games." I grabbed up some clothes and my coat and hat and went down the hall to Bobbi and Don's room. I walked in, grabbed a paper bag off the floor, and stuffed some of my things in it. Then I scooped up her sleeping bag and marched down the stairs.

I met Bobbi and Don on the second flight. Don was yelling at Bobbi and yanking her arm by the wrist as if he wanted to pull it out of its socket.

"You guys can have my bed," I said, storming past them, not caring what happened to Bobbi and her arm. I kept on walking, right past the kitchen, past Aunt Colleen and her leprechaun, out the door and down the slope to *my* cabin.

I heard Pap calling to me but I didn't answer. I slammed open the cabin door and threw my things on the floor.

It didn't take long before Larry came running down the slope after me, shouting, "O'Brien, if you lay a hand on that table, I swear—"

I'm in control, I told myself, taking a deep breath and stepping over to the table to wait for Larry. I tried to steady my legs, which trembled so much I feared they'd buckle under me.

Larry burst into the cabin and I stood running my hand over the table's surface, trying to act as calm as could be.

"Get out of here, O'Brien." Larry panted. His eyes looked wild.

"You've got the house," I said. "You win. It's all yours, Larry. But I need someplace to go and I'm going here. I'll just take this little cabin." I tapped the table.

He lunged at me and swiped my hand off his table. "Get out of here! I'm not kidding."

"Neither am I." I grinned. I could feel myself grinning and I couldn't help it. I hadn't meant to smile. I wanted to look tough, to feel tough, but I felt scared, shaken. I didn't feel in control at all anymore. Larry's eyes burned with a strange light, an anger, and I could feel mine burning, too, but my burning spoke of fear, my grin, alarm. I clenched my fists but kept them down by my side, and took a prepared stance, one foot in front of the other.

Larry saw this and cocked his head to one side. "Hey, look, we were just kidding around in there."

"Yeah, I know. You like doing that, don't you?"

Larry shrugged. "You're an easy target, O'Brien."

"Yeah? Give me your best punch and let's see who the easy target is, because I'm not leaving this cabin. My cabin. My mother, my house. Your parents didn't want you, remember? Your whole family didn't want you, did they? Your father—"

Larry rammed his fist into my stomach, taking me by surprise and knocking the wind out of me. I fell back against the table and tried to suck in some air. I felt a wave of panic come over me. I couldn't breathe. I grabbed on to the table and Larry stood watching, his chest heaving, but a look of concern spread over his face.

"Hey. Hey, I didn't mean it. Are you okay?" He reached out for me and I took my first good breath and doubled over. "You keep away from me," I said. "I'm not moving. This is my cabin." And I thought to myself, *It's all I have*—but even then I knew it, too, belonged to Larry.

Chapter Twenty

★

I GUESS LARRY felt bad about knocking the wind out of me, because he left me in the cabin—but not before he'd checked his table for damage from my fall against it. I wished the whole thing would have collapsed, but it was too sturdy. He gave me another warning about staying away from the table, a less belligerent one, and then left.

I lowered myself onto the floor and leaned my back against the wall. I closed my eyes and cursed, first at Larry, then at the cabin and the house and all of New Hope, and then at my mother, and finally at Dr. Mike. Somehow, it all came down to the whole thing being his fault. He'd encouraged Mam to enter the contest in the first place. He'd encouraged Mam to sell Grandma Mary's house. And there he was in Switzerland with Mam while I sat on the floor of a cold cabin. I'd never hated a person the way I hated Dr. Mike. I hated Larry and his buddies and the way they teased me, but they were all a part of this Dr. Mike thing, too. They wouldn't be here if Dr. Mike hadn't come along. If I had any guts at all, I really would kill him.

I crawled onto the sleeping bag and lay down on my back. "If I had any guts at all," I said to the ceiling.

I don't know how long I lay there daydreaming. The back of my mind registered the workers getting in their cars and leaving, and then the leprechaun saying good-bye to Aunt Colleen and leaving. I heard Aunt Colleen calling to Pap, trying to coax him down off the roof before she left, but she didn't succeed and she drove away. Before too long, day had turned into night, and I was still working on my plan to get rid of Dr. Mike.

Then I heard Jerusha calling to Pap and my mind snapped back to the present. Pap needed to be inside. It was cold out. Too cold to stay still without more cover than he had. I'd had to climb into Bobbi's sleeping bag with my down coat on to keep from freezing.

I listened to Jerusha's coaxing and felt guilty about what I'd said to her when I shoved the casserole at her that afternoon.

I listened awhile longer and I knew that the way Jerusha was going at it, Pap would never go inside. I climbed out of my sleeping bag and went to see if I could help.

I stepped out of the cabin and looked up at the lighted figures on the roof. I knew Pap was sitting behind them, but I couldn't see him, and I supposed Jerusha had climbed out the window and sat beside him because I couldn't see her, either.

I called up to Pap and felt foolish because I knew it looked as if I were talking to the Nativity set.

"Pap," I said, "I know I'm not yer mam or anything, but see, Grandma Mary said to me that it was time for you to go inside now because Mam won't be coming tonight."

I felt bad lying to him, pulling a Larry stunt, but I figured it was better than his getting frostbite.

Jerusha stood up then and turned toward the window.

"You don't have to leave," I called up to her.

"Yeah, I got things to do," she said, and then she stepped through the window and disappeared.

I cleared my throat. "Pap? Are you up there?"

"Yup, I'm here, but you know what? It's cold." Pap spoke through chattering teeth.

"Grandma Mary is angry that you're still up there. She says you're acting stupid."

"Hey, down there, I'm not stupid and yer me own boy, remember, and I'm not stupid."

"Then how come you're sitting up there waiting for Mam when you know you should be taking a hot shower and eating a big dinner and going to bed?"

"'Cause I need to talk to her, is why. Where is she, James Patrick?"

Pap's whining voice coming from behind the Virgin Mary sounded so pitiful to me.

"Pap, she's in Switzerland, remember? What do you need to talk to her about? Could you maybe tell me?"

"Maybe."

"I'm listening, Pap."

"I feel funny, James Patrick." Pap's voice was quiet and slow, his chattering had stopped.

I stepped closer to the porch, then, seeing even less than

before, stepped back again. I felt ashamed of my unwilling-ness to go inside and climb out onto the roof with him, but I didn't want to run into anyone in the house.

"How funny, Pap? Sick-in-the-body funny, or funny-in-your-thoughts?"

"Yeah, funny in my thoughts, 'cause like, are you still me little boy down there?"

"Of course I am, Pap. I'll always be your boy."

"But, see, you got taller than me. James Patrick, you're taller than me now."

"I know, Pap, but I'm still your boy. I'm just growing up, but you'll always be older than I am."

"James Patrick?"

"Yeah, Pap, I'm here." I shifted to my right, trying to see Pap's shadow between the plastic figures.

"James Patrick, that's a good thing. Don't you think? Don't you think it's a good thing you'll always be me boy?"

I smiled. "Yeah, it's good. It's a sure thing."

"I like that," he said.

"Yeah, me, too," I replied. And I did. It had never oc-curred to me before. I'd never noticed the steadiness of our relationship. I'd never seen the order in it, the perfection of this single thing. I'd looked everywhere for some bit of sta-bility, and here it existed with Pap. I would always be his son, he would always be my father. The thought comforted me and the comfort surprised me. I tucked my hands in the pocket of my coat and hunched up my shoulders.

"James Patrick, down there, I want to know, will Erin al-ways be me wife?"

I shivered. "Yeah, sure, Pap," I said, hoping I sounded

more certain than I felt. This thought, too, had never occurred to me. I couldn't see beyond the affair itself, and I couldn't really see that. I hadn't allowed myself to believe that Mam was doing anything more than going to operas and museums with Dr. Mike. I'd accused her, but inside I held tight to the hope that I was just overreacting, as she herself had said to me. Now here was Pap, knowing in a way that the rest of us couldn't, that his relationship with Mam was in trouble. He understood from some feeling he had inside that he could lose Mam, and only he dared to see beyond the facts to the unthinkable: that they might not always be together.

"How come she's not here, James Patrick? How come she's with Mike now?" Pap called down to me.

"She's taking a vacation, Pap. You know what a vacation is, don't you?"

"Sure." Pap raised his hand and slapped it back down on his thigh. I saw the hand flap above the Virgin Mary's head and heard the slap.

"It's okay. Pap? Everything's okay. But while Mam's away you've got to take care of me and everybody. You're the father around here, and a father takes care of his children."

Pap stood up, coming out from behind the figures. "Yeah, but I forget. Am I everybody's father?"

"Not really. Just mine. You're just my father, Pap."

Pap nodded. "Good, 'cause I can take care of you okay."

"You sure can, Pap, and you know what I need? I need some food. I'm starving." I twisted around to the cabin and twisted back. "I'm living out in the cabin now, but I don't have any food out there. Could you go in and bring some out for me?"

"Yup. I can do that, and I'm hungry, too, so I'll have some food, too."

"Yeah, but Pap, don't forget about me. Go in and get enough for both of us and we'll have a picnic outside in the cabin, okay? I'll try to find Grandma Mary's old kerosene heater and that old lamp of hers."

Pap scooted to the window and stuck his leg through. "Okay, James Patrick, okay."

I waded through all of Pap's junk in the garage, hunting for the lamp and the heater and finally for some kerosene. At last I found all three and hauled them to the cabin. I got the lamp going first and looked around at the cabin walls, hoping I wouldn't set such a tinderbox on fire. I started up the heater and then checked my watch. Pap had been gone a long time. I decided he wasn't coming and climbed back into my sleeping bag. I wished I had had the foresight to bring a pillow and mat down with me. The cabin floor felt hard against my back, especially my tailbone, and I knew I couldn't rest my head on my arms all night.

Then I heard Pap calling to me. "Here I come, James Patrick." I scrambled out of the bag and peered out the window. I could see him jogging down the slope with a stack of blankets in his arms, but no food. I felt glad for the blankets but disappointed about the food. I sat back down on the sleeping bag.

Pap banged open the cabin door and stepped inside.

"Jerusha said that I should bring you these blankets 'cause it's going to be freezing tonight."

"Thanks, Pap. I've got the old heater going, though, see?"

Pap glanced at the heater and dropped his load of blankets.

"Yeah, I remember that, I do. That's mine from when I was a wee lad." Pap got down on his knees and held his hands up near the heater.

I got up and closed the cabin door and heard my stomach growl. "Pap, what about dinner? Did you forget?"

Pap turned and smiled at me. He started to say something, but he got interrupted by a knock on the door.

"What?" I said in an unwelcoming tone.

Jerusha said, "I brought you your dinner."

"Oh. Oh, sorry, come in." I grabbed the door and opened it for her and she stepped inside with a tray loaded down with my chili con carne casserole, steaming hot, a Thermos, and some rolls wrapped in plastic.

"Here's dinner," she said, clomping across the floor in a pair of heavy hiking boots and setting the tray down on Larry's table.

I thought I should say something about not using the table, suggesting that she set it on the floor, but what were tables for, anyway?

Jerusha slipped out of the pack she had on her back, swung it around in front of her, and pulled silverware and plates and cups out of it. She set these on the table, too.

I didn't know what to say. I felt ashamed of what I'd said to her earlier, how I'd always treated her. To try to make it up to her I said, "Why don't you join us? You brought plenty. I mean, thanks for bringing all this."

Jerusha turned around to face me. She smiled and her brown eyes looked bright and sparkling beneath her bangs.

"I'm glad you offered," she said to me, digging her hand back into her pack. "I happened to bring an extra set of silverware, *and*"—she paused for effect—"my own plate. Tah-dah!"

"Hey, all right!" I said. "This is my lucky day. Jerusha eats off her own plate, alert the media."

"Tah-dah!" Pap said, lifting his arms in the air.

Jerusha bent down and picked up one of the blankets. "Come on, help me spread this out."

Pap and I both took ends of the blanket, and the three of us spread it out on the floor. Then we set the food and the rest of the things on top and sat down to eat.

While Jerusha served our plates I said, "So, look, I'm sorry about what I said in the kitchen this afternoon. I don't know why I said that. I didn't mean it. I mean, you're not ugly at all." I could feel myself blushing when I said this.

"Jerusha is tah-dah!" Pap said, enjoying the word.

I nodded. "Yeah, you're tah-dah."

Jerusha laughed. Then she shrugged her shoulders. "I look at it this way. You gave *me* the casserole."

"I did, didn't I?"

She handed me my plate.

"Anyway," she added, "you needed someone to take your anger out on, so you chose me."

"Yeah, but why didn't I choose Larry or Harold, someone who was giving it to me? Why didn't I give it back to them? You weren't even saying anything."

Jerusha handed Pap his plate of food and took up her own. "Look," she said, "there were six or seven of them in there. It was an uneven fight. You chose me because I was the safest one. You knew I wouldn't fight back."

I took a bite of my chili and nodded. "Yeah. Yeah, that

sounds good—I mean, that's right. I didn't mean it, but yeah, you were safe." I nodded again. "You were easy pickins. That's what Larry said to me. I'm easy pickins. I'm safe."

"Exactly." Jerusha nodded and her whole upper body bobbed up and down. "You know, this is really good," Jerusha said, loading up another forkful of the chili.

"Yeah," Pap said. "It's me mam's dinner. I miss it, James Patrick."

I smiled and took another bite. It *was* good. It was the best thing I'd eaten in a long time. I knew if I closed my eyes I'd be back home, sitting at the old kitchen table with Grandma Mary across from me.

We ate in silence for a while and I thought about Jerusha. She was the only one out of all of them who didn't get into fights with any of the others. Everyone else seemed to be feuding with someone, but Jerusha managed to stay out of it.

"Doesn't anything ever bother you?" I asked her.

She looked up surprised. "Yes," she said, yanking off a piece of her roll with her teeth. She shrugged. "I just don't have to take my frustrations out on other people."

I looked down at my plate of food. "Maybe that's because nobody picks on you."

"You did, this afternoon," she said, still chewing on her mouth full of bread.

I looked up. "Oh, right, I forgot for a second."

"See, I thought about it, how everyone's always trying to razz you, and I knew your feelings were hurt. I knew you weren't really wanting to hurt me personally, just someone."

"Yeah, but you shouldn't just let people walk all over you. You should have given it to me."

"What good would that do? Anyway, I don't let people walk all over me."

"You let me," I said.

"You think so? I've practically got you eating out of my hands." Jerusha grinned and tossed me another roll.

I laughed. She was right. She'd made friends with the enemy, bringing me the food and sending Pap down with the blankets—but Larry and the others, that was different. I couldn't let Larry just take over the whole place. I had to at least put up a good fight. No casserole would settle our differences.

Pap held out his plate. "I'm finished with that much, but I want some more."

I grabbed the serving spoon and dug into the casserole dish. I scooped out another helping for each of us; checked Jerusha's plate, expecting to see it still full, and was surprised to find it almost empty.

She held out her plate and I scooped some more chili onto it. She took the plate and hunched over it. "You're a good cook, JP, you should do more of it."

"And I can make soda bread with raisins," Pap said.

I nodded. "It's good, too. We'll have to cook you up a real special dinner one of these days."

"With a chocolate cake," Pap said.

"All right, that's a deal," Jerusha said, taking a sip of the peppermint tea she'd brought us in the Thermos.

I thought again about what Jerusha had said. I thought about making a dinner for everyone, the whole crew. Would they say they hated it just to make fun of me? Would Larry get angry and think I was taking over the kitchen—his kitchen?

I shook my head. "We're all fighting over the stupidest stuff. Maybe we're all just bored. You know? Nobody's doing much of anything around here. It's just a lot of posturing and posing. Larry and his scarf and English accent and..." I stopped. I'd forgotten about Jerusha and her suits and ties.

"We're all just trying to find our way, JP, that's all. Even you. Even Pap and your mother. You need to give people a break, give yourself a break." Jerusha took another sip of tea and set her cup down and looked at me. "I look at this house as the great incubator, and all of us—your mother, Larry, Harold, Bobbi, all of us—we're all eggs waiting to hatch. We're trying out different ideas, trying on different hats to see which one fits. That's why I took a year off from college. I wanted time to figure out what I really want to do with my life. It's great how your mother has opened her house to all of us. JP, it's great that she's willing to share all this with us."

I set my plate down on the blanket. "I guess so. I just wish she'd be a bit more picky about who she lets in."

Jerusha shook her head and set her plate down across from mine. "Then it's too predictable. Predictable gets boring."

"Then I guess I'm boring," I said, hoping Jerusha would contradict me.

Instead she nodded with her upper body and took another sip of her tea. "On the outside you are, because you're holding it all in, playing it safe. No one with a brain like yours, though, could be boring on the inside. You just have to let more of that out."

"I'm interesting," Pap said. "Lots of people say I'm very interesting because I'm different, is what they say."

Jerusha leaned forward and tapped Pap's leg. "You're the most interesting person I've ever met, Pap," she said, and I found myself wishing she'd touched my leg and said those words to me.

"I know that already," Pap said.

Jerusha took one last sip of her tea and then started cleaning up. I scrambled to my knees and helped her, wondering at the same time how I could be more unpredictable.

Jerusha paused and looked about the cabin. "It's nice here," she said. "The lamplight's nice, all the shadows. I like it here, don't you?"

"Yeah, it's really nice, especially with you here." I said it without thinking, then realizing what I'd said, I felt myself blush and hurried to pick up the rest of the dishes.

"Hey, I wasn't through with that tea, ya know," Pap said when I grabbed his cup.

"Sorry," I said, setting the cup back down. Then I had a thought, an idea, an unpredictable idea.

Jerusha stood up and held open the plastic bag the rolls came in. "Here, stick the dishes in here," she said.

I slipped the plates in and said in as nonchalant a tone as I could deliver, "So, since you like it here, why not stay the night here with me?" I glanced at her, felt myself blushing again, and turned to Pap. "You too, Pap. Let's have a sleep-over party out here."

"All right!" Pap said, getting to his feet and spilling his tea on the blanket.

I turned back toward Jerusha.

"Sounds good to me. I'll go take these dishes up and get some more blankets and pillows. Pap, you can help."

"Right," I said, feeling the grin on my face move through my whole body—a whole delighted body grin. I could get used to this unpredictability.

While they were gone I busied myself with arranging three places to sleep. I made a pallet out of one of the blankets and set it next to the sleeping bag. I spread the other blanket out over Larry's table, making sure the wet spot from Pap's tea didn't touch it. I knew when Pap saw the tentlike setup he'd choose it instead of one of the other two, and then Jerusha and I would be side by side.

When I heard Pap's voice outside, I opened the door to wait for them. I looked up and saw three people coming down the slope—Jerusha, Pap, and Leon. Leon carried Jerusha's cello in one arm and a foldout chair under the other. Pap and Jerusha carried blankets and pillows and two rafts.

"Leon suggested some music," Jerusha said when they reached the door.

"It's going to be a real party," Pap said.

"Sure is," I said without enthusiasm, stepping back to let everyone in. I hadn't figured on unpredictability being a two-way street.

"Hiya," Leon said, stepping into the cabin. "Place looks bigger on the outside," he added after looking around.

"That's because of all the people inside," I said. "Be careful of the heater."

Leon scooted out of the way and moved to the other side of the room.

Jerusha set her blankets on the table and unfolded the chair Leon had leaned against the wall. Then she grabbed her cello and said, "I'll have to tune this thing up again. All these changes in temperature aren't good for it."

"Jerusha's going to play," Pap said, and then discovering the tent I'd made him, added, "Hey, neat. I call I get the tent to sleep under." He grabbed a pillow and a couple of blankets and crawled under the table.

"I can hear you, Jerusha," he said. "I can hear you playing your music instrument all the way from under here."

Leon and I fixed up the other beds, placing rafts under two and just folding a blanket under the sleeping bag I had brought down.

Leon chuckled. "I don't know what everyone else is going to do tonight, I think we got all the blankets." He crawled onto one of the rafts and spread out on his back, folding his arms behind his head. "If music be the food of love, play on," he said to Jerusha, quoting Shakespeare.

I sighed and climbed into my sleeping bag. At least Jerusha would be sleeping between us.

Jerusha warmed up with some scales and I realized I'd never paid much attention to her playing before. I thought her scales sounded pretty good. Then, before she finished with the scales, we heard voices outside, and then loud knocking on the door.

"Fee, fi, fo, fum," Susan called out. "We're going to huff and puff and blow your house down."

"Hey, it's Susan," Pap said, rising from under the table and banging his head. "Ouch!"

The door opened and in paraded Susan and Harold. Harold had a large bowl of popcorn in his hands and Susan had her guitar and another folding chair.

"Impossible," I said. "We'll never fit."

"O ye of little faith," Susan said, stepping over me and setting her chair in front of Jerusha so she'd be facing her when they played. Harold stepped over me and sat down on Jerusha's bed, lowering himself in one movement so that he ended up cross-legged, the bowl of popcorn held high in his hands. He lowered it and Pap came out from under the tent and joined him on the blanket. Both of them blocked most of my view of Jerusha. I sat up. Jerusha tapped the edge of Susan's chair with her bow and said, "Quiet, please. I will now play Bach's Prelude, Suite number one."

And just like that, we hushed and Jerusha played. Her whole body moved with the music. She kept her eyes closed, and as she moved her hair swung into her face and away again. Then she came to a place in the music where the notes escalated, climbing and climbing, and her torso moved in circular breaths and I found my own breath changing to fit her rhythm.

When she had finished I had no breath left; I just held it. I didn't know what to do. I didn't want anyone to move or speak. I wanted her to play it again, but I didn't want to have to tell her, I didn't want to interrupt the spell with words. Then Susan began the same piece on her guitar and Jerusha joined her and they played it through again. Susan didn't play as well as Jerusha, but still it sounded beautiful. Jerusha was beautiful and I found myself falling in love again, in love with Jerusha and Bach's Suite no. 1.

Chapter Twenty-One

★

THE SIX OF us stayed up most of the night. Jerusha and Susan played a mixture of classical, folk, and jazz. Then Susan strummed the guitar while Harold recited one of his poems about his father, a father he never knew, and about how he planned to be there for his own children, be responsible, capable, accountable. I liked it because it came across as more powerful, more personal than some of his other poems. I decided I liked Harold better after hearing it.

I thought about it again later that night, or really, the next morning, when we had all settled down and were falling off to sleep. His poem revealed something about him, just the way Bobbi's singing and Jerusha's cello playing revealed something about them. They were sharing something of themselves with their art and it made me understand them a little more. It made me like them, and I wondered what I had to share. What could I do to reveal who I was? I had already tried with computers and the Game of Life, but they weren't interested. Why was it I could listen to their poetry and music, but they couldn't care less about my interests? How could I make them care? I didn't have any idea, and I fell asleep thinking about this, lying on my opened-up sleeping bag, sharing a pillow with Harold, who shared a blanket with Leon and Susan, who shared a pillow with Jerusha. All six of us lay spread out across the cabin floor, sharing blankets and pillows and breathing in the kerosene fumes.

Just a couple of hours later my watch alarm went off. I groaned. I had to get ready for school. I left the others sleeping and lumbered up the slope toward the house, hoping Larry would still be asleep and I could get dressed and eat breakfast without running into him. I made it through my shower and got dressed and was halfway through making breakfast when Larry shuffled into the kitchen. He squinted in the light and, catching me standing over the stove, paused. He scratched his head, then shuffled forward again, over to where I stood.

"Smells good. What you making?" he asked.

I thought about saying, *What does it look like, stupid?* but I changed my mind and said, "My grandmother's pancakes. I know I used some of your buckwheat flour, but that's the only flour we've got."

Larry dug a cigarette out of the pack in his breast pocket and nodded. "We don't have any syrup," he said, lighting up the cigarette and shuffling to the table and sitting down.

"I know. I made some sauce with a couple of your oranges and your cinnamon and—"

"Okay, cool it with the *my* oranges stuff. We were just fooling around. You have a right to the kitchen if you want it."

I didn't say anything. I flipped my pancake, one large one

that filled the skillet, just the way Grandma Mary's always did. It looked a lot darker than hers, from the buckwheat flour, but it smelled the same. I lifted it out of the pan and put it on a plate. Then, feeling a mixture of excitement and embarrassment, I took it over to Larry and set it down in front of him.

He looked up at me and I said, "It might not be so good made out of buckwheat. Try it and see what you think."

I grabbed the sauce I'd made off the counter and handed it to Larry. He stubbed his cigarette out in a coffee mug left over from some other day and pulled his chair up closer to the table. "Thanks," he said.

I handed him a fork and knife and he cut a slice and ate it. While he chewed he nodded. "Excellent," he finally said, cutting another piece. "Excellent."

"Want coffee or what?" I asked. "I've boiled some water."

He glanced up at me, then back down at the pancake. "Well, normally I have herb tea, but since I'm eating this, why not go whole hog—sure, hit me with some coffee."

I went back to the stove and ladled some pancake batter into the skillet for myself. Then I fixed Larry's coffee, smiling to myself. Maybe I could share this with the others. Maybe I could cook up more of Grandma Mary's recipes.

I sat down with my own pancake, and while I poured on the sauce Larry said, "Sorry about yesterday. That was stupid."

I shrugged. "What are you going to do with that table?" I asked. "Sell it?"

"Nah." He took a sip of his coffee and poked in his pack for another cigarette. "I thought I might, I don't know, give it to my family."

Larry's face got red. He shook his head so that his hair fell into his face. He lit his cigarette, took a drag, and closed his eyes. "Wonder what they're all up to these days."

"Why don't you go find out? Why don't you take them the table as a . . . as an Easter gift? Easter's coming up soon."

"Yeah, I could do that," Larry said, but his voice sounded uncertain.

I took a bite of my pancake. Even buckwheat couldn't destroy Grandma Mary's recipe. "I'll go with you," I offered, hoping I'd be in just as generous a mood when the time came. "I could visit your brother," I added.

Larry nodded. "Okay, we'll see. Thanks." He turned to me and gave me a light punch on the arm. "It's complicated, but we'll see."

I wondered what he meant by "complicated," but I didn't have any time left to discuss it with him. I had to get to school.

It was the first time in my life I had ever dreaded going to school. For one thing, I'd had all of two hours' sleep, and for another I hadn't done my homework. I expected a lot of yelling and a lot of zeros for the day, but all the teachers were understanding. I could do the homework that night and turn it in a day late.

Instead, I skipped my hour helping at the computer lab and did it in the library, handing the assignments in by the end of the day. Then, feeling pleased with myself and my good day's work, I decided to stop by the chorus room and pick up Bobbi and walk with her to the veterinarian's office, maybe talk to her about things.

When I got to the chorus room, though, I found Don

standing just outside the door, peering in through the small square of glass.

"Hi, Don," I said.

He twisted his neck and glared at me. "What's she doing in there?"

I peeked through the window. Bobbi stood on a platform with Andrew Weinfeld. The two of them were singing to each other, holding hands.

I looked at Don. "It's just a duet. They're acting."

He shoved me aside. "Yeah, well, I don't like it."

"Believe me, Bobbi doesn't like Weinfeld. The guy's a nerd."

"Yeah? Then what's she doing with her head next to his, huh?"

"They're acting, I told you."

"Well, she's done acting."

The singing stopped and I heard the teacher announce something, and then the door opened. Don could hardly wait for Bobbi to get out. He pushed at the kids filing out of the room, grabbed Bobbi by the arm, and pulled her out into the hallway.

"Hey! That hurts. What's wrong?" Bobbi said. Then, seeing me, she added, "Hi, JP."

I walked behind them, not sure what I should do. Don held on to Bobbi's arm and hurried her out of the building. I scooted along behind them. He pulled her out to the parking lot, yanking on her arm if she dragged too far behind. Bobbi kept asking, "What's wrong? What did I do?"

Don wouldn't answer. He just kept marching her toward his pickup.

Thinking I could slow things down a little, I said, "Hey, Don, could I get a ride home?" I bobbed about in front of the two of them, and Don shoved me out of the way without answering.

"Get in," he said when we'd reached the truck. Bobbi looked at me, then opened the door.

"Bobbi—" I stepped forward and held the door while Bobbi climbed into the front seat. "Wait, I—I need some help at the office—uh, they told me to see if I could get someone to help me today, and I thought maybe you—"

"Look, JP, stay out of it, okay? I know what you're trying to do, but just butt out. I can take care of myself."

Don shouted from the other side of the truck, "Shut the door!"

Bobbi reached out for the handle and pulled the door shut.

Then Don jumped in and peeled out of the parking lot, and I saw Bobbi looking back at me a second before her body jerked toward Don's. He had yanked her hair.

I wanted to run after the truck, do something. If Bobbi could take care of herself, why didn't she?

★

WHEN I GOT home later that day, I found Pap had climbed back out on the roof, Aunt Colleen was flirting with the leprechaun, and the workers were loading up their truck. I could find no one else around. I called up to Pap to ask how long he'd been sitting on the roof.

"I just got out here, 'cause I went to work and I have a new plant, see?"

Pap stood up and held up a spider plant. "Soon I can make me a wildflower garden with Bobbi. They said so at the Center, that I could do it soon 'cause the ground is getting unfrozen."

"That's good, Pap. What are you doing up there?"

"I'm just talking, JP, so don't you be telling me what to do. I have things to say now, so you go away."

I waved. "All right, Pap." I left him and decided to walk down to the cabin. I wanted to relive the memories of the night before. I wanted to recall Jerusha's eating dinner with me, and her music, and Harold's poem, and all of us, including me, squeezed in under the blankets, getting in a few jokes before we all fell silent and drifted into our separate thoughts. I had loved being a part of it all. I loved that they had come down to me—maybe not to be with me, but I was the reason they were at the cabin and not in the house. And it didn't seem weird and uncomfortable and Bohemian at all. It felt easy and relaxed. I felt glad the others had come down after all.

I stepped inside and started up the heater. I had decided to do my homework in there among the blankets and pillows and bask in the warm feelings from the night before.

After a while Aunt Colleen came down and checked on me before leaving, and I watched from my window when she pulled out in her car behind the leprechaun's truck. I wondered if they were going to get dinner together somewhere. I told myself not to get bothered by it. *Ignore it. It's none of my business. Butt out,* as Bobbi would say.

Then, just after thinking about her, I heard Bobbi yelling, "I already told you, okay? I told you."

Then I heard Pap shout, "Yeah, she told you already."

I looked back out the window and saw Bobbi and Pap standing up on the roof. Don stood leaning halfway out the window. I hadn't even heard them come home.

He shouted at her and Bobbi shouted back and Pap echoed Bobbi. Back and forth they went. I shrugged and told myself to butt out. I sat back down to do my homework, but I couldn't concentrate.

"She's a big girl. She can handle it herself," I said, but I kept listening. Then I heard Bobbi squeal, "Stop it! Stop!"

I jumped up and Pap shouted, "You're bad. You're a bad man! Stop that now, 'cause you're hurting her," while Bobbi kept shouting, "Stop it!"

I saw Don out on the roof wrestling with the two of them, and all three were knocking into the Nativity set. I dropped my notebook and flew out of the cabin, shouting at them to watch out, but I was too late. Pap's feet had gotten tangled up in the electrical cord. I saw him look down and try to get out of the way of it. I called out to him and he looked up, twisting his body slightly, and over he went with the whole Nativity set falling down on top of him.

Chapter Twenty-Two

★

PAP'S BODY LAY sprawled out on the grass, the Nativity set in a tangle of wires all around him. I felt a flash of relief that he'd fallen off the side instead of over the front onto the driveway, but then I saw how still he was lying, how lifeless he looked, and I panicked. I ran to Pap, shouting up at Don, "I swear if he's hurt, I'll kill you! I swear I will."

I fell on my knees, knocking the Wise Men out of the way, and called to Pap. "Pap! Pap, are you okay?" He had his left leg bent from the knee, up under him.

Bobbi cried, "You killed him! Look what you did, you killed him!"

I kept calling to Pap, placing my ear to his chest and listening for a heartbeat.

Again Bobbi yelled, "You killed him!" and I shouted for her to shut up and call an ambulance. "Do it now, Bobbi!"

A minute later Don ran out of the house and hustled toward his truck. Pap had opened his eyes, but when I saw Don trying to escape I shouted, "I will hunt you down, you bastard! I swear I will. You're dead!" The man tore out of the driveway and sped off down the road.

I returned to Pap. "Pap, are you okay? Say something."

"Kerplooie!" he said, lifting his head and shaking it. "I fell off the roof!" He tried to rise up onto his elbows, but I held him back. "James Patrick, you're getting tears all over me face, you know, and I've got to move, 'cause me leg is in very great pain." He tried again to move and bellowed, "Owww! Who-ee, this hurts! James Patrick, get off of me with your tears."

★

BOBBI AND I rode with Pap to the hospital. While we waited in the waiting room, I lectured Bobbi.

"What is wrong with you, anyway? How could you take up with someone just like your father? Don's exactly like him! You're just asking for it. You said you could handle it—well, why didn't you? Why didn't you fight back? 'Stop it! Stop it!'" I whined, imitating her, flapping my arms. "Why didn't you haul off and flip him, or kick him? You could have at least done that, instead of acting like a limp noodle. You sure had no trouble flipping me to the ground last spring, remember?"

"Yeah, but I didn't *love* you!" Bobbi said, jabbing at my chest with her finger, her face red with fury.

I felt stung by her words, but I ignored my hurt feelings and shot back, "Love? Love? You call that love? Are you crazy?"

"What would you know, O'Brien?" She squinted her eyes. "You've never loved anyone in your life, and no one loves you. You're like a piece of deadwood. Don has passion and fire, but you wouldn't know about that, would you? You think you've got all the answers because you're so smart, you read all those books—but you don't know anything about real life."

"Oh, and real life's letting someone beat on you? You can have it!"

I could see out of the corner of my eye people watching us. I turned away from Bobbi and waited for Pap by myself near the nurses' station, mulling over her words. She didn't love me. Well, I supposed I'd known that all along—but to hate me? I could see the hate in her eyes. Did everyone hate me? She said I had never loved anyone and no one loved me. Just a couple of months ago she had said I'd always had my parents' love, that I had been surrounded by love but couldn't love back. I thought her earlier judgment was more accurate, but I knew, too, that she had never loved anyone, either, not with real love.

Then I saw Pap hobble down the hall toward me on crutches with a cast running all the way up his thigh. He was jabbering away with the nurse, explaining to her that he had broken his leg in two places, and watching him, I thought, *I do, too, love someone.* I loved Pap. Until that moment I had never realized how much, but I did. I loved Pap with all my heart.

It was late when Larry and the others picked us up at the hospital and brought us home, and as soon as we all walked in the door, Bobbi got on the phone and called around looking for Don. She finally found him at a friend's house and asked him to come pick her up. Pap and I were working our way up the stairs to Pap's bedroom when Bobbi came down with her grocery bag filled with her belongings. She made sure I saw the bag, and I shrugged and said, "It's none of my business what you do."

Bobbi stopped on the steps and said, "It's about time you figured that out." She switched her bag to her other hip.

"But how you could go off with that maniac instead of staying here, where it's safe, is beyond me."

"Everything's beyond you." Bobbi marched down to the bottom of the steps and Pap, who sat on his bottom inching his way up the stairs backward, said, "Are you leaving us, then, Bobbi?"

Bobbi stopped and turned back around. "I love him, Pap," she said in the meek tone she used with Don.

"Well, congratulations," I said, shaking my head and nudging Pap to continue up the steps by poking him with one of his crutches. "You've turned out just like your mother."

I heard the door slam shut behind me.

"There goes Bobbi," Pap said.

Larry shot out into the hallway. "Was that Bobbi leaving?" he asked.

"Yup," Pap said.

He hurried outside and joined Bobbi on the porch. I could hear the two of them arguing, and I said under my breath, "Good luck."

I'd gotten Pap settled in his bed with everything he wanted, including his Winnie-the-Pooh stuffed toy, when I heard Larry come back inside the house. "I can't believe it!" I heard him shout.

"Believe it," I said under my breath, and Pap said, "What?"

"Nothing, Pap, just lie back and take it easy and tomorrow I'll make you one of Grandma Mary's special meals with a chocolate cake, and you can lick the bowl, okay?"

"Yeah, okay, but I make the soda bread with raisins," he said, smoothing back his wild mass of hair and exposing a pale and tired face.

I patted his arm. "You'll be okay, Pap," I said, searching for some kind of comforting words to say, more for myself than him.

Pap nodded and slid down in his bed, wrapping an arm around his Winnie-the-Pooh. "Yup, I know it. And you know what? The nurse said I'm very handsome, like a model."

"'Night, Pap," I said.

★

AFTER SCHOOL THE next day I stopped by the bank and took out some money and bought groceries for the dinner I'd promised Pap. When I got home I discovered the workers had already left and, stepping inside, I found the place all cleaned up, smelling everywhere of fresh paint and furniture polish.

I could hear Aunt Colleen explaining something about the piano to someone in the parlor. I set my groceries down in the kitchen and went to find her. She sat on the piano bench and beside her in another chair, with his broken leg resting on the bench, sat Pap.

They both looked up when I came in.

"Hiya, James Patrick, and I'm getting a real piano lesson so I don't make that awful noise, 'cause Colleen says."

Aunt Colleen stood up. She had on a lace shirt and green skirt—no overalls. She seemed tired, maybe sad even, but I felt pleased to see the old Aunt Colleen back.

"Well, James Patrick, what do you think of the place? It's all done. Do you think your mother will be surprised?"

"Sure, it's great." I looked around the room at all that she had had done and all that she had paid for, the fresh paint, the shored-up floor, a couple of new pieces of furniture—chairs with a floral print. I nodded. "Yeah, it looks like something out of a decorator magazine. How did you get the place cleaned up so fast?"

"Easy, I hired a clean team to come out this morning."

"Well, yeah, it all looks great, thanks. Everyone's going to love it. So"—I twisted toward the kitchen and then back—"I've got some groceries to put up and a dinner to prepare."

I eyed Pap, and he struggled to get up. I rushed over to help him, and Aunt Colleen and I got him up on his feet.

Aunt Colleen wiped her hands together and said, "Well, then, I'd better get going. I'll still stop by each day and keep Pap company until your mother comes home. I thought we wouldn't try going back to the Center just yet."

I nodded and began to lead Pap out of the room, then stopped.

I turned back to Aunt Colleen. "So, uh—why don't you stay for dinner," I said. "We're celebrating Pap's recovery from his fall. I'm going to make a cake, and anyway, we owe you a lot. I mean"—I started to blush, I could feel the heat rising up my neck—"I mean, how could we possibly thank you? Mam's going to go into shock when she sees how great this place looks."

Pap cheered. "Chocolate cake and Aunt Colleen!"

Aunt Colleen perked up. "Yes. Yes, that would be very nice, James Patrick, thank you." She brushed at her skirt with her hand and followed us into the kitchen, and I felt proud of myself for thinking to invite her.

I got started on the cake while Pap worked on the bread, and Aunt Colleen offered to make the salad. But after twenty minutes of watching her peeling one cucumber and feeling my blood start to boil, I took a deep breath and asked her if she might like setting the table more.

She looked relieved.

"Make it look festive," I added.

"Festive is what I do best," Aunt Colleen said, setting the knife and cucumber down on the counter and rinsing her hands.

Soon the others began filing into the room, and before they could get on my case about using the kitchen, I assured them I planned to make enough for everyone this time.

Melanie ran a finger around the emptied cake-batter bowl, licked it, and raised her eyebrows in surprise.

"Not bad, JP. When did you learn how to cook, anyway?"

I smiled. "I didn't. I'm just following my grandmother's recipes. I guess watching her all those years paid off. Anyway, it's easier than I thought, kind of like doing a biology experiment."

Susan said, "That's JP, always has to bring science into it."

I decided to take her comment as a joke and laughed, and the others laughed, too, and got to talking about something else.

I watched them from my side of the counter while I sliced

potatoes for the soup. The others sat around the old kitchen table, talking and kidding one another, and even though the counter separated us I felt a part of them. I felt included. I joined in the conversation now and again and they didn't attack the things I said any more than they did anyone else's.

Larry and Ben arrived and I caught a flash of annoyance crossing Larry's face when he saw me dumping the corn and potatoes into the big pot on the stove. I guessed he thought it was fine for me to take over the kitchen for a meal or two, but this was three meals in a row, and he must have figured I planned to crowd him out.

I glanced over the remaining vegetables on the cutting board in front of me and grabbed up a bunch of garlic cloves.

"Hey, Larry," I said, leaning over the counter toward him with the cloves in my hand. "I was wondering, could you make us some of that salad dressing you made once? That garlic one everyone loved so much? I'm fixing a celebration dinner for Pap."

Larry blinked a moment, glanced at Ben, and then shrugged. "Okay, sure," he said, and he moved right on around the counter and joined me.

I grabbed a paper towel and wiped at my sweating face. I noticed the sweat under my arms had soaked the sides of my T-shirt as well. Making friends was tense work.

The rest of the group continued to chat around the table while Pap and Larry and I prepared the dinner and Aunt Colleen set the dining room table.

At one point Melanie said, "I don't know what it is, maybe getting the house all fixed up or something, but I've got this feeling like something exciting's about to happen."

The others agreed and spoke about the changed atmosphere in the house—less fighting going on, less competition, more camaraderie. I agreed. I knew the constant tension I had felt since we had moved to the house had lifted off my shoulders at last. Aunt Colleen had brought a bit of order into the house, making us pick up after ourselves and getting the repairs that we had always meant to do, done.

That night at the dinner table everyone had second helpings of the corn chowder and salad and bread, and then while we were eating ice cream and cake, Jerusha spoke up and said, "You know what this is? This is comfort food. JP makes great comfort food."

The others nodded and Susan said, "You notice how we've all been talking as a group all night instead of in separate groups or over each others' heads?"

"Or fighting," Harold added. "JP, what did you put in that soup, anyway?"

"Yeah," Susan said, "I feel like confessing all my deepest darkest secrets."

"It's the lighting," Aunt Colleen said. "I always think candlelight is the best way to eat an evening meal."

Everyone got quiet for a moment, and we all stared into the candlelight. Then Leon said, "Man, I used to be so afraid of the dark when I was a kid."

Larry nudged him and said, "You still are, who you trying to fool?"

Larry laughed, but Leon nodded and said, "It's true, I am. I still hate the dark."

"I hate the dark, but I love the dark cake," Pap said, "and I love Harold."

Everyone laughed, and Pap wanted to know what he'd said that was funny.

Harold asked if anyone at the table had ever been to an all-black gathering?

Melanie confessed that she knew she'd feel weird. "I mean, I don't think anything about you being with us, Harold, but I know I would feel really out of place if it were the other way around."

We had a long discussion about white and black America, and Harold confessed he acted white around us because he didn't think we were ready for the total African American experience, and Jerusha said, "Then you're cheating us of learning from you and, worse, you're cheating yourself. Give us a chance, Harold."

Larry said, "Hey, we all act different than we really are. Like Leon said, we're all afraid of the dark—no pun intended, Harold."

Then Aunt Colleen, who had been quiet during this whole discussion, set down her fork and said, "I've left my husband."

I choked on the cake crumbs in my throat and took several swallows of water while everyone else consoled my aunt. Tears rolled down her cheeks, leaving streaks in her powdered face. She dabbed at her face with her napkin.

"We haven't been getting along for a long time. I've been putting up with him, he's been putting up with me, but coming here every day and seeing what Erin has here—not that I want this life exactly, but seeing that there are other lives I could be living, that I didn't have to feel dead inside—well..." She shrugged and more tears fell.

I thought I should say something, but all this baring of

the soul felt too touchy-feely for me. I wanted more than anything to announce that I had homework to do and take off the way I usually did, but I had started the whole thing with my comfort-food dinner. I knew I couldn't back out.

We listened to Aunt Colleen a long while, and we all said we wanted her to stay at the house now that she'd fixed it up so nicely. At long last we convinced her to stay with us, and Larry offered her his room since he never slept there, anyway, and she sniffed her last few sniffs and dabbed at a few more tears and thanked us, and we grew silent again. I thought it would be a good time to stand up and clear off the table and end all the confessions, but then Larry said, "I know I have to try to make it up with my parents, but I don't know—I don't think they'll ever accept me, even if I do give them the table I made. The drugs were bad enough, and not playing football and dropping out of school." Larry laughed, but it was a pained laugh. "What do you think they'd say if I told them about me and Ben?"

I dropped the fork I was fiddling with in my hand. It clattered on my plate. "What about you and Ben?" I asked.

"Take a flying guess, O'Brien," Ben said.

Susan added, "I can't believe he didn't know. You're blind, O'Brien."

"But—but that's—sick! In this house? In my house! You guys are—"

"Spit it out, O'Brien," Ben said. "You can say it, *homosexual*. Repeat after me, *homosexual*."

"See what I mean?" Larry said, rocking back in his chair and gesturing toward me with his hand. "Here before you is a prime example of my family's reaction."

"But what is that you're saying?" Pap asked. "I don't get it."

Aunt Colleen patted his hand, and Larry said, "Ben and I love each other, Pap, that's all."

"Well, I love you, too," Pap said. "I love everybody at this table and I love Bobbi, who's not at this table, and Erin, me own wife, who is in Switzerland."

I tried to pull myself together, to remind myself of all the good times and good feelings: the night in the cabin, the dinner before me, my desire for friends, but it wasn't enough. No way could I accept Larry and Ben as a couple. Forget friends and family and excitement in the air; it was just plain impossible.

Chapter Twenty-Three

★

I HAD CUT out early from my job in the school office so that I could cook my meal for the crew at home. After Larry's surprise announcement, though, I decided to go back to my old routine of school, work, and homework. I decided to get back to where I belonged. I didn't want to cook anymore, anyway, because Larry cooked. Homosexuals cooked. I gave Larry the jeans he'd worn of mine and the rain forest T-shirt of mine he liked to wear. I didn't like the idea of sharing clothes with him, or sharing anything else. I stayed away from both Larry and Ben as much as possible. I stayed away from all of them when I could, even Jerusha. I had decided that my love for her was just an infatuation. I was in love with beauty and perfection; not her, just her music. If anything, I told myself, I was in love with Bach's Prelude, that's all.

Whenever I thought of that night when I had cooked dinner and they all sat around telling their deepest darkest secrets, I had to shake my head in wonder. I had been foolish to think I could ever fit in. I had been crazy to even think I wanted to become a part of the gang.

Even Aunt Colleen fit in better than I did. Since moving in with us, she had taken charge of tending to Pap. Aunt Colleen, who had recommended that Mam place Pap in a home after Grandma Mary died, who couldn't stand being around him for more than a few minutes, was now with him all day long. She saw to it that he stayed off his leg when it got to hurting him or when his foot started to swell. She had the idea of fixing the broken lightbulbs and bringing the Nativity set inside and placing it in Mam and Pap's room, so Pap could see it from his bed. She worked with him on the piano every day and got him to play the first three notes of "Three Blind Mice." He played them over and over, and she never told him to stop. She laughed when he said something she thought was funny and let him hug her and didn't make the sour face she used to make whenever he said he loved her. Instead she patted his head or hand and smiled and got on with the lesson. She gave him plenty of lessons. She had the piano lessons, the set-the-table-the-right-way lessons, the shake-hands-with-strangers-instead-of-hugging-them lessons, and the proper-way-to-pronounce-just-about-everything lessons. Pap, for his part, taught Aunt Colleen how to make Irish soda bread and how to take care of and sing to plants, and how to have fun in a garage full of junk.

Then Larry decided the time had come to take the table to his parents and introduce them to Ben.

"Hey, you're an ex-football star; they've gotta love you," he said one night at the dinner table. "I'm going to call them right now and see when a good time would be to go over there." Larry got up from the table and so did I. I took off for the safety of my room, hoping he wouldn't remember my offer to go with him when he took the table to his parents' house. He had Ben, anyway, and I was on his parents' side, so I didn't think it likely he'd want me around.

Maybe he didn't, but Tim Seeley wanted to see me.

Larry called me downstairs and handed me the phone. "My brother wants to speak to you," he said, not looking at me.

"Yeah, thanks," I said. I took the phone and turned away from him. I wiped the receiver before speaking into it.

"O'Brien, why don't you come by when Larry comes? Man, I haven't seen you in ages."

"Not since we moved," I said.

"Right. So hitch a ride."

"I don't know," I said, trying to think up a reason not to go. I thought I'd like to see Tim, see for myself if he'd really changed as much as I thought he had, or if there was still some connection between us. I needed a friend. I needed my old friend to talk to. I thought about unloading all the stuff that had been going on, the way he had always done with me, and although the idea was really tempting, I didn't want to ride in a car alone with Larry and Ben. Not that I thought they'd attack me or anything. I just didn't like the way they made me feel when I was around them. I felt weird and embarrassed.

"I think I've got a big test to study for." I tried to laugh. "You know me, gotta be class valedictorian next year. I got a B on a history test. I bet—"

"Right, just thought I'd ask. Save the excuses, O'Brien. I thought we were friends. Fact is, I thought I could talk to you about something."

I hesitated and then said, "Okay, sure, I'll be there. Yeah, I want to come. I've got some stuff to tell you, too."

"Good, then see you on Saturday. We'll play a little football or something. It'll be great."

★

SATURDAY DIDN'T START out great, however. First, when Ben, Larry, and I went down to the cabin to fetch the table, Larry inspected it one more time and found a nick on the corner where I had fallen against it the night he punched me. He had a fit about it and looked at me as if it were all my fault, and I said, "You were the one who punched me, remember?"

Ben tried to calm him down by rubbing his back and saying soothing words.

"Oh, please, don't make me puke," I said, turning away from the two of them. How had I gone so long without noticing how queer they acted? Susan was right, I had to be blind not to have noticed. They wore matching earrings, even, and Larry had dyed his hair a lemon color to match Ben's.

Larry sanded the teeny-tiny nick and stained it and then, at last, we loaded it onto the roof of the van. We had blankets set on top of the van, blankets wrapped around the table, and blankets on top of the table, all tied with thick ropes and knotted inside the van so that I couldn't close the doors all the way. We had to tie the doors as closed as we could get them after we had climbed inside. I sat in the back, in charge of watching the knots to see they didn't loosen around the table, and Larry and Ben sat up front.

Ben drove the van and Larry sat in the passenger seat, moaning and whining and saying every minute or so, "Maybe we should just turn around. I'm not ready."

"Sure you are." Ben patted his hand, and I rolled my eyes. "Look, you've got your act together," he continued. "You've got a steady job, right? You know what you want. Don't let your parents mess you up. Your father's got to be pleased with the table."

Despite Ben's encouragement, Larry got more nervous the closer we got to the old neighborhood. I could see sweat beading up on the side of his face every time he turned to look at Ben for reassurance. Even with the doors open some, it had begun to stink inside the van. It smelled like stinkin' fear, and I had to admit, I felt a little sorry for Larry. He kept shifting in his seat, clearing his throat, pulling his hair back in a ponytail, and taking it out again.

Just as we approached the entrance to the neighborhood, Larry said, "Stop! Stop the car."

Ben slammed on the brakes, and the driver behind us gave us the finger as he drove past.

Larry jumped out of the car and ran to the side of the road toward the creek. He disappeared behind the O'Learys' house and Ben nodded. "He's sick to his stomach. I told him he shouldn't have had that orange sauce."

"What orange sauce? My orange sauce?" I asked.

"What?" Ben twisted around to face me. "Yeah, that sauce you showed him, and the pancakes. He loves the stuff. You're a good cook, O'Brien. He says his don't taste the same as yours."

I shrugged. "I just follow my grandmother's old recipes."

Ben turned back around and watched out the window for Larry and so did I.

"I don't think science was Larry's favorite subject," Ben said. "What does 'two eggs, separated' mean, anyway?"

I laughed. "Tell me he didn't take two eggs and put them in separate bowls."

"I don't know. I didn't watch."

I sat back in my seat. "I grew up watching my grand-mother cook. I guess that's the difference."

"You're a natural." Ben nodded.

It had to be the nicest thing he'd ever said to me. I guessed he was forgetting to be mean because he felt worried about Larry.

"Where the hell is he?" he asked, resting his head on the window.

"Maybe he decided to drown himself in the creek," I said.

"Don't even joke." Ben unlocked his door and was about to get out when Larry came jogging back toward the van.

He hopped in all out of breath and said, "Okay, ready."

"We thought you'd drowned," Ben said.

"Nah," Larry cleared his throat. "Thought about it, though."

Ben patted his hand and started up the car.

It felt strange coming into the old neighborhood. Some of the houses had been painted, some looked the worse for wear, and they all looked smaller, much smaller than I'd remembered.

Our house had been repainted. We had left it white, but the new family had painted it a dull salmon color. "There ought to be a law," I said when we passed it, and Ben chuckled.

When we pulled up to the Seeleys' house, Larry said under his breath, "Help me, Lord," and I found my own heart beating a little faster. I busied myself with the knots, first the ones on the doors and then the ones across the ceiling above me. While we were lowering the table off the roof, Tim and Mr. and Mrs. Seeley came out of the house and stood on their steps, watching.

"What in the world?" Mrs. Seeley said when we turned the table right side up and began unwrapping it.

"Come see for yourself," Larry said. He brushed his hair back off his face with his fingers and blew out his breath.

Tim jogged ahead of his parents and gave Larry a pat on the back. "Good to see you, Larry."

"Real good to see you, kiddo," he said. I saw tears in his eyes, and I looked down at the table and pretended to brush some sawdust off the top.

Larry turned to his mother, who had come up behind him, and he hugged her, then shook his father's hand. "Hi, Dad," he said, and cleared his throat.

Then everyone said hi to me, with Mrs. Seeley hugging me, and Mr. Seeley slapping my back and asking me about basketball season. Then Mr. Seeley nodded at Ben and, eyeing the table, said, "So what have we here?"

Larry twisted around to Ben. "Oh, sorry, this—this is my friend Ben, here. He's my friend."

Mr. Seeley took one of his hands out of his pocket and pointed at the table. "I meant the table. What's this for?"

"It's for you." Larry looked around. "It's for all of you. I made it. I made it all myself. See, I'm thinking of going—"

"We've already got a table, Larry. I bought it twenty years ago, and it's still as sturdy as the day I got it," Mr. Seeley said. He stepped forward and tried to jiggle the table.

Larry glanced at Ben, then back at the group. I could tell he wanted to cry. His face had turned red about the cheeks and forehead, but around his eyes and mouth he'd gone dead white. He kept blinking and rubbing his sweaty palms on his thighs. I looked down at the ground and kicked at one of the blankets.

"It's wonderful, Larry. Sturdy as can be," Mrs. Seeley said, running her hand over the top. "Just real nice."

Mr. Seeley nodded. "Yeah, real sturdy, but where we gonna put it?"

Tim nudged me and said, "So come on, let's go to the creek."

I followed him across the street and around the Polanskis' house toward the creek. Before we got out of hearing range, I heard Larry say, "Ben's an ex-football player from Doylestown, Dad."

When we got to the creek, Tim and I stood at the edge of the bank and looked into the water. "Still the same old creek," I said, watching the water spill over the rocks, clear, clean-looking water with streams of sunlight running through it.

"Still the same old everything," Seeley said, his hands on his hips.

I turned to him. "No, you're different. You lifting weights?"

"Yeah, I stay in shape. So, what's it like living up in New Hope?"

"Come see for yourself sometime."

Seeley picked up an acorn and pitched it into the water. We watched it ride the flow, then disappear beneath the surface.

"No offense, but it's not exactly my kind of crowd—Larry and Bobbi and all."

"I thought you liked Bobbi. She said you did."

Seeley shrugged. "I heard you've got a whole house full of weirdos, huh?"

I sat down on the ground and Seeley joined me. We stretched our legs out toward the bank and automatically started moving our feet side to side, heels planted. It was something we used to do as kids. If we started moving our feet in the same direction it meant we were in agreement, but if one started left and the other right it meant we were in disagreement. My feet knocked against his and we stopped.

"Man, word sure travels," I said. "Who told you about everybody?"

"Bobbi, over the holidays. Remember? She came home?"

"She called us weirdos?"

Seeley sat up and crossed his legs. "No, but I do. Reading poetry—give me a break—and sleeping on top of each other and shooting baskets at midnight—well, that's cool, except Larry and someone else are wearing those queer mime costumes."

I nodded, laughing. "Yeah, Ben, the guy you just met."

"Bobbi said she sleeps in a sleeping bag on a raft."

I nodded again and remembered the night I slept with some of the others in the cabin, sharing blankets and pillows. "It's not so bad," I said, surprising myself.

"Right, and roasting weenies outside on Christmas Eve—just your average American family." Seeley kicked my leg. "Good old Pap."

I laughed. "Pap's plants are taking over the place. He takes them into the parlor and plays the piano for them. I mean he bangs on the piano for them. What's amazing is that the things grow like crazy. I think Mam must sneak around at night feeding the plants some secret formula or something."

Seeley shook his head. "Poetry."

"It's not so bad," I said again. "They're getting better. One girl, Jerusha, is really good, I think. She's less showy with hers. And she plays the cello like nothing you've ever heard. She could be a professional."

I thought of tall, skinny Jerusha, with her big eyes and her hoarse voice. I thought of her playing the cello, her movements as she played, her hair quivering and swinging to the music. I thought of the men's suits and the Disney ties she wore, and I missed her. I missed the way she sat with the group but apart from it, too, watching, listening, putting in her two cents' worth only after everyone else had spoken, and always using logic and compassion. I thought that had to be a rare combination, logic and compassion. The rest of them just used passion. All of them acted out of passion, without thinking things through.

"What are you smiling at, doofus-face?" Seeley cut into my thoughts.

"I was just thinking about Jerusha. She's nice."

"Great body, eh?" Seeley nodded and pulled at the grass by his feet.

"Great person," I said.

Seeley sniffed or snickered, I couldn't tell which, and we fell silent for a minute or two. I closed my eyes and listened to the sound of the water spilling over the rocks. I inched closer to the bank and listened again. With my eyes closed, it felt as if the water were flowing right through me. I could hear the sound of the rushing water on my right and a separate sound on my left, softer, more babbling, and it all passed through me, as if I absorbed some of the sound and passed the rest on; as if I were water, too, a part of the creek. I wanted to capture this feeling, think about it, think about being a part of the flow of things. I knew there was something in it, some neat idea about chaos and flow, but Seeley broke into my thoughts and I knew he wouldn't understand if I shushed him.

"So who's this Ben guy Larry brought with him?" he asked.

"You really want to know?" I kept my eyes closed, listening half to the water, half to him.

"I knew it!" I heard Tim get to his feet. "That idiot's going to make one of his famous announcements, isn't he?"

I opened my eyes and stood up, too. "Yeah, why? What?"

"What is it? What's he going to tell Mom and Dad this time? As if I didn't know."

"Well, if you guessed that Ben's his boyfriend, as in *love interest*, as in *little cupcake*, then you guessed right."

Seeley staggered backward as if I'd just given him a blow to the head, and I felt bad, first for Seeley, for how stricken he looked, as if he hadn't guessed at all—but also for Larry and Ben. I felt as if I was betraying them, telling their secret and saying it in that way, making fun of them. It was a secret that belonged to them, to the house in New Hope, our house.

I felt in that instant that we had come there as a team, Larry, Ben, and I. I was surprised by this thought, surprised by all the thoughts that had come to me that afternoon. I realized we weren't just a team, we were a family. We were part of that large and strange family that came from that farmhouse on the hill, and I had told a family secret that should have stayed on the hill until Larry and Ben decided to tell it.

"Dad's going to piss steam!" Seeley said, still reeling. "He's going to blow a gasket! That idiot! That loser! It figures. We all knew he was coming back for something. He never just visits. That stupid table of his. What's that supposed to be, his peace offering? That piece of junk!"

"Hey! If anyone in your family had bothered to notice, or had any aesthetic sense at all, they would have seen that that piece of junk is a work of art."

"Listen to you! Next you'll be telling me *you're* a homo."

"Me? Listen to you! You're freaking out like it's the end of the world."

Tim punched his fist into the oak tree beside him. "What a loser!"

"Why don't you just cool it with the *loser* stuff. Larry's only a loser when he's here, when he's around you guys. He cooks our dinners, plans our meals, everything. He writes poetry. He even has one real good one about the Waste Land. He's smart, Seeley. He taught himself—"

"Shut up! Just shut up! Okay?" Seeley slapped the tree. "You don't get it. You don't get it at all."

"So fill me in, and don't tell me to shut up."

"Dad's going to explode."

"You think he'll hit Larry, or what?" I asked, still not understanding why Seeley was in such a rage.

"Try a heart attack. Dad had a stroke about a month ago. He's on all this medication for high blood pressure and high cholesterol. Just fifty-one years old. We're not supposed to upset him, but nowadays every little thing upsets him."

"So what are we doing standing here? Let's go stop Larry," I said.

Seeley pounded the tree one more time and took off. I ran behind him, but I could tell as soon as I rounded the front of the Polanskis' house that Larry had already broken the news to his parents about Ben and him.

Mr. Seeley stood on the front stoop, waving his newspaper at them and bellowing something about how all faggots should be shot, while Mrs. Seeley pulled on his arm and tried to calm him. Larry and Ben were in the van, tying down the table, and in their hurry, getting their hands all tangled up in it. I jumped in the back with them and said, "I'll do it. You guys just drive."

Ben didn't need any more direction. He squeezed into the front seat, started up the car, and we took off, doors swinging wide open, Larry flying forward against the front seat, and me holding on for dear life to the rope above my head.

Chapter Twenty-Four

★

WE SPED DOWN the street and into the McDonald's parking lot across from the neighborhood. Ben stopped the van and I secured the table and tied up the doors. We didn't say much, and when we got going again we didn't say anything for the longest time. Larry sat with his body leaning up against the door, his head resting on the window. Every once in a while I'd hear him sniff, but from where I sat behind him I couldn't tell if he was crying or not. Ben reached over and touched his leg now and then, and Larry would nod to him, but they didn't speak.

I sat back in my seat and thought about Tim and the rest of the Seeley family, how they wouldn't give Larry a chance, how they couldn't see past old history. Then I thought about what Jerusha had said the night in the cabin, that we were all just trying to find our way, and that our house was like a great incubator. At the time I thought she made us all sound as if we were some kind of prisoners of the dark who couldn't see what was right in front of us. I'd known I wasn't like that. I could see all too plainly. It was everyone else who was blind.

Then, riding in the van that afternoon with Larry and Ben, I realized that I was just trying to find my way, too. I had believed the chaos tumbled all around me, that it didn't touch me, because I wouldn't let it. I was the only thing stable, unchanging. I believed that I could hold myself to my ideas, hold on; but just by spending that brief time with Tim, I realized I too had changed, the molecules had shifted and rearranged themselves inside me without my noticing it. I didn't belong in that neighborhood anymore. I had outgrown my past, just as Larry had outgrown his. I still wasn't exactly on Larry and Ben's side, but I knew I couldn't be on Mr. Seeley's side, either. I thought maybe there didn't have to be sides. Maybe I could just learn to care about Larry without making a judgment either way—maybe.

I leaned forward and tapped Larry's shoulder. "Sorry," I said.

Larry lifted his head.

"Really," I said. "I'm really sorry."

He nodded and lowered his head again.

Larry, Ben, and I lugged the table back to the cabin when we got home, and then Larry said he wanted to be left alone for a while. Ben and I closed the cabin door behind us and left him standing over his table, his hands dug into the pocket of his jeans.

That night I helped Larry and Pap prepare dinner. I sang "I've Been Working on the Railroad" along with Pap while he kneaded his bread, and Larry kept to the dinner preparations, smoking his cigarettes, saying little, deep in thought.

I stayed at the dinner table with the rest of the crowd after I had finished eating. We sat around the table, again with the candlelight, and talked about Mam coming home soon, and how surprised she'd be with the house and Aunt Colleen living with us. I thought how surprised she'd be when she saw the change in Aunt Colleen, and I hoped, too, that she would find me changed as well. I had resolved to be more accepting, more tolerant of her attempts at finding her way. I looked around at the group seated at the table and smiled to myself. I resolved to be more accepting and tolerant of all of them.

★

I TRIED TO speak to Bobbi in school. I wanted her to see how I had changed. I wanted her to know that I was willing to be there for her, without judging her. This was more of my resolve. I wanted Bobbi back home with us, where I felt she belonged. Larry had told me she'd moved with Don into some nearby apartment. After Pap's accident she'd skipped school a couple of days and I thought that maybe she wouldn't be coming back at all, but she did, only she wouldn't talk to anyone except a few girls who hung around with her. I had noticed she had dropped out of chorus and that Don waited for her at the main exit every day after school.

Monday, I found her at her locker by herself, and I went up to her.

"I just want to know if you're all right, that's all. I just want you to tell me how you're doing once in a while."

Bobbi slammed her locker door. "It wasn't his fault, you know."

"What?"

"Pap got tangled up in the cord. Don didn't push him. He wasn't trying to hurt him, so I'm sick of everyone thinking it was his fault."

"Hey, he was hurting *you*, remember? Listen to yourself trying to stick up for him. You're making excuses for him."

Bobbi shrugged. "I made him mad."

"So what does that mean? He should try to toss you head-first off a roof?"

"No! He just wanted me to come inside. He never would have pushed me off."

"He just wanted you to do what he wanted. He just wants complete control over you. I see him waiting for you every day."

"Sounds a lot like you, O'Brien."

Bobbi started to leave and I said, "Thanks, and the family's just fine, so glad you care."

Bobbi halted, started to turn around, changed her mind, and strode away down the hall.

★

LATE THAT NIGHT, after Leon, Jerusha, and Melanie had read some of their poems, Larry stood up and I thought he planned to read us one of his poems, but instead he held up a magazine he had in his hand. He no longer wore the scarf around his neck. He didn't speak with an English accent. I couldn't recall when he'd changed. He just wore jeans and a sweatshirt and talked like the old Larry.

He stood with the magazine in his hand and said, "I have an announcement to make," and I thought about what Tim had said about Larry always making some upsetting announcement.

Larry cleared his throat and said, "I've come to a decision. As soon as I can get into a class, I'm going to the Fox Maple School of Traditional Building in Maine. I'm going to learn how to build timber-framed homes."

"What are those?" Melanie asked.

Larry opened up the magazine titled *Joiners' Quarterly* and passed around a picture of a room with large exposed beams up near the roof, no ceiling.

"It's the way our house here was built," Larry said, "only most of our beams and posts are hidden by plaster." Larry took the magazine back and set it on the table next to him. He leaned over the picture and placed his index finger on it. "These houses are built to last," he said, tapping his finger. "I've been reading all about them. They've got integrity, and so do the people who build them, and I'm going to become an apprentice up there in Maine and learn how to build them." He raised his voice, his eyes widened. "I'm going to build houses, great, big, beautiful houses, and mountain retreats—and . . . I'm going to build a career out of it. This is what I'm going to do with my life. I've decided. I'm going to do it!" Larry grabbed the magazine and sat back down.

Harold clapped his hands and the rest of us joined in. I knew Larry had been thinking of his father when he spoke. The determination in his voice, the pride, the spirit, all were meant for his father. If our house was, as Jerusha claimed, the great incubator, then I figured Larry had become our first hatchling.

★

THE NEXT DAY Mam came home, arriving a day earlier than she had planned. She rode up to the house in a taxi, appearing tired and dazed and even more so when she took the tour of the house and learned that Aunt Colleen now lived with us.

"Of course, I'll leave whenever you say, Erin," Aunt Colleen said, and Mam, coming out of her stupor for just a moment, reached out her hand and grabbed Aunt Colleen's arm. "No, I'm so glad you're here. It's perfect. Everything's perfect, thanks."

Then she hugged Aunt Colleen, and Pap hugged them both and almost fell, and Mam cried. I thought it was because of Pap and his leg. Every time she had looked at him her face had clouded over, her mouth turned down as if she was trying to hold back her tears, and then when he hugged them both she let go.

"What is it, Erin?" Aunt Colleen said.

Mam shook her head. "I'm just so glad to be home." She looked around at all of us, wiping her eyes, trying to smile. She reached out and took Aunt Colleen's hand, then released it and laughed. "It's just good to see you all, but I am tired. It's been a long day." She looked at all our faces, then frowned again.

"Where's Bobbi?" she asked.

We explained the rest of the Pap-and-his-broken-leg story, and Mam nodded, but I knew she didn't hear a word of it.

"Well," she said, letting out a big breath of air, "I think I'll get myself a bath in my newly repaired bathtub, thanks to Colleen, and get a good night's sleep." Mam took Aunt Colleen's hand again. "Colleen, will you come with me?"

The rest of us tried to figure out what had happened, why Mam had come back early, why she'd arrived in a taxi and not in Dr. Mike's car. We all agreed Mam and Dr. Mike must have had a fight, and I couldn't help but feel pleased inside, even if I had resolved to be more accepting of their friendship.

★

THE NEXT MORNING I got up early so I could fix Mam breakfast in bed before I left for school. I wanted to tell her so much about what I felt, what I had been thinking about, how I had learned to let go of things a little bit, how I understood her need to have friends, how I had made a real effort to fit in. I didn't think I could really tell her all these things, but I figured bringing her breakfast in bed could be a peace offering. I thought she'd understand without my having to say anything.

I knocked on Mam and Pap's bedroom door and she called for me to come in. She sounded as if she had been crying.

I opened the door and found Mam sitting on the edge of her bed with her back to me. She had drawn the curtains and turned on the lights of the Nativity set, which Aunt Colleen and Ben had hauled upstairs and placed in front of the fireplace. The set filled that whole side of the room. Mam turned around to face me when I came in. She saw the tray, closed her eyes, and shook her head.

"JP, could you get that out of here? Quick."

"What's wrong? It's just eggs and toast and—"

"Please!" She put her hand up to her mouth.

"Sure." I turned around and set the food on the floor outside her door. I stepped inside and closed the door behind me.

"You okay?"

Mam nodded and backed herself onto the bed, leaning against her propped-up pillows.

"Where's Pap?" I asked.

"He slept downstairs. I think in the parlor in one of the chairs Colleen bought."

"Are you sure you're all right?" I asked again, stepping closer.

Mam nodded and reached for a cracker. She had a package of saltines on the bed beside her, where Pap should have been.

"What's that?" I asked.

"What, this?" Mam held the half-eaten cracker up. I saw her blush. "A cracker."

"You don't eat crackers." I stepped closer to her bed. I didn't know much about such things, but I had heard that women eat soda crackers when they have morning sickness, when they're pregnant.

"Now I do. I had them all the time while I was in Switzerland. I guess I've just gotten into the habit." Mam tried to smile, but her voice sounded defensive and she looked frightened. Her shoulders were hiked up, her eyes looked everywhere but at me. She had her hair pulled back off her

224

forehead, and I saw that the hair around her temples was wet.

"I can't believe it," I said, breaking my resolve to be more accepting and tolerant.

I pointed my finger at her and raised my voice, "You're pregnant! Aren't you? Aren't you?"

"JP, calm down."

"Calm down? I haven't even begun to get upset."

I paced in front of her bed, my arms waving and shaking and gesturing all over the place. "How could you? How could you? I can't believe it. You're pregnant. Are you pregnant? Just answer me, Mam."

"Yes, JP. I'm pregnant."

"You are not!" I said, making no sense at all and not caring. "I can't believe it. I'll kill him. How could you be so stupid?"

Mam sat up. "Now, that's enough! You asked and I told you. I'm pregnant."

I stopped pacing and looked at her. She sat with her eyes wide, breathing hard, almost panting.

"Maybe you're not. How do you know for sure? You need to see a doctor."

"I saw one in Switzerland."

"How could they tell so soon? You need to be tested by a real doctor."

"JP, I didn't get pregnant in Switzerland if that's what you think. I'm eleven weeks along already and for most of that time I thought I was getting sick again. I thought I was sick, JP, but I'm not. I'm just pregnant."

"So what are you saying? This isn't Dr. Mike's? This is Pap's?"

Mam closed her eyes and sat back against the pillows again. She cocked her head strangely and said, "Yes. Yes, of course."

I didn't believe her. I took a deep breath and then, pointing at her, I shouted, "You cannot be pregnant!" I stormed toward the door. "You cannot be pregnant!" I opened the door and slammed it behind me, and charged downstairs and out the door.

Chapter Twenty-Five

★

I RAN TO the woods not caring that I'd be late for school. I shouted at the trees, at the sky. I cried and shouted some more. I wiped at my tears with the back of my hand and my damp hands felt raw in the nippy air. I stared at them. I held them in front of me and stared at my red knuckles and blinked back more tears. "I hate her," I told my hands. "I hate them all. I've tried. They've never tried. They don't try. It's always me having to make the effort. Why? What for? Why should I try to fit in all the time? Forget it. I refuse to accept this. Mam pregnant! I refuse. I won't accept it." I jammed my hands in my pockets and shouted at the trees again. "I refuse to accept her!" Tears ran down to my chin and landed on my shirt.

I marched deeper into the woods. I thought of the times when it worked, when I fit in, when I made it work, the time I cooked the dinner for everyone—comfort food, they had called it—and the ride back from the Seeleys' with Larry and Ben, when I had been willing to see past their relationship. I tried, damn it! And there was the night in the cabin listening to Jerusha and Susan play their music and sleeping six across, and even Christmas Eve with Bobbi.

I wanted that. I wanted more of those moments, but they always got ruined by someone doing something stupid, messing up. It wasn't worth it. I stopped walking and shouted to the sky, to all the world, "It's not worth it!" I shook my head and continued walking. "Who's she kidding? Pap's baby. I could kill that doctor. I really could. Mam's just trying to find her way, Jerusha? Well, she's thirty-seven years old. A little late to be finding her way, don't you think? Why'd she have me? I must have been her first accident. She's no mother. She's a child. She's like some wild teenager, always getting herself in trouble. She doesn't even have enough sense not to get pregnant." I looked back up at the trees. "I hate her! I hate her! I hate her!" I threw myself against a maple and sagged to the ground and cried, hugging myself.

I cried a good while, cried and shivered and shuddered. I was still in the T-shirt I had slept in and the wind blew through it as if it weren't there. "Good," I said, and then, "I can't, I can't love her. Pap's baby. Yeah, right. Right! I'm sure!"

I sat shivering at the base of the tree a long time, letting the same thoughts circle in my mind. Then finally I knew what I would do. I would talk to Dr. Mike. I would confront the bastard. I stood up and brushed my hands off on my pants. "Let's just see whose baby it really is."

I marched back to the house and went straight to the phone. Mam had written Doctor Mike's numbers on the pad we kept by the phone. I dialed his home number first. No answer. I called the hospital and they put me on hold for close to twenty minutes. I stood rapping a pencil on the pad, keeping my rage going, keeping my courage up.

"James Patrick?" Dr. Mike said when he got to the phone.

"It's about time," I said. "I've been waiting at least twenty minutes."

Dr. Mike sounded irritated. "I do have patients, you know."

"Yeah, and I've got no patience," I said. "I want to talk to you, face-to-face. Today."

"I'm busy today. I've got my patients this morning and I'm picking someone up at the train station this afternoon, and then—"

"I'll meet you there."

"Where? No, that's ridiculous. We can talk another time."

"What time you going to be at the station?" I said, with more force in my voice.

There was a long pause, and then he let out a heavy sigh. "All right, if you insist, why not. I'll be there around three-fifteen."

I slammed the phone down.

★

THAT AFTERNOON I cut my last class, borrowed Jerusha's bike, and left in plenty of time to meet Dr. Mike. It felt good to get out on the bike and feel the cold air on my face. It helped to clear my mind. I knew just what I wanted to say. No shuffling around—get right to the point, catch him off guard. I made a fist and took a jab at the air.

I had about ten minutes to kill when I reached the deserted station. No one was around in the middle of the day.

Long grass grew up from beneath the stones in the center and along the edges of the tracks, and they looked as if they could have been tracks from twenty years ago. They were timeless, silent. I leaned Jerusha's bicycle against a bench and began pacing and planning just how I would say what I wanted to say, and the whole time thoughts of Mam and Dr. Mike in Switzerland, sharing a hotel room, and sharing a bed, kept playing in my mind.

I remembered all the dates, to galleries, dinners, operas, plays. I wondered how many were really plays and operas and how many were evenings spent at Dr. Mike's place, or did they go to hotels? I could feel myself tensing, my hands in fists, my teeth biting into my lower lip, my eyes burning from staring without blinking as I paced. Memories of early days with Mam, days of discovery along the creek, days in winter when she taught me how to build a snowman and later, after a giant storm had dumped so much snow on top of an already record-breaking winter of snowfall, when she taught me how to make a real igloo. Would she be teaching the new kid about igloos? Mike's baby? Would she teach it about making vent holes in the roof of the igloo to keep carbon monoxide from building up? Would she show it how to smooth down the sleeping platform so that when it froze you wouldn't have lumps and bumps under your sleeping bag? Would she teach the child about chlorophyll, explain to it how the leaves weren't really green at all, that the chlorophyll absorbed most of the bands of light and only reflected back the green and yellow wavelengths? Would she share our private universe with some other child, the universe she'd tossed away when Grandma Mary died?

I could feel the tears building up again and a lump had formed in my throat that wouldn't go away. I brushed at the tears and told myself to get mad, get angry. *Forget about the past, forget all that. It's long gone.*

I saw Dr. Mike's BMW rolling down the road. I stopped pacing and waited, glaring at him through his dark windshield.

Dr. Mike got out of the car and walked toward me, striding as if he thought he were a god. I spread my hands out, then clenched them in fists again.

"All right, James Patrick. I have about five minutes," he said when he'd gotten close enough. "What is it you wanted to discuss?"

I wondered if he spoke to his patients that way: *I have five minutes to tell you you're dying of cancer and explain the rest of your life. Now, any questions?*

"My mother's pregnant." I said, swallowing hard, trying to get rid of the lump in my throat. He stood facing me, and I wanted to stare him down but I couldn't. I looked away.

"Yes, that's correct."

I turned back to him. He nodded at me and walked onto the train platform. He gazed down the tracks, acting as if he were dismissing me.

I stepped up onto the platform with him and asked, "Is it your baby?"

Dr. Mike turned his head and gave me half a smile, maybe a smirk. "Ah, that's why you wanted to talk to me. Well, now, don't you think you should ask your mother that question?"

He stood there so smug, the doctor-god.

"I did ask her."

I saw a train coming down the tracks, its big light glaring like the sun. Dr. Mike got closer to the edge of the platform and watched.

"I did ask her," I repeated, raising my voice. I could feel heat rising in my head, and a heaviness there, and then, staring at the back of Dr. Mike, I had this sense of sparking lights shooting off behind my eyes. I wanted him to pay attention, to stop dismissing me.

"Hey!" I shouted.

He jerked his head in my direction.

"She said it was Pap's."

He raised those bushy black brows of his, surprised. Then he broke into a smile and laughed. "Well, then, there's your answer, isn't it?"

"Is it?"

"You have your answer," he said, turning back to the train, dismissing me again—smug man.

The train was coming too fast. It wasn't his train. It was going to go through, not stop. I heard it coming, saw it speeding along the tracks. Dr. Mike didn't know yet that it wasn't his train. He moved closer to the edge. Idiot-god.

Then I heard a voice inside my head tell me to push him. *Push him. Quick. Hurry. No one will know. Perfect crime, perfect murder. Hurry! Do it!*

The train kept coming, getting louder, faster.

Do it! Go on. Push him. Do it! Do it! Do it now! Now! Now!

"DO IT!" I hollered and closed my eyes, but I saw my hands in front of me, fragmented by the sparking lights. I saw my arms, saw him standing there, still waiting, watching the train, saw me push him off the platform, in slow motion, in strobe motion, saw the train go by, run right over him, it kept going, the train kept right on going. The lights sparked along the track behind it.

I felt someone shaking me. I opened my eyes. Dr. Mike stood scowling, shouting something at me. What was he saying?

I looked down the tracks. I saw the train in the distance, speeding away. I turned back to Dr. Mike. He had his hands on my shoulders. I could feel their weight, their heat, all the life still in them. I felt so relieved I broke down. I sank to the ground and cried, hugging myself and rocking and crying like a baby.

"What is it? Look here, are you okay? I thought for a second you were going to jump. I didn't mean to hurt you. Your arm okay?"

I looked up at him standing over me. I shook my head. "I was trying to kill *you*, not me, you bastard!"

"You'd have to get a lot closer to me, then. And it would help if you got behind me when you pushed me over."

"What?"

"You weren't going to push me."

"I was!" I cried. "I was—but I chickened out. 'Cause I'm a coward. I'm a damn coward!"

Dr. Mike knelt down in front of me. "No, son," he said. "A real coward would have pushed me."

Chapter Twenty-Six

★

I DIDN'T KNOW what had happened. One minute I was in my right mind, and then, in an instant, a flash, a spark, I had gone insane. I didn't know why I hadn't pushed him, what had saved me, saved him. Was it true what he said: A real coward would have pushed him? I wanted to think so.

Dr. Mike had left with some woman—sister, wife, patient? He asked if I would be okay. I shrugged away from him. I stood up and left. I crossed the tracks and boarded the next train. It took me into Philadelphia, into the Thirtieth Street station. I thought about what had happened. I couldn't close my eyes without seeing my hands pushing Dr. Mike onto the tracks. I heard his voice. *A real coward would have pushed me.* But I *was* a coward. I was afraid of everything. I was afraid of living a life without Grandma Mary. I was afraid of the people who lived in my house. I was afraid of the person Mam had become, and I was afraid because I knew I had outgrown my past before I could see a path to my future.

I found myself standing in the middle of the Thirtieth Street station with a giant pretzel in my hand. I must have purchased it, but the sight of the pretzel, with the mustard running toward my hands, made me sick. It reminded me of squished worms and bug splat on windshields. I tossed the pretzel in the garbage. I returned to the platform and waited for the train to take me back home.

I got off at the stop near my old house. I hadn't meant to do this. I watched the train pull away and stood watching it disappear, and then when it did, I still watched. The sun reflecting off the tracks burned my staring eyes. I turned away and walked down the familiar streets, past Saint Ignatius and my old house with the new salmon paint and on to the Seeleys' house, where I stopped. Were they all in there? I didn't want to find out. I looked across to the Polanskis' house. Nothing had been done to the outside of the place in years. Paint peeled, steps sagged, and a washing machine older than I sat rusting out on the porch. I headed toward the house, then cut around back, remembering how just a few days earlier I had stood at the creek with Tim. I remembered the feeling I had had when I heard the creek water rushing past me, and how it felt as if it ran right through me, as if I were a part of the creek, too. I wanted to feel that again. I wanted it to bring me back to my senses.

This time I climbed down the bank and stood, beat-up basketball shoes and all, in the water. I held my arms up and listened.

"JP?"

I dropped my arms and twisted around. Bobbi stood above me.

"What are you doing here?" I asked, stepping out of the water, feeling foolish.

Bobbi laughed and edged down sideways to join me. "What are you? I saw you going around the house. I thought you were coming to see me."

"I didn't even know you were in there."

"Yeah, we came yesterday. Daddy's got bleeding ulcers."

"Sorry—I guess. So is Don here?"

Bobbi, with her arms crossed in front of her, looking cold, twisted around as if she expected Don to be standing above her. Then she returned to me. "Yeah, he's at McDonald's right now." She hunched her shoulders. Her voice had gotten quieter.

"Couldn't he trust you to get here by yourself?"

Bobbi shook her head and stared down at her feet. She had on a flimsy pair of toeless slippers, and I saw she'd painted her toenails black. "No, he barely lets me out of his sight."

"Sorry," I said again, and meant it more this time.

She looked up at me with a pleading in her eyes I couldn't bear to see. I faced the creek.

"He's everywhere now," she said, almost whispering. "He's on me for the least little thing. He used to be so sweet, remember? Remember all the little gifts he'd bring me?"

I didn't say anything. I never thought he was sweet.

"He never showed any sign that he was like Daddy. He never lost his temper, not at me at least. Not at first." She paused and then asked, "How do you know the way somebody's really going to treat you?"

I shrugged. "You just do."

"I don't."

"I noticed."

We stopped talking. We stared into the water. Then I caught sight of both of our reflections and I stirred them up with my foot.

"I think he's crazy," Bobbi said, almost whispering.

"You still love him?" I asked, and I couldn't keep the bitterness I felt out of my voice.

Bobbi didn't answer at first, she just stood with her head lowered. Then I saw her tears dropping into the water.

I stepped back so that I stood closer to her, but I kept my hands stuffed in my pockets.

"I understand him," she said at last, and then added, "I'm not excusing him, I just—I just understand him. And my father. People don't get it at all. They say he's a drunk. They think he gets drunk and then beats us."

"Well, doesn't he?"

"No!" Bobbi said, as if she were shouting at an imbecile. "He gets drunk *because* he beats us. The drinking comes after. He's so ashamed of himself. He's so helpless."

"Helpless, that's a new one," I said.

Bobbi stooped down and ran her hand through the water. "It's all so easy for you, O'Brien."

I stood above Bobbi, thinking how much I hated that she always thought everything was so easy for me. The scene at the train station flashed through my mind. Then a crazy thought came to me. I could push her. I could push her in the water. Why didn't I? The only answer I had was that I didn't want to. I didn't need to. With Dr. Mike I had wanted to push him. With every part of my being I wanted to push him, but maybe I didn't need to. I didn't know why I didn't, but maybe it had to do with the difference between the kind of life I had led and Don's life. I knew Don would have pushed him. Maybe there was a difference between being a coward and just being afraid. Maybe, but if so, I knew that a very fine line existed between the two, and that I had come closer than I wanted to stepping over that line.

It scared me to realize this. To realize how easy it was to become the very person you never wanted to be. Bobbi had become like her mother, and I guessed Don and Mr. Polanski were a lot like their fathers.

Who had I become? Who was I like? I had thought it was Aunt Colleen, but I realized it wasn't, not totally. I had become the male version of Grandma Mary. Order had reigned in her house. Pap always did as she said. Mam lived the way Grandma Mary wanted her to. She became the dutiful daughter, the playmate for Pap. Grandma Mary always had the answers, always knew the way. Were these bad qualities? We all loved her. She was also loving and generous and warm. She was comfort and stability and safety. She demanded a lot from all of us and she got it, but her spirit was all love. She made our house a home, something I hadn't felt in the new house. No, she had so many good qualities, many which I knew were missing in me, but I saw, too, how much we had depended on her to solve all our problems, to be everything to us, and for us. All our love had been directed at her because she gave us everything we needed, she told us what we needed. But she forgot to show us how to love each other. When she died we felt alone, abandoned, because we'd never learned to love one another, just her. Her strengths made us weak. I was weak because I loved too little, and Bobbi was weak because she loved too much, the wrong person, the wrong way.

I stooped down next to Bobbi.

"Mam's pregnant," I said.

Bobbi nudged me. "Real funny, O'Brien."

"Not funny, true," I said.

She looked at me. "Are you serious?"

I didn't say anything. I stuck my hand in the icy water and stared at its whiteness, waiting for it to turn red.

"Is she okay?"

"I guess. It's Dr. Mike's baby."

"Oh."

That's all she said, and she said it as if I had said, *Looks like it might rain.*

"Yup, life's easy," I said.

"You wanna trade? My life for yours?" Bobbi asked.

"No!" I pushed her shoulder and she fell over sideways and laughed.

"Here, try this," I said, standing up and stepping into the water. I lifted my arms out to my side and closed my eyes.

"The Wright brothers already tried that. You need better wings, and a propeller."

"Ha, ha. Just try it."

Bobbi stood up and kicked off her slippers. She stepped into the water, groaning and picking her feet up out of the water a few times before she settled down.

"Okay, what's supposed to happen?"

"Just listen."

We stood together in the water a moment, and I realized she was blocking part of the sound.

She opened her eyes. "What am I supposed to hear?"

"Stay there." I backed up. "Now try it." She closed her eyes again, and I said, "Listen to the water. Listen to the sounds on either side of you."

"Okay," Bobbi said, waiting.

"Doesn't it feel as if the water is running right through you? Like you are the water? Listen."

"No, it doesn't feel—"

"Just stand there and be quiet a few minutes."

I moved away from her and took up my own spot, behind her, and waited, watching her.

"Hey, yeah! Yeah, I do. Wow!" Bobbi said. "It's washing right through me. I feel so—so powerful, like all this water is rushing through me."

"Told you," I said, thrilled that she could feel it, that I could show her a moment of discovery, the way Mam used to with me.

"It's great. It's like that song we used to sing with Sister Patricia, remember? 'Roll on, Columbia'—about the Columbia River?" She opened her eyes and looked at me. It was the nicest look she'd ever given me. Her smile was for me, truly for me this time—a thank-you smile. I smiled back and we laughed, and then we heard Don's voice calling.

"Bobbi?"

"Shh," Bobbi said, alarm distorting her smile. She grabbed her slippers and headed up the embankment. "Don't follow me," she said. "Go away, hurry, down toward your house."

"Bobbi?"

I could hear the temper in Don's voice. I wanted to go with her, defend her if I needed to, but I knew my being there would only make it worse for her. She knew more about protecting herself than I did. But I couldn't run away. I couldn't just abandon her. I couldn't move at all. I stood still and tried to listen above the sound of the water. I heard Bobbi calling to Don. She sounded out of breath.

"Look what I found. I wanted to try to find some real flowers to pick, but forsythia's pretty, don't you think?"

"Get on inside. You're in your slippers! Don't you have any sense?"

"I thought they'd look nice on the table," Bobbi said in a saccharine voice.

"Just go on, your burger's getting cold. And leave the flowers. You probably killed the bush picking those."

Bobbi said something, but I didn't catch it. They had moved on toward the house.

I sloshed through the water and picked a spot close to where the water washed over a set of large rocks. Then I lifted my arms up and listened, but all I could hear was the sound of a train hurtling down the tracks.

Chapter Twenty-Seven

★

I DECIDED TO go home. I thought about hitchhiking my way back, but I didn't want to have to talk to anyone, so I boarded yet another train, chose an empty seat, and sat down. I gazed out the window and watched the blur of grass and concrete as the train sped toward home. I didn't know what I would do when I got home, what I would say. I didn't know what I wanted from Mam anymore. I wanted to tell her I knew she had lied, I knew Dr. Mike was the father of her baby, but every time I rehearsed this in my mind my throat would close up as if I had stuffed a balled-up sock down in it.

I couldn't believe Mam had lied to me. That was the worst of it for me. She had never lied before. It proved how far apart we had grown in the past year. I remembered how Mam used to say, "Just me and you, JP," and I understood that she didn't mean to exclude the others, she just meant that we had something special between us. Maybe we did love one another once. Maybe we didn't save it all for Grandma Mary—but when she died, when she abandoned us, we all lost our way somehow, and I wondered if we'd ever find our way back to each other. How could we if Mam lied to us?

I sat picking at the skin along the side of my fingernail, chewing at it now and then, and trying not to think about Mam and me.

At last the train pulled into the station. I stepped out onto the platform and went to the spot where I had left Jerusha's bicycle. The bike was gone. I heard a car horn and then Jerusha's voice.

"James Patrick O'Brien, are you deaf?"

I looked up and saw Jerusha sitting at the wheel of Larry's van. She waved.

How could I face her? I'd lost her bike. I turned away and walked along the platform and then hopped onto the tracks behind the retreating train.

"JP?" Jerusha had gotten out of the van and pursued me down the tracks. She caught up with me and said, "Hey, come on. Everybody's been looking for you."

I kept walking and she walked beside me, her long legs matching mine stride for stride. "You okay?" she asked.

I stopped and faced her. "I lost your bike!" I shouted, sounding angry at her, as if I hated her.

She blinked at me, drawing her head back as if my words had slapped her. "No, you didn't, I've got it in the van."

"What?"

"Sure. I came by here earlier and picked it up. Mike called and said you were down here. He said you were quite distressed, and I guess you are. You look a wreck."

"Thanks." I swept my hair back off my face.

"Come on." Jerusha took my hand and we turned around and headed toward the van.

"Have you been waiting for me all this time?" I asked, when we had reached the van and I saw the bicycle lying across the backseat.

"No. I've been combing the whole town for you, JP. Everybody has. I need to get you home and call off the hunt. It's getting late, in case you hadn't noticed."

I hadn't noticed, but I did then. I saw the pink sky and the dark shadows in the trees.

"Sorry," I said. I climbed into the van, and Jerusha backed out of the parking space.

"Mam's been a wreck, too," Jerusha said once we got on the road.

"She deserves it," I said. "I'm glad she's worried about me."

"Oh, she isn't, not about you at any rate." Jerusha bit her upper lip. "Sorry, if that's what you wanted," she added.

"Figures." I crossed my arms in front of me and slid down in my seat.

Jerusha shook her head and her hair slapped at her face. "No, it's not what you think. She said you were too practical to run off or do anything stupid. She has confidence in you, JP, that's all."

"Yup, that's me. Dependable, responsible JP." I sat up and turned toward her, as much as my seat belt would allow. "You know, I almost pushed Dr. Mike in front of a train today. I came just a millimeter away from doing it. I swear I did."

Jerusha laughed.

"You don't believe me?"

Jerusha shook her head again, and I watched her dark hair

fly. "Never in a million years would you have done it," she said, so sure of herself that I felt I hated her again. Then she added, "You know, JP, sometimes it's good to be the kind of person others can always count on. Actually, most of the time."

"Thanks," I said, feeling myself blush and turning to face forward in my seat. Man, I loved her.

We turned onto a street where workers were repairing potholes. Jerusha slowed down and said, as if it were just the tag end of our conversation, "Your mam's moved out of the house."

I turned to look at her and felt lightheaded. I told myself to be calm, act calm. "Yeah?" I said. "Where is she? Or do I need to ask? She's run off with the good doctor, right? Of course, I knew it. It's what I expected." My words were calm but my heart was pounding. I slammed my head back against the seat and it felt good to direct my energy somewhere. I wanted to punch something. Instead I slammed my head back against the seat again.

Jerusha touched my arm. I glanced down at her long fingers. She took her hand away. "No, she's still at the house, just outside. She says she's going to live outside from now on." Jerusha turned onto our street and accelerated up the hill.

"That makes good sense," I said. "About as much sense as Pap sitting out on the roof all day." I knew I sounded angry, and I meant to, but inside I felt relief. I looked up at the roof of the van and asked it, "Why can't we have a normal family?"

Jerusha laughed, and I smiled. It felt good to make her laugh.

We turned into the drive. I saw in the last light of dusk the aluminum lounge chair with the plastic weave stretched out on the lawn. Mam wasn't in it, but I saw signs that she had been there. The afghan from her bed, one Grandma Mary had made Mam and Pap when they were first married, hung off the side of the chair, an empty plate and a mug sat on a plastic table set up beside it, and Mam's binoculars stood in the grass.

I climbed out of the van and headed toward the chair, rehearsing what I had planned to say to Mam. I clenched my teeth and told myself to just blurt it out. Just accuse her as soon as I saw her. Tell her that I knew the truth, call her a liar.

Then I saw Mam coming out of the woods and I braced myself, folding my arms across my chest, my feet wide apart. She saw me, but she didn't quicken her pace, didn't wave or even look happy to see I'd come home safely, and I felt all the energy and the tension that had expanded inside my body suddenly collapse, leaving me tired, more tired than I'd ever felt in my life. My arms fell by my side, too heavy to hold themselves up anymore.

I hadn't realized Jerusha had come up behind me until I heard her speaking in my ear.

"Mam thinks she's going to die," she said.

I turned my head and saw Jerusha nod. "She's sure this pregnancy will kill her."

I turned back to Mam. She had paused to gaze up at a bat that had just swooped past her head.

I took notice of the bat and then returned to Mam, to the stranger with a baby growing inside her and a self-proclaimed death sentence hanging over her. How dare she? Grandma Mary, Pap, and I had spent a lifetime fearing every time she got sick that this was it, this was the one, she was going to die on us, and now she was planning on it. She was planning on dying having *Mike's* baby. The whole idea was too much for me. She wasn't going to die. She just had a guilty conscience.

I watched her standing out on the lawn, following the bat's flight, ignoring me, too guilty even to face me. My desire to speak with her and accuse her of lying to me had vanished. What was the use? She didn't care about how I felt. She didn't care about me. I realized there was nothing for me to do but turn and walk away.

Chapter Twenty-Eight

★

THAT SPRING AND summer, Mam and I stopped talking to each other. It wasn't something we had agreed on. It just happened. At first I felt too angry to speak, and too confused by her behavior. Why was she living outside? What was going on with her? And where was Dr. Mike? What did it mean that he wasn't coming around anymore? Then later I felt too depressed to speak. Depressed because I had figured Mam would notice my silence and seek me out, try to make things up to me, explain herself; but she didn't. She answered my silence with a silence of her own.

No one else seemed to notice. I felt sure they thought everything was fine between us. Mam stayed outside and I stayed inside, both of us busy, both of us using the others like a wall and shield to keep from having to deal with each other, to even notice each other existed. I did this on purpose, suddenly making extra efforts to fit in, to be one of the crowd. Larry had taken a second job as a waiter in a high-class restaurant to help pay for his house-building course, so I took over the job as head cook, and the others would often gather in the kitchen while I prepared the food. They'd sit at the table or lean against the counter and talk to one another and to me. They said they loved coming home and smelling something wonderful cooking, they couldn't resist coming into the kitchen, and so I made sure I always had something on the stove or in a Crock-Pot, a soup or stew, that could be simmering all day until I got home to take over my duties. Even if I got home late, I could find them in there, and often someone would be sampling the dish and then, seeing me, would lower the lid and give me an innocent look, backing away from the stove. I'd just smile and get to work, pleased that they were waiting for me and not outside with Mam.

I wanted her to know I was fitting in. I wanted to hurt her with the knowledge that everybody wanted my comfort food. I wanted her to be there when Jerusha and I set up our chess game out on the porch table and when Leon and I shot baskets, when we played one-on-one. I wanted her to know that her silence didn't bother me at all, and anytime we did happen to be in the same place at the same time, I made sure she saw what a great time I was having. I talked louder, laughed harder, always keeping that wall of others between us, always so, so busy. I had to study for final exams. I had my jobs in the computer lab and the school office. I found it easy not speaking to Mam, and yet all my busy-ness did not block out my awareness of her. I watched her more than ever. I knew where she was, what she was doing, who she was with, more than I ever had, and I noticed she, too, had become extra-busy. She lived outside, just as she had said she would, sleeping out on the lawn each night and escaping to the porch when it rained. She even had Jerusha buy her groceries that would keep outdoors and that she could use to make easy meals.

I learned from Aunt Colleen that Mam had declared she didn't want to miss another moment of the life around her. She felt that by living outside, by studying the soil or a blade of grass, by watching the ants working their way across the bottom porch step each morning, she could slow down time, she could soak up every last bit of life before it was over.

She began working on the wildflower garden that Bobbi and Pap had planned that past autumn, digging up the lawn and bringing home plants of all kinds from the Center.

Pap tried to act as helper, but Mam wouldn't let him do much of anything. He wanted all the flowers to be yellow, and he wanted the tall flowers in the front and the tiny ground cover ones hidden in the back. He wanted foreign plants that he'd seen pictured in a book instead of the native ones Mam insisted on planting.

"I hate you today, Erin," Pap often would say, throwing down his trowel in frustration and storming off. I saw his frustration as an opportunity to get Pap on my side. I'd call him in to bake a loaf of bread for dinner or to sing with me while I cooked or to join the gang in the living room, anything to make him want to stay inside with me. Then I came up with the idea of having a garden of my own. Why not? Let Mam stop me, if she wanted to. I created a garden for Pap, and we planted only tall yellow flowers, and Pap hugged me and bragged to Mam that he had his own garden now, so "Na, na!" And I felt somehow that this was a victory for my side.

Then Mam invited the students from her classes on a field trip to the house to help her work on the garden, and they arrived in a couple of vans and spread out over the yard, planting flowers, vegetables, and even a few trees and bushes. I knew Pap felt jealous of the others, and I felt sorry for him that afternoon when I saw him dashing from one end of the yard to the other, claiming that they were on his property and those were his tomato plants and his daisies. "Hey, that's mine!" he'd exclaim, and then with a hurt expression look to Mam and say, "Erin, that's mine they're using now."

Mam made a halfhearted attempt at appeasing Pap by handing him back the garden tools Bobbi had given him. But Pap wanted more, he wanted them off his property. Mam flopped down in her chair, bowing her head in her hands. She remained that way until Aunt Colleen came along and put some order into the activities, placing Pap on a team with two others and putting him in charge.

Everyone agreed that there was something strange going on with Mam. She wandered off on long hikes through the woods or went down along the towpath or out to Washington Crossing State Park to wander through deeper woods and Bowman's Hill Wildflower Garden.

I said to Aunt Colleen once, "If Mam really thinks she's going to die, why isn't she spending more time with us? Don't people who are dying usually do that?" Really what I wondered was why, if she thought she was dying, she didn't try making up with me. Why didn't she try to set things straight?

Aunt Colleen said, "Oh, your mother's just nervous. She got this way when she was pregnant with you, too. Don't worry, she's not dying."

"Oh, believe me, I'm not worrying," I said, rocking back in my chair. "I just think she's acting awfully strange for a dying person, all this living outside. It's like she doesn't even want to be around us anymore."

Jerusha had come into the room by then, and she agreed with me. "She's giving us the brush-off, all right."

Aunt Colleen waved her hand in front of her face, dismissing our notions. "You've got to understand how it is for her. You know, JP. Your mam spent her whole childhood cooped up indoors because she was too sick to play outside. I remember she used to say that if she ever got well she'd go outside and never come in again. I guess she's living out her old fantasy. Your mam's not like the rest of us, never has been, much as I've tried to change that. I think she equates the indoors with sickness and hospitals, and fresh air and sunshine with health and vigor." Aunt Colleen smiled at us and patted my hand. "And don't worry, she's not really giving you the brush-off, she's just concentrating on the baby, that's all. She'll be back to normal after the baby's born, you'll see."

"I told you, I'm not worried, but if you ask me, it's more like she's concentrating on herself," I said, and Aunt Colleen nodded.

"Same thing."

So Mam and I didn't see each other much at all, never spoke, and yet I thought about her all the time. I felt her absence as an even greater presence than that of all the others gathered in the kitchen around me each evening. To me, her absence was like a hot spot in the room, this space she should have been taking up. When we ate dinner, this hot spot hovered over the dining table and it was as if we all had to talk around it, pretending we didn't notice it was there. When I played basketball with Leon it filled the yard behind me, whether Mam stood behind us or not.

When I studied, hunched over my desk, memories of her dancing to Mozart with Pap in the old house, twirling in and out of the room, disrupted my work even more than it had done back then. And late at night, when I crawled into bed, exhausted, the hot spot hovered close, keeping me awake, alert, stirring up more memories, drawing me to my window to look out over the lawn and find her dark form sitting up in the lounge chair or stretched out on the ground.

By the time school let out for the summer, our household was in the midst of yet another transition. Without telling any of us, Jerusha had applied to the university, for pre-med, and had gotten in for the summer term. She left us to live on campus and only visited on occasional weekends. I was surprised how much I missed her. After she left, and after I had taken over her job as waiter at the Railroad Restaurant, where everybody still talked about her, I realized she had become my best friend. I wanted her back home. She belonged with us, at home.

Larry and Ben had planned to hitch a ride to Maine with some friends toward the end of August, but then Mam decided that with the Center closed for a few weeks it would be the perfect time for her and Pap to visit her brother, John, at the monastery up in Portland. Then Aunt Colleen said she wanted to go, too, and invited her leprechaun friend to join them. So they all piled into the van and off they went, shrinking the household down to just five people.

The place felt deserted. I wandered the house, moving

from room to room. Jerusha's cello stood in the living room like a dateless man at a dance. Larry's poetry books, his last box of cigarettes (he had finally quit smoking), and his mime costume were left in a pile in the parlor, where Aunt Colleen and the leprechaun's sewing project had been abandoned.

The leprechaun had come back into Aunt Colleen's life after she'd reassured him it was over with her husband. He started coming to the house again, spending his evenings teaching Aunt Colleen how to sew. They had set up the sewing machine and cut out the pattern in the parlor. The half-finished tennis dress lay on a table next to a box of pins and several spools of white thread, and the sheets of the pattern used to cut out the material still lay spread out on the floor.

Pap's plants sat on top of the piano in order from biggest to smallest, and he'd left the vacuum cleaner out on the rug, its hose set to suck up Aunt Colleen's paper pattern the second it got turned on.

Each room in the house was cluttered with clothes and shoes and other objects left behind, and still the place felt empty, as if everything had been cleared out. The house felt ridiculously large with only the five of us left.

Leon came into the kitchen one evening when I was tossing together something for us to eat, looked around the deserted kitchen, and said to me with his eyebrows raised, "And then there were none." He laughed, but I didn't find it funny. I remembered the Agatha Christie mystery Bobbi had brought home with that title. It was the story about ten houseguests who were killed off, one by one. That's what this felt like. It felt like a death, and memories of losing Grandma

Mary just a little more than a year ago kept pushing their way into my mind, and despite the clutter of thoughts, I felt as emptied out inside as the house felt to me on the outside. When Susan joined a folksinging group and left to tour with them in Pittsburgh, I panicked, deciding everyone was going to take off until there was just me, alone.

One afternoon I went out onto the porch and found Mam's binoculars, her sketchpad, and several familiar old field guides sitting on the checkerboard table. I sat down and picked up the binoculars. I stared out at the yard, at Larry's cabin, at the woods. I tried to see if I could see the road through them. I couldn't. I set the binoculars down and picked up a guide to birds and flipped through it, then closed it and squeezed it in my hands.

I didn't care about whose baby she carried, or whether or not she had lied. I wanted Mam back. Larry had said Mam and Dr. Mike had agreed to go their separate ways, but I didn't even care about that anymore. I didn't care about any of it. I just wanted her back.

I wanted everybody back. I wanted chaos. Mam had been right, stagnation was death, and I wanted life, I wanted chaos. I was ready to let go of the old life with Grandma Mary. I wanted the house filled with people. I missed Bobbi marching into my room and yelling at me for something trivial like leaving the toilet seat up in the bathroom. I missed Larry and his English accent, and Ben and his mime act. I missed the bodies asleep on the floor when I came down each morning and Jerusha eating off my plate at night. I missed staying up late with Pap and watching the Nativity set. I missed the poetry and the music and the loud voices, and I missed Mam. I wanted to hike through the woods with her, go fishing, make dinner for her, take her back to the creek and have her stand in the water with her arms up and feel the water running through her body. I wanted her to wear my boots when she couldn't find her own. I wanted her to need me, to want me around again.

I remembered when she won the house the reporter had asked Mrs. Levi why she picked Mam's essay over all the others, and she had said how she liked the Harpo Marx line Mam had used about wanting to see a face in every window when she came home each day. I wanted that, too. I wanted to see a face in every window, and I wanted one of the faces to be Mam's.

Chapter Twenty-Nine

⭐

I WOKE UP Saturday morning to an empty house. Harold, Leon, and Melanie had already gone to work. I couldn't stand the quiet. I didn't know what to do with myself. Nothing seemed worth doing. I picked up a book and tried to read, but I couldn't concentrate. I made myself a huge bowl of cereal, mixing four different brands together the way I liked it, then ate only two bites before I lost interest. I started out for a walk in the woods, but the birdcalls sounded so lonely and depressing I turned back and went inside. I went into the parlor and turned the vacuum cleaner on with my foot. The suction wasn't strong enough to take up the dress pattern on the floor, after all. I turned it on and off a few times and then left it on.

I ran my fingers over the piano keyboard, then sat down and shouted over the noise of the vacuum, "I will now play for you; please be quiet." Then I lifted my hands and crashed them down on the keyboard. I smiled. I did it again, then again. Then I announced, "I will now sing for you." I sang "My Darling Clementine" and banged away on the piano, striking any note, any chord. I sang "I've Been Working on the Railroad" and "You're a Grand Old Flag." I belted out the songs. I pounded the piano. Nothing had felt this good to me in a long time. I felt the tension leave my shoulders. I felt my chest expand and I noticed my breathing suddenly, as if I had just begun to breathe after months of holding my breath. I sang "From the Halls of Montezuma" and "Marching to Pretoria," and then for Bobbi, "Roll on, Columbia, Roll On." I loved it. I loved acting like Pap. I felt as if I had discovered a great secret, a secret Pap had been keeping all to himself. I could picture him laughing at us all because we didn't know what he knew. We didn't know how easy it was to be happy, how simple it could be.

I jumped up from the piano, turned off the vacuum, and still singing went up to Mam and Pap's room, and one by one, carried the Nativity pieces back out on the roof. When I had arranged them the way Pap liked them, with the Three Wise Men closest to the Baby Jesus, and hooked it all up and plugged it in, I stood back, lifted my arms up, and declared to the sky, "I am the Three Wise Man!" I shouted it louder, "I am the Three Wise Man! Ho, ho, ho, I am the Three Wise Man!"

I stood holding my hands out, lifting my face to the sky, and I felt such a longing for Pap and Mam that the words "Wise Man" broke in my throat. I swallowed and stared at the clouds. I stared until my arms, still out, began to ache. I lowered them, but in that silence, watching the sky, a thought came to me. It was more than a thought, it was an urge, a feeling as if a hand were pushing me along, and a voice were whispering, *You have to go to Maine.* I didn't know where the urge came from, but I felt overcome with the need to go, to see Mam and Pap.

I started to sit down, to think things through. I wanted to decide if this was a good idea, plan when and how, figure out where the urging was coming from, but then I stopped myself. "Just go," I said. "For once, just go. Be spontaneous."

I packed a suitcase, took the money I was once again saving to buy a computer with out of the bank, and called Jerusha, who borrowed a friend's car and drove me to the airport. I had never flown before, so Jerusha came with me to the counter to purchase a ticket and led me through the airport to the boarding gate. We didn't speak at all once we sat down to wait for the plane, but we held hands and sat in the comfortable silence of a close friendship. When the call came for the passengers to board the plane, we stood up and hugged each other. I hesitated, wondering if I were acting silly heading off to Maine, but Jerusha pushed me forward and said, "Go on," and I left, glancing back only once to see Jerusha still waving at me.

Once I was on the plane, after the excitement of takeoff, the need to see Mam and Pap, to be there now, grew stronger. The plane couldn't fly fast enough. A new thought had come to me: I just knew something was wrong with Mam. As soon as I thought it, my heart pounded against my chest and I started sweating. I checked my watch. We had thirty more minutes till we landed. The thirty minutes dragged by. The woman sitting next to me patted my hand and asked, "Is this your first time flying?"

I didn't answer. I gripped the armrests and stared out the window. "Don't die, Mam," I said to myself, and thought about how many times we had almost lost her in the past. I feared her luck had run out.

Her sickness had always made me angry. Every time she went to the hospital I blamed her, and I knew it was only because I loved her and I needed her so much. "I'm sorry, Mam. Please wait. Don't die this time. Please be all right."

Then I told myself I was jumping to conclusions. She was fine. Of course she was fine. I would have heard. I was being silly.

We had begun our descent. I sat back and tried to take a couple of deep breaths. I decided I would call the monastery from the airport. *I can let them know I'm on my way, maybe speak to Mam for a second.*

As soon as we landed I headed for the nearest phone and called Information for the number of the monastery. Then I punched out the number and waited.

"Saint John of the Cross, Brother Andrew speaking," came the deep voice on the line.

"Yes, this is James Patrick O'Brien. My uncle, John Murphy—"

"Yes, I remember you, James Patrick. Your uncle is at the hospital—Maine Medical Center. I'm afraid your mother—"

I dropped the phone and ran through the airport, searching for an exit. At last I found one near the baggage claim, and I ran out to the street to hail a taxi. I felt like a character in a movie when I said, "I'll pay you ten dollars extra if you can hurry it up."

The driver looked at me in the rearview mirror and said, "Son, ten dollars won't pay for my speeding ticket. Don't worry, I'll get you there in plenty of time."

I wanted to ask, *In plenty of time for what?* What did he think I was hurrying to the hospital for?

I tapped my fingers on the armrest until the driver told me to stop. Finally I saw the hospital up ahead and almost told him to pull over, I'd run the rest of the way, but then I decided his driving had to be faster than my running. I sat forward in my seat and watched out the front window. He signaled to turn into the hospital entrance and waited for a van to pull out.

"Hey! That's Larry's van," I said.

"Huh?"

The van had pulled out and was going down the street, back the way I had come. I caught sight of Aunt Colleen and Ben and several other heads, but I couldn't tell if Mam was in there with them. I thought about telling the driver to follow that van, but he had already pulled into the parking lot.

I paid the driver and ran into the hospital. It seemed like forever before the front desk could locate what floor and room Mam was in, but at last they found it and they said as far as they knew, she was still there.

I took the elevator, got out, and stared up at the sign to see which way Mam's room was, but my eyes blurred so, I couldn't read it. I ran to the nurses' station. "Which way is room three twenty-eight?" I asked the smiling woman at the desk.

She pointed to my left and then asked, "Who are you looking for?"

"Mrs. Erin O'Brien," I said.

The nurse stopped smiling. She stood up and said, still with her pleasant voice, "Just a minute, let me see if she's still there."

She had a computer in front of her, but she left the desk and went over to talk to someone else.

I could feel my legs trembling and in my chest the trembling turned into a sound that came out of my mouth, a cry. I looked around to see if anyone else had heard me. Then I didn't care. What was wrong? Why were they just standing there talking to each other? Where was Mam?

I called out, "What's going on over there? Is she here or what?"

The nurse came back to me. She smiled.

"Yes, she's here, but she's been moved. They had quite a scare with her last night. High blood pressure and—"

I shouted at her, "Is she here or not?"

The nurse smiled and nodded. "Yes, but she's been moved to room five-oh-eight."

I ran to the elevator, got off on the fifth floor, and read the signs myself this time. I hurried down the corridor and found the room. The door was closed. I didn't know whether to knock or just go in. I hesitated for a second and then pushed down the handle and opened the door. I stuck my head in the door and saw Mam. "Mam?" my voice croaked.

She turned her head, saw me, and burst into tears. She help up her arms and I fell into them, sobbing.

She ran her hand over the back of my head and then held me close, and we cried.

Finally she said, "JP, I'm so sorry."

"You wouldn't talk to me," I said, standing up and wiping my eyes.

Mam reached out for my hand and I gave it to her. She squeezed it. "You weren't talking to me. I could see in your eyes that you hated me. You hated me for going to Switzerland."

"Because you went with Mike."

Mam nodded. "I know. At the time, all I could see was that I was getting a chance to fulfill a lifelong dream, but once I got there all I could think of was you and Pap, and I knew I had made a mistake."

Mam pulled my hand forward and kissed it. She looked up at me, tears still trickling from the corners of her eyes, and gave a weak smile. "I realized I couldn't just live for myself anymore, I had to think of you and Pap, but then I found I was pregnant and all I could think about was myself, my fears. That's when I needed you most, but by then you hated me too much. I'd lost your love and your trust. What could I do but wait, JP? I knew you had to decide for yourself whether you could love me as I am or not. I was just giving you the space to do it."

"Sorry it took me so long," I said.

Mam nodded. "And me, too. I'm sorry."

She shook my hand. "Me and you, JP." She smiled.

I nodded and said, "And Pap, and Aunt Colleen, and the leprechaun, and Larry, and..."

Mam laughed, wiping the tears off her face and said, "And Mary."

I nodded. "And Grandma Mary," I said, but Mam, looking past me, lifted her chin and repeated, "And Mary."

I turned around, and there was Pap standing with a nurse in the doorway, and in Pap's arms was the tiniest baby I'd ever seen. And Pap, my dear Pap, with his heart so full he couldn't even speak, came forward and placed the baby, our baby Mary, in my arms.

HAN NOLAN is the author of the National Book Award winner *Dancing on the Edge*, the National Book Award finalist *Send Me Down a Miracle, Born Blue*, and several other acclaimed novels. She and her husband live in the South.

www.HanNolan.com